The
Dialectics of
Creation

THE
DIALECTICS OF
CREATION

Patterns of Birth & Regeneration
in *Paradise Lost*

by MICHAEL LIEB

THE UNIVERSITY OF MASSACHUSETTS PRESS

For Roz & John

Acknowledgments

MY DEBTS ARE too many to acknowledge sufficiently here, but I should like to thank those whose assistance has been of particular importance to my work. I have greatly benefited from the detailed and sympathetic criticism of Professors John T. Shawcross, Barbara K. Lewalski, Thomas R. Edwards, Maurice Charney, G. Stanley Koehler, Leon Barron, and Frank Evans. Their time, stimulation, and encouragement are certainly appreciated. But to Professor Shawcross goes my deepest appreciation, not only for his untiring attention and advice regarding matters both large and small, but also for his having first taught me how to read Milton. Finally, I am grateful in a very special way for the assistance I have received from my parents and from my wife Roslyn.

Williamsburg, Virginia
April 1969

Contents

The
Dialectics of
Creation

Introduction

The Dialectics

WHEN MILTON REFERS to "this great Argument" (l. 24) in the proem to Book 1 of *Paradise Lost*,[1] we can hardly overemphasize the fact that the polemicist of the prose tracts is now asserting himself poetically. That is, we cannot overlook Milton's decidedly persuasive stance as an epic poet. Indeed, by stressing his "great Argument" almost immediately, Milton does not allow us to forget that he will assume the posture of one who argues in order to convince, except that now he will argue as a poet rather than as a prose writer. This means that as a poet his "adventrous Song" will transcend the realm of prose (and, in fact, of all previous poetry), that it will "soar / Above th'Aonian Mount, while it pursues / Things unattempted yet in Prose or Rime" (1, 13–16). Or, to borrow a metaphor from the prose, Milton will use his right hand rather than his left in order to write. Therefore, his objectives in the poetry will be more nearly universal and sublime than they are in the prose. He will argue not so much about the fate of a nation, as he does in his tracts, as about a higher province, the fate of man and the world.

Despite the vehicle Milton chooses to express his convictions and the degree to which his objectives differ from one form of writing to the next, however, his role as polemicist and the fundamental assumptions upon which he bases the conduct of his "great Argument" do not change. (What does change, of course, are his argumentative tactics, his recourse to the principles of decorum,[2] a point I shall stress later.) Indeed, we might proceed one step further and say

---

[1]All references to Milton's poetry in my text are to *The Complete English Poetry of John Milton*, ed. John T. Shawcross (New York, 1963).

[2]For a full study of Milton's decorum, see Thomas Kranidas' *The Fierce Equation* (The Hague, 1965).

that a preliminary means of discovering Milton's own attitude toward argumentation is to resort to the prose, for there his polemical views are made explicit. From a brief examination of the prose, I think, we will discern more fully how Milton accommodates his polemical vision to the writing of epic poetry. And no more eloquent statement of his beliefs concerning argumentation exists than *Areopagitica*.[3]

The need for argumentation, or the active engaging in disputes to ascertain the truth of an issue, lies at the heart of Milton's plea for the liberty of publication. Central to *Areopagitica* is the idea that man cannot know what is right unless he is willing to entertain views that are alien to his own. Such an attitude, of course, is based upon the assumption that man's fallen nature will not allow him to experience good without experiencing evil also. Milton suggests that "perhaps this is that doom which *Adam* fell into of knowing good and evill, that is to say of knowing good by evill" (II, 514). Because the experience of one requires the experience of its opposite, man can begin to arrive at a knowledge of Truth only by subjecting his notions to what is "contrary" (II, 515).

Since Truth is by its very nature controversial, man must not remain content with received knowledge and accepted maxims. Rather, Truth and Falsehood must undergo some kind of rhetorical warfare before one can attain to a higher knowledge. "Where there is much desire to learn," Milton says, "there of necessity will be much arguing, much writing, many opinions; for opinion in good men is but knowledge in the making" (II, 554). This is dialectic: it assumes that, because the knowledge of Truth is always "in the making," forever arising dynamically out of the contention of opposing views, argumentation will be neither aimless nor destructive. On the contrary, disputation will be the constructive means

---

[3]All references to Milton's prose in my text are to the *Complete Prose Works*, gen. ed. Don M. Wolfe (New Haven, 1953–).

of uniting opposition in a superior perspective.[4] Dialectically, one might express Milton's attitude in this manner: one side of the argument confronts the opposing side, and these oppositions, in turn, manifest themselves in a higher union. Milton conceives of the idea metaphorically in *Areopagitica*, first as an image of resurrection and then as an image of construction.

The "search" for the mangled and torn body of Saint Truth underscores the first image. That search, of course, will not be complete until the "second comming," when Christ "shall bring together every joynt and member, and shall mould them into an immortall feature of loveliness and perfection" (II, 549). But until then, the seekers after Truth will attempt to "unite those dissever'd peeces which are yet wanting to the body of Truth" (II, 550–551). Implicit in the image is the dialectical process of synthesizing those diverse aspects of Truth that comprise the contrary positions of an argument. The process takes on an architectural dimension in the second image. There, the nature of controversy is such that its oppositions will "joyn" and "unite" in a kind of "spirituall architecture" (II, 554–555). In the construction of God's Temple, "there must be many schisms

---

[4] See Kranidas, p. 77. The idea is integral to Milton's thinking. If we consider the following statement from *The Reason of Church-Government*, we shall see that controversy is basic to Milton's outlook as a writer:

> If sects and schismes be turbulent in the unsetl'd estate of a Church, while it lies under the amending hand, it best beseems our Christian courage to think they are but as the throws and pangs that go before the birth of a reformation, and that the work it selfe is now in doing. For if we look but on the nature of elementall and mixt things, we know they cannot suffer any change of one kind, or quality into another without the struggl of contrarieties. (I, 795)

Such an assertion foreshadows much of what I shall say about Milton's technique in *Paradise Lost*. Here, as in the epic, Milton refers to his subject through a language of birth: he envisions a higher unity emerging creatively out of the "turbulence" of "elementall and mixt things." The point is that Milton views the world as process: the "work" (whatever its nature) is always "in doing," forever undergoing constructive "change" through the "struggl of contrarieties."

and many dissections made in the quarry and in the timber, ere the house of God can be built" (II, 555). Only after this process will a "reformation," or a re-forming of what was originally destroyed as a result of man's fall, occur. Only through the dialectical method of engaging in the "sublimest points of controversie," Milton maintains in *Areopagitica*, will man experience Truth as a transcendent thing.

Indeed, Milton envisions the process of ascertaining Truth dialectically in extremely emotional terms. By means of dialectic, man in the pursuit of Truth will undergo a spiritual rejuvenation; he will cast off the "old and wrincl'd skin of corruption . . . and wax young again, entring the glorious waies of Truth" (II, 557). He will rouse himself from his stupor of accepted ideas and kindle his "undazl'd eyes at the full midday beam; purging and unscaling [his] long abused sight at the fountain it self of heav'nly radiance" (II, 558). Such is the experience that the poet of *Paradise Lost* would allow man to undergo by enacting in full the dialectical assumptions of his "great Argument." In *Paradise Lost*, however, the dialectical process is extended to many other levels, the implications of which are complex and far-reaching.

Despite its polemical nature, Milton's epic argument must be examined within a poetic context. That is, although Milton's intentions are stated immediately in the proem to Book I, the argument itself does not move axiomatically but dramatically. Milton's "great Idea" is not fulfilled through a straightforward presentation of answerable propositions and verifiable conclusions. On the contrary, the argument finds expression through a complex mode of indirection and nuance, in which each statement, whether figurative or structural, has relevance for the whole. Indeed, what may be called the "systematic oppositions" of conventional dialectics[5] appear as dramatic events in *Paradise Lost*. The development of the argument conforms to Kenneth Burke's definition of dialectics in general as the "interplay of various

[5] Mortimer J. Adler, *Dialectic* (New York, 1927), p. 241.

factors that mutually modify one another, and may be thought of as voices in a dialogue or roles in a play, with each voice or role in its partiality contributing to the development of the whole."[6] Thus, in one respect, the role of the Son finds its counterpart in the role of Satan, and we cannot begin to understand the function of one without a complete awareness of how the other functions.[7] In another instance, God's act of creation operates most significantly when viewed in the light of its opposite, the defeat of Satan in Heaven. Carrying the idea still further, we can see how the Son's entrance into Chaos and return to glory in Book VII is contrasted with Satan's entrance into Chaos in Book II and return to ignominy in Book X. Or, to cite a critical commonplace, the contrast between the holy Trinity of God, Son, and Spirit and the unholy Trinity of Satan, Sin, and Death allows us to see how the divine world is parodied by the degenerate. As obvious as these contrasts might appear, they serve to indicate the importance of dialectical reasoning to *Paradise Lost*. Indeed, Milton's reference in *Areopagitica* to the necessity of learning by what is "contrary" should determine the very way in which we approach Milton's epic. For to understand the polemical nature of *Paradise Lost* is to come to terms with the essential oppositions that manifest themselves on all levels.

With the dialectical approach as the basis of my study, then, I propose to discover a common referent by which the oppositions of the poem find expression. That referent, as I shall argue, has to do with the idea of creation in all its aspects: conception, pregnancy, birth, and offspring (both sublime and degenerate). I shall suggest that Milton as a poet speaks in a language of birth in order to dramatize such events as the warring of good and evil, the fall of angels and men, the redemption of man through grace, God's creation of the universe, and the poet's creation of the poem.

[6]*A Grammar of Motives and a Rhetoric of Motives* (Cleveland, 1962), p. 403.
[7]For a full explanation of this idea, see John T. Shawcross, "The Son in His Ascendance: A Reading of *Paradise Lost*," MLQ, XXVII (1966), 388–401.

To dramatize briefly Milton's dialectical practices in this respect, we might consider some specific relationships. The association of "reduce" and "return," for example, is revealed in at least two ways, both of which become significant through the contrast of sublime and degenerate meanings. Normally, "reduce" and "return" refer to the idea of becoming less, in the first case, and going back to a beginning point, in the second. In *Paradise Lost*, however, the concepts are fused to form a meaning whose referent is in the idea of creation.

On the sublime or deific level, God himself is paradoxically "reduced" to the condition of the angels through the glorification of his angelic offspring (v, 842–845). That is, the result of the angels' adoring God is the "reduction" of God as a ruler to the state of those who obey. The antithesis of the sublime experience is the degenerate experience: Satan also is "reduced" through the glorification of his host. He laments rather than celebrates the fact:

> While they adore me on the Throne of Hell,
> With Diadem and Scepter high advanc't
> *The lower still I fall*, onely supream
> In miserie; such joy Ambition finds.
> (iv, 89–92; italics mine)

We could not begin to understand the irony of these lines were we not aware that they represent the dialectical counterpart of the divine state of "reduction." Even with an awareness that "reduction" has sublime and degenerate references, however, we are still not in full possession of the way in which Milton articulates his "Argument."

"Reduce" in *Paradise Lost* relates not only to the idea of becoming less but, through its Latin derivation, to the idea of returning to a source. On the deific plane, God's "reduction" which results from glorification repeats on a minor scale the apocalyptic "reduction": then the Son as the agent of God will "lay by" his "regal Scepter" with the result that "God shall be All in All" (iii, 339–341). In that grand moment of regeneration, the world shall be "reduced," that is, "led back," "returned," to the source from which it came and from which it first received life (III, 333–338).

On the degenerate plane, however, Satan's purpose will be to enact an antithetical "reduction," in other words, to "reduce" what God has created "To her original darkness" and the "sway" of Chaos and Night (II, 982–986). "Reduction," then, is associated with the idea of "return": both come to have meanings which reveal themselves within the context of generation (and ultimately regeneration). When applied to God, "reduction" and "return" have positive and life-giving significance. When applied to Satan, on the other hand, their generative implications are reversed.

"Reduce" and "return" are only two of the many terms that have creative possibilities in the poem. But even a preliminary discussion of these terms has revealed, I think, how pointedly Milton as a poet uses words that reflect major patterns and basic antitheses. And for a full understanding of what these antitheses imply, one must become as receptive to the degenerate overtones of the creational imagery as he is to the sublime overtones. That is, he must be willing to consider the idea of creativity in all its aspects.

Kester Svendsen was one of the first critics who saw in *Paradise Lost* the major importance of creativity. Svendsen notes:

> Fecundity and creativity, extolled as early as the elegy on the coming of spring, form a dominant motif in *Paradise Lost* in the opposition of Christ and Satan. The emergence of life from the dust of the earth, the origin of Adam and Eve, the dynamic opulence of the garden, indeed, the whole narrative, symbolize the struggle between positive and negative creativity.[8]

What Svendsen states here is that primal opposition through which the dialectics of the poem operate. The sublime creative world of God is reflected in and parodied by the

[8]*Milton and Science* (Cambridge, Mass., 1956), pp. 187–188.

degenerate and obscene world of Satan. And that world of Satanic creativity is obscene in the fullest sense of the word. As Svendsen states:

> When Milton reached the composition of *Paradise Lost*, he had had long experience in formulating analogies from animal and human reproduction. The motifs of miscegenation, hermaphroditism, and disnatured conception occur in the prose and have their counterpart in the epic.[9]

Since Svendsen referred to that basic antithesis in the poem, however, no one has followed his lead and performed a full study of the topic.[10]

A glance at the polemical attitude in the prose will give us some indication of the extent to which Milton draws upon a language of degeneracy to humiliate his opponents. In his chapter entitled "The Human Body," Svendsen has catalogued a series of Miltonic invectives, from "canary-sucking" prelates and vomiting and belching conservatives, who cause God himself to vomit, to a henpecked Salmasius, who is at once an hermaphrodite and who publishes dunghills and resembles a "true cock."[11] As early as *Of Reformation*,

---

[9]Ibid., p. 188.

[10]I am hardly suggesting that the idea of creativity has never been the subject of analysis. Among others, W. B. C. Watkins, *An Anatomy of Milton's Verse* (Baton Rouge, Louisiana, 1955), A. S. P. Woodhouse, "Notes on Milton's Views on the Creation: The Initial Phases," *PQ*, xxviii (1949), 211–236, and Grant McColley, *Paradise Lost: An Account of Its Growth and Major Origins* (Chicago, 1940) have considered the topic. Because creation is so important to the action of *Paradise Lost*, most scholars have had something to say about its presence in Milton's epic. Yet to my knowledge, no one has fully analyzed creativity from the dialectical point of view. (See, however, Balachandra Rajan, *Paradise Lost and the Seventeenth-Century Reader* [London, 1947], esp. pp. 39–52.)

[11]*Milton and Science*, pp. 182–190. For further references to Milton's use of invective, see John Milton French, "Milton as Satirist," *PMLA*, li (1936), 414–429; Allan H. Gilbert, "Milton's Defense of Bawdry," *SAMLA Studies in Milton*, ed. J. Max Patrick (Gainesville, Florida, 1953), 54–71; Edward Le Comte, "Milton as Satirist and Wit," *Th' Upright Heart and Pure*, ed. Amadeus Fiore, o.f.m. (Pittsburgh, 1967), pp. 45–69; and Don M. Wolfe, "Introduction," *Complete Prose Works*, i, 914–916.

Milton employs a dialectic with imagery foreshadowing the sublime and degenerate antitheses culminating in *Paradise Lost*. The sublimity of the Reformation (compare the idea of regeneration in *Paradise Lost*) contrasts with the degeneracy of the prelates, who become the type of Satan himself (I, 524–525).

Milton resorts to a language of uncompromising vilification to characterize the Antichristian dignitaries. In one instance, he compares prelacy to a "huge and monstrous Wen little lesse then the Head it selfe, growing to it by a narrower excrescency" (I, 583–584). Allegorically, the Wen is questioned by a "wise and learned Philosopher": "Wilt thou (quoth he) that art but a bottle of vitious and harden'd excrements, contend with the lawfull and free-borne members . . .?" After a reply by the Wen, the Philosopher continues:

thy folly is as great as thy filth . . . thou containst no good thing in thee, but a heape of hard, and loathsome uncleannes, and art to the head a foul disfigurment and burden, when I have cut thee off, and open'd thee, as by the help of these implements I will doe, all men shall see. (I, 584)

The parasitical and excremental imagery fused in the figure of the Wen is further developed in the course of the tract. As parasites, for example, Milton's opponents become leeches that "suck the Kingdome" (I, 589), "hungry and ravenous Harpies" that cause corruption (I, 591), and breeding vipers that "eat through the entrals of our *Peace*" (I, 614). Moreover, the image of excrement is associated with the "excessive wast of Treasury," the "Idolatrous erection of Temples," and the "insatiate desires" for wealth and appearances (I, 589–590). Such filth culminates in a reference to spontaneous birth out of corruption:

What can we suppose this will come to? What other materials then these have built up the *spirituall* Babel to the heighth of her Abominations? Beleeve it Sir

> right truly it may be said, that *Antichrist* is *Mammons* Son. The soure levin of human Traditions mixt in one putrifi'd Masse with the poisonous dregs of hypocrisie in the heart of *Prelates* that lye basking in the Sunny warmth of Wealth, and Promotion, is the Serpents Egge that will hatch an Antichrist wheresoever, and ingender the same Monster as big, or as little as the Lump is which breeds him. If the splendor of *Gold* and *Silver* begin to Lord it once againe in the Church of England, we shall see *Antichrist* shortly wallow heere, though his cheife Kennell be at *Rome*. (i, 590)

Invective here descends to the depths of defilement; indeed, it becomes almost visionary in its depiction of a world concerned with sexual perversion, gastronomical disorders, sordid and monstrous diseases of the skin, plaguing parasites, and filth of the worst sort. And that world expresses itself finally in a vision of birth: out of a putrefied mass of corruption arises a Monster that will wallow in the loathsomeness of its own desecration.

In discussing the prose, I have devoted so much time to the degenerate aspects of Milton's argumentative stance because I wished to show to what depths Milton as a polemicist would go in ridiculing his opponents. Milton's own defense of such ridicule from "The Preface" to *Animadversions* will be useful here, first in establishing his view of satire and second in making the inevitable transition from mockery in the prose tracts to mockery in the epic. I suggest that in reading Milton's statement we substitute the word "Satanism" for the word "Prelatry" with this consideration: if the prelates, who are merely the types and shadows of evil, are subject to the kind of castigation we have seen in *Of Reformation*, how strong, then, will be the vilification of the arch-exponent of evil, Satan himself!

> *And although in the serious uncasing of a grand imposture (for to deale plainly with you Readers, Prelatry is no better) there be mixt here and there such a grim laughter, as may*

*appeare at the same time in an austere visage, it cannot be
taxt of levity or insolence: for even this veine of laughing
(as I could produce out of grave Authors) hath oft-times a
strong and sinewy force in teaching and confuting; nor can
there be a more proper object of indignation and scorne
together then a false prophet taken in the greatest dearest
and most dangerous cheat, the cheat of soules: in the dis-
closing whereof it be harmfull to be angry, and withall to
cast a lowring smile, when the properest object calls for
both, it will be long enough ere any be able to say why those
two most rationall faculties of humane intellect anger and
laughter were first seated in the brest of man.* (I, 663–664)

By using epithets like a "false Prophet" who engages in the
"cheat of soules," Milton might easily be referring to Satan.
As the object of scorn in *Paradise Lost*, Satan will be viewed
from the standpoint of both anger and laughter. Toward
God's enemies, the epic poet will adopt none other than
God's attitude, which appears so strong in Milton's trans-
lation of "Psalm 2":

> he who in Heav'n doth dwell
> Shall laugh, the Lord shall scoff them, then severe
> Speak to them in his wrath.
>
> (ll. 8–10)

Anger and laughter: with that combination, we may expect
to find the entire world of invective loaded upon Satan's
head.

Like his counterparts in prose, Satan will exist in an
environment of filth, disease, and moral and sexual perversion. He will not only be made to experience such an environment, but he will be the devotee of that environment. All
his actions, all his speeches, all his motives, will reveal
themselves as part of his damnation. His creations will be
the symbolic equivalents of Salmasius' dunghills; he and his
fallen crew will become the "vitious and harden'd excrements" and "loathsome uncleannes," the parasitical wens

and leeches and vipers that must be purged lest they "eat through the entrals of our *Peace*." With their thrones, wealth, and erection of temples as symbols of their putre-faction, their corruption will cause unnatural and monstrous births. And were anyone to assert that such a vision of Satan is unbecoming to the sublimity of Milton's epic purpose, Milton would reply that "Christ himselfe speaking of unsavory traditions, scruples not to name the Dunghill and the Jakes" (*An Apology*, 1, 895) and that "God who is the author both of purity and eloquence" descends to use obscenities "as fittiest in that vehement character wherein" he sometimes speaks (*An Apology*, 1, 902).[12]

Viewing Milton's treatment of Satan in this manner recalls my earlier statement that we cannot divorce the poet of *Paradise Lost* from the polemicist of the prose tracts. We can, however, suggest the way in which vituperation will differ from one mode of writing to the next. Invective will descend as low yet will remain forever aware that it is operating within a poetic rather than a political atmosphere. That is, the epic decorum governing the images will make the invective content more covert, especially when obscene. Ridicule and insult will become dramatic, so that the effect will be one of divine mockery, tempting man to side with the devil and re-enact his fall. That the drama may succeed, Satanic devices will be made as attractive as the upper portions of Sin. The repulsive and vilified underportions of Sin, however, will also be latent in each Satanic image and in each Satanic statement. A failure or unwillingness on our

---

[12] Cf. Gilbert's statement (in "Milton's Defense of Bawdry," p. 63): "Milton holds that an obscene subject may properly be dealt with in obscene terms by the most honorable and modest men. Indeed, he asserts [in *Pro se defensio*] that it is not 'out-of-the-way and immodest for an author in the same [work] to assail baseness with sharpness of wit . . . and also to think about God.' " In his defense of "tart rhetoric" (*An Apology*), Milton establishes the fact that the "spirit of God, who is purity it selfe" will descend to vehemence and obscenity when necessary and admonishes those "fools who would teach men to read more decently than God thought good to write" (1, 901–903). Milton, then, continues to defend laughter and derision as proper methods of exposing and degrading evil (1, 904–905).

part to recognize these "underportions" at every instance will result in our failure to read the poem properly. Milton's prose openly invites one to participate in the ridiculing of the opponent; if, for dramatic reason, the poetry is not so overt in its invitation, it is nonetheless as urgent (if not more so) in its purpose. With Milton's polemical approach in mind, therefore, I shall discuss the way dialectic manifests itself in *Paradise Lost*.

Prolegomena

The Dark World

TO DISCOVER WHAT any argument is about, one should locate the basic issue which is at the source of opposition, and if we are viewing the argument of *Paradise Lost* polemically as a dramatization of opposing attitudes, we might also do well to locate the center of opposition in the epic. Accordingly, we must concern ourselves with the nature of Chaos, whose apparent importance to *Paradise Lost* Milton indicates in at least two ways. First, he mentions the Abyss twice in the proem to Book I (ll. 10 and 21), which supposedly contains in brief all matters essential to his proposed epic purpose; furthermore, he represents Chaos in various ways (most obviously through Satan's journey in Book II and the creation in Book VII) as contributing to the fable upon which the action of the epic is based. If nothing else, then, the narrative presence of Chaos attests to its relevance.

But there is more: as I shall discuss in greater detail, Chaos becomes the referent through which the powers of God and Satan, of creative Deity and destructive anti-Deity, work their way. On the one hand, Milton causes the Abyss to become the aboriginal realm out of which rises the entire visible creation (I, 9–10). On the other hand, he causes that realm in the course of the poem to participate in an antithetical occurrence: the returning of creation to its uncreated state. The first instance becomes an account of God's act; the second, of Satan's. Consequently if each power resorts to the Abyss in order to manifest itself, an initial investigation of Chaos is of prime importance to an understanding of Milton's epic argument.

Chaos embodies two possibilities: one productive and one destructive. The Abyss is not inherently evil, although it can be put to evil use. Nor is it inherently good, although it can be put to fruitful use.[1] The chaotic realm is imbued with the potentiality for glorious production and inglorious destruction. It becomes the original medium out of which fruition is effected, in the case of God; and it becomes the resulting medium into which fruition may be reduced, in the case of Satan. It remains with God to cause the elements to become the means of future offspring (II, 915–916), and it remains with Satan to defile and debase that which has already been divinely created into the aboriginal "dark materials" from whence creation came.

The vocabulary through which Milton refers to the center of such opposing forces is one of generation and destruction. He describes Chaos as the "Womb of nature and perhaps her Grave" (II, 911). From God's point of view, Chaos is a "Womb" out of which new creations may arise. Thus, although the Abyss itself is in an uncreated state (II, 912), it has the potential for production, since significantly all four elements are "in thir *pregnant* causes mixt" (II, 913; italics mine). In the act of creation, God need only extend his virtue into Chaos, which is nothing more than that part of himself from which he has withdrawn his influence (VII, 168–173).[2] From Satan's point of view, on the other hand, Chaos is a "Grave" into which God's creations may be returned. This raises an important point: although we may use the terms "destruction" and "uncreation" interchangeably, we should remember that destruction constantly implies the reversal of its opposite. Satan's activities are not merely destructive in the usual sense; they always take into account the nature of God's creativity.

The ambivalent qualities of Chaos—its potential for

[1]A. B. Chambers, "Chaos in *Paradise Lost*," *JHI*, XXIV (1963), 69.

[2]See, for example, Woodhouse, "Notes on Milton's Views on the Creation," p. 228: "So far, then, from creation's entailing the withdrawal of God's active goodness, it results . . . from the putting of it forth." See also Walter Clyde Curry, *Milton's Ontology, Cosmogony and Physics* (Lexington, Kentucky, 1957), pp. 42–43. For a review of the scholarship concerning the opposing (but discredited) retraction theory, see Balachandra Rajan, *Paradise Lost and the Seventeenth-Century Reader*, p. 139n.

productivity as opposed to destructivity—assert themselves in the personifications of Chaos and Night. The inherent sexuality of the Abyss is represented in these two figures, the first male and the second female. Through them we are presented with a new perspective of how God works procreatively and of how Satan works destructively.

As the most ancient bearers of offspring, Chaos and his "Consort" Night are "Enthron'd" on the "wasteful Deep" (II, 960–963). Implicit in Milton's handling of the personifications is a variation of the myth in which Day is the daughter of Chaos and Night.[3] Allegorically, the union of Chaos and his consort in *Paradise Lost* suggests that through God's influence the coition of two negative qualities results in the birth of that which is positive. Such a pattern repeats in small the major pattern of the poem: out of darkness will spring forth light; out of disorder will spring forth order; out of evil will spring forth good.

Chaos and Night, however, also have destructive overtones, for the monarchs "hold / Eternal Anarchie, amidst the noise / Of endless Warrs, and by confusion stand" (II, 894–897). Here, the elemental qualities are in endless conflict "and to Battel bring / Thir embryon Atoms" (II, 889–890). The destructive qualities of Chaos are dramatized by a military metaphor that is reiterated thematically throughout the epic. Thus, when Satan and Sin first view Chaos, the opening is so wide that "with extended wings a Bannerd Host / Under spread Ensigns marching might pass through" (II, 885–886).

The repercussions of the chaotic conflict are dramatized in Book VI. The War in Heaven, as I shall discuss, represents the reduction of what has already been created to its elemental existence. Creation undergoes uncreation, a sort of metaphorical loss of identity, and resembles in its anarchic state

[3]That Night in the myth is also the offspring of Chaos, so that Day results from an implied incestuous relationship, offers a parallel to the infernal Trinity of Satan, Sin, and Death (John T. Shawcross, "The Balanced Structure of *Paradise Lost*," *SP*, LXII [1965], 715).

the "Battel" of the "embryon Atoms." The Heavenly conflict is compared to the breaking of "Nature's concord" and the springing up or birth of "warr" among the "Constellations" (VI, 311–312).[4] Moreover, like the noise of Chaos, the confused "hubbub," which has its birth in the "womb" of the "hollow dark" (II, 951–953), all Heaven resounds with the dire noise of the conflict (VI, 211–217).

And Satan's professed purpose is to effect such a state upon all creation. He promises the personifications of Chaos and Night to reverse the process of creation by reducing what was God's dominion "to her original darkness" and the "sway" of the elemental monarchs (II, 977–984). Satan thereby reveals his particular way of thinking: he can envision the concept of origins only insofar as there is a reduction of what has been created to its original constituents. In that sense, his thinking is "uncreative." Unlike God, who employs Chaos as a focal point for his creativity, Satan employs Chaos for his uncreativity.

From the Satanic point of view Chaos becomes a place of devastation and waste (compare "wasteful Deep" [II, 961]). Isabel MacCaffrey cites the primary example of its wasting power as that of the Deluge (Chaos is, of course, an "illimitable Ocean" [II, 892]), which causes paradise to become "an Iland salt and bare, / The haunt of Seals and Orcs, and Sea-mews clang" (XI, 834–835).[5] But "waste" also implies the antithesis of "bareness" and devastation: it likewise expresses itself in indiscriminate and uncontrolled overproduction. Even the overwhelming abundance of unfallen Nature in Eden would result in "waste" were not Adam and Eve constantly to temper its productivity.

The lack of such temperance has its counterpart in the need to devour whatever is in sight, whether in the form of knowledge or food. These two "objects" of possible intemperance complement each other in Milton's mind. And we can easily discern what degenerate qualities Milton attributes

---

[4]Cf. *PL*, VI, 209–210, 668–669, 693–694.
[5]*Paradise Lost as "Myth"* (Cambridge, Mass., 1959), pp. 88–91.

to the "waste" of intemperance, for he has Raphael warn
Adam and Eve:

> But Knowledge is as food, and needs no less
> Her Temperance over Appetite, to know
> In measure what the mind may well contain,
> Oppresses else with Surfet, and soon turns
> Wisdom to Folly, as Nourishment to Wind.
>
> (VII, 126–130)

"Waste" (or, here, "Surfet"), then, is very decidedly
associated with the transformation of that which is healthy
("Wisdom," "Nourishment") to that which is unhealthy or
debased ("Folly," "Wind"). And the mode of that debasement has to do metaphorically with the digestive process.
"Wind" or the unhealthy production of stomach gases is
the counterpart of "Folly." The relationship is not merely
metaphorical, however, for we shall see the "Wind" of that
"Folly" buffet Satan about first in Chaos, where all such
currents originate, and then in the Paradise of Fools.

I have noted here some of the many meanings of "waste":
there are certainly more.[6] My immediate purpose, however,
has been first to explore the Satanic view of Chaos through
one word and, second, to show in a preliminary way what
associations the consideration of a single word can evoke.
From a discussion of "waste," we can see that Milton causes
his language to have "low" or debased connotations. They

---

[6]An even further connotation of "waste" is that of tedium. The fallen angels,
for example, are made to "waste Eternal dayes in woe and pain" (II, 695) as part
of their damnation. Indeed, as Chambers notes, the Greek derivation of Chaos
is "to yawn" (p. 56). (Cf. Hell's "yawning" to receive the fallen angels [VI,
874–875].)

Interestingly enough, the comic aspect of wasting one's time in the boredom
of fruitless activity becomes a dominant motif in The Dunciad. I refer to that
poem especially because in a number of ways Pope, it seems to me, read Paradise
Lost as I am attempting to read it now: from the point of view of negative
creativity. Thus we have in the fourth book of The Dunciad Dullness' universal
yawn, which penetrates the kingdom until the empire of Chaos is restored
(ll. 605–656). (References are to The Poems of Alexander Pope, ed. John Butt
[New Haven, 1968].)

are part of Milton's verbal richness. The texture of *Paradise Lost* is so tightly integrated that one word may contain a multitude of reverberations throughout the entire epic. I shall explore those "reverberations" more fully in the course of my discussion.

If there are vast differences between the Satanic and deific attitudes toward Chaos, these attitudes converge in a single means of expression: the idea of birth. Obviously, Milton uses words that connote generation in order to describe God's creativity: the very presence of "Womb" (as opposed to "Grave") as an epithet characterizing the process of divine creation testifies to that. What is not so obvious, however, is that Milton draws upon a language of birth to formulate with overwhelming irony the position of Satan. "Grave" becomes not merely a term suggesting destruction but a womb whose properties are the exact opposite of creativity. To understand the significance of Chaos as it is negatively conceived, we must investigate how Satan and his cohorts respond to their fallen condition. The debate in the council scene will provide a fitting point of departure.

Because the angels have fallen, they are obliged to come to terms with the Abyss. Their fall has forced them to become part of a precosmogonic state, and all their actions will therefore reflect a chaotic environment. In their folly they react to their situation as if they have been initiated into the secrets of the Abyss.

Responding to Moloch's nihilistic willingness to have himself reduced to a state of nothingness in a further defiance of God (II, 96–97), Belial denies that God would "spend all his rage" on the rebel angels and reduce them all to non-existence (II, 144–154). Rather, Belial argues that God's plans are to subject the fallen angels to endless punishment. Arguing against open war, Belial invokes the world of Chaos and its dark constituent Night through a language of generation. He considers annihilation as the state of being

> swallowd up and lost
> In the wide womb of uncreated night,
> Devoid of sense and motion.
>
> (II, 149–151)

From God's point of view an entrance into a "womb" implies eventual egress in a renewed state. And yet to Belial that identical activity implies just the opposite. The Abyss as Belial envisions it is not a place of potential creation but a world into which things are reduced and "swallowed up." "Womb" ironically suggests the annihilation of life or the causing of life to be without (that is, "*devoid*" of) "sense and motion."

The area of generation receives what has already been created into its nothingness and uncreates it. From the Satanic point of view, "womb" is a place which negates generation. It manifests itself in images of swallowing rather than in images of giving forth, in images of entering into wide openings rather than in images of exiting from openings. Such is the diabolic attitude toward Chaos: it envisions the Abyss not as a world out of which things come newly arisen but as a world into which things go to lose their "being" and never come out again.

Beelzebub further characterizes the nature of Chaos (II, 404–410) through his fear of its emptiness and darkness. For the fallen consciousness, both characteristics are related to the idea of generation. The palpable obscurity of Chaos indicates not only a physical deprivation of sight but a symbolical deprivation, which by its very nature prohibits discovery. Whoever "tempts" the Abyss must "find out" his unknown way, that is, discover or invent a means of productive egress. The emptiness that surrounds the discoverer threatens him with a complete loss of security. The sudden or abrupt vastness of the Abyss suggests both its complete vacuousness (compare II, 932) and, to the fallen consciousness bent on destruction, its unfruitful and barren wastefulness. Chaos, as Beelzebub conceives it, therefore, is a realm whose obscurity coupled with its vacuity produces absolute negation.

Satan's view of Chaos resembles Belial's and Beelzebub's: the act of traversing the Abyss becomes one of entering a nonproductive opening and of risking there complete loss of identity. If one can get beyond the prison of Hell with its "huge convex of Fire" and "gates of burning Adamant" (II, 434–437), then

> the void profound
> Of unessential Night receives him next
> Wide gaping, and with utter loss of being
> Threatens him, plung'd in that abortive gulf.
> (II, 438–441)

As the dark Abyss is "uncreative" to Belial, it is "unessential" to Satan. "Unessential" here has the same implications as "uncreative." If, as William B. Hunter, Jr., suggests, "essence" implies individuality,[7] then "unessential" describes a world that indicates the complete absence of individuality. Chaos becomes a realm which reduces the "essential" or quickening aspect of existence to the "unessential" or complete negation of existence. It, therefore, "threatens" whoever enters it "with utter loss of being," with a complete reduction of his identity to that substratum of which Chaos is composed.

The "unessential" quality of Chaos has even further overtones in its association with the epithets that Satan gives to the Abyss in the tenth book. When Satan boasts that he has been able to traverse the "unreal, vast, unbounded deep" (X, 471), the "unreality" of the Abyss may be related to its "unessentiality": that which lacks being or identity is somehow illusory in its makeup and it can only be given a sense of reality when a creative presence endues it with essence or being. Moreover, the "unessentiality" and "uncreativity" of the Abyss are complemented by still another descriptive

[7]"Some Problems in John Milton's Theological Vocabularly," *HTR*, LVII (1964), 353–365.

trait. Satan describes himself as having been

> plung'd in the womb
> Of unoriginal *Night* and *Chaos* wild.
>
> (x, 476–477)

The dark Abyss is "unoriginal" not only because nothing existed before it, but because Chaos itself contains no being, no essence, and is therefore "unoriginated."[8] Within the "uncreative" context, Satan's use of "womb," like Belial's, implies not the promise of productivity but the threat of annihilation. Again "womb" refers to its opposite: a "wide gaping" hole into which one is "plung'd" in hopelessness. And if there are any suggestions of procreation, they are characterized by the fact that the "womb" which Satan encounters is "abortive" (ii, 441). Birth from the diabolic "womb" must ultimately be unnatural and monstrous.

We are not surprised that the fallen angels conceive of Chaos in a nihilistic manner, considering their own recent devastating experience of having fallen "headlong" from the heights of Heaven to the depths of Hell (see, for example, Sin's description of the event [ii, 771–773]). The downward motion and the inverted position of the body contrast with the upward motion of the "Heav'ns and Earth," which rise out of Chaos (i, 9–10). Divine birth from Chaos finds its antithesis in the "destruction" of the angels, who are plunged into a "wide womb" of uncreativity.

That "destruction" is described as part of the angels' defeat in Book vi, when they observe to their terror the very wall of Heaven open. In that moment they are bereft of all security previously provided by the confines of the paradisiacal world (vi, 860–862). They are initiated suddenly into the horror of an opening and the horror of a descent, and they fall headlong into an infinite and bottomless realm, whose opening is hideously exaggerated: "Hell at last / Yawning receiv'd them whole, and on them clos'd" (vi, 874–875). Here the Satanic crew undergoes the experiences

[8] Shawcross, ed., *Complete English Poetry*, p. 434n.

that it attributes both to Hell and the Abyss. The metaphor of being devoured is fused with the idea of being swallowed up in a womb. The "yawning" mouth opens as wide as possible to chew and swallow its food.

Satan characterizes the feeling of being swallowed and devoured in a hole just before he penetrates the confines of Eden:

> Which way I flie is Hell; my self am Hell;
> And in the lowest deep a lower deep
> Still threatening to devour me opens wide,
> To which the Hell I suffer seems a Heav'n.
>
> (IV, 75–78)

That Satan does "escape" temporarily from the physical confines of Hell and is able to voyage to earth in no way contradicts his inability to escape from the moral and psychological confines of his own damnation. Indeed, even after he "succeeds" in overcoming his physical imprisonment, he laments that he has not escaped at all. His soliloquy reveals an essential ambivalence that confronts the unregenerate consciousness: the inability to escape the torments of the fallen self as opposed to the diabolic horror of self-annihilation. Despite the depth to which the fallen soul has been thrust, it must always face the danger of another fall and of a deeper hole. By its very nature, the fall precludes all hope of egress, of discovering an exit through the hole which will allow for the freedom of an ascent. No exit exists: the hole is self-contained, sealed up, and cannot be opened except for the purposes of a further descent. And yet Satan persists in penetrating places where he does not belong.

The first instance of such a penetration occurs as the result of Satan's successful temptation of Sin to open the gates of Hell. The "infernal dores" suddenly fly open "with impetuous recoil and jarring sound . . . and on their hinges grate / Harsh Thunder" (II, 876–882). The stealth with which the act is performed is undermined by the astonishing noise it occasions. Sin is powerless to close the gates because the consequences of her disobedience are unretractable. After the gates are opened, Satan and Sin confront the "secrets of the hoarie deep" (II, 891).

The implications of their peering into the Abyss before Satan embarks upon his exploratory journey are ignoble. C. S. Lewis' observation that Satan in spying upon Adam and Eve is no more than a "mere peeping Tom"[9] is fore-shadowed in his earlier activities. The privacy of the Abyss as a womb is violated in Satan and Sin's perverted indis-cretion. Their act takes on the character of a sexual offense to a realm associated with impregnation and procreation. For through that medium, the Spirit of God in utmost secrecy gives birth to the universe.

Ironically, Satan is at great pains to deny his perversity. When he tries to convince the personifications of Chaos and Night that his intentions are noble, he reveals that aspect of himself which is most despicable. He assures them:

> I come no Spy
> With purpose to explore or to disturb
> The secrets of your Realm.
> (II, 970–972)

However, these are the qualities that most aptly describe the Arch-Deceiver. He has already seduced Sin into revealing the secrets of the "nethermost Abyss," and his mission of exploration has about it the undertone of perversion. Indeed, the forced opening of the gates accompanied by the violation of privacy becomes a central aspect of Satan's degeneracy.[10]

And yet the "Anarch old" succumbs to Satan's temptations

---

[9] *A Preface to Paradise Lost* (New York, 1961), p. 99.

[10] The need to bore holes and create openings in previously closed areas (cf. Satan's "forced" entrance into Chaos and, later, into Eden) is, according to C. G. Jung (*Psychology of the Unconscious*, trans. Beatrice M. Hinkle [New York, 1927], p. 175) sexual in its implications. If Satan's perversions border upon "voyeurism" in one context (see n. 9 above), his "boring" activities coupled with his need to create a fantasy world in which his own image is omnipotent border upon onanism.

and allows Satan to pass through his kingdom, so that the Arch-Deceiver "staid not to reply,"

> But glad that now his Sea should find a shore,
> With fresh alacritie and force renew'd
> Springs upward like a Pyramid of fire
> Into the wild expanse.
>
> (II, 1011–1014)

Satan's confidence is renewed: the "sea" of his insecurity is given a "shore," a boundary which the fallen Angel may see in the distance and to which he may now aspire. The feeling inspires him, and he experiences a sense of rebirth which allows him to spring upward like fire. But even in that very motion he is defeated by the associations of the language that describes his ascent. Because the common (and erroneous) derivation of "pyramid" in the seventeenth century was "pyre,"[11] Milton employs that derivation as a means of undercutting Satan's act. For when we see that "pyramid" puns on "pyre," we can also understand that Milton comically associates Satan's springing upward with the idea of self-immolation. Satan's ascent is simultaneously the motion of his own destruction. In that way Satan will deliver himself and his cohorts from perdition.

To understand fully the significance of Satan's journey through Chaos, we must realize that an unexpected reversal in meaning also occurs. We have become acquainted with the following assumptions. From God's point of view, Chaos is a "Womb" to which God resorts in order to create, while from Satan's point of view, Chaos is a "Grave" into which Satan (theoretically) reduces God's creations. To counteract God's creations, which "rise" out of Chaos, Satan would cause those creations to "fall" or "descend," as he was made to fall, into a state of uncreation. Implicit in the last statement, however, is the assumption that if

---

[11] See the *OED*, "Pyramid B.4, 1651, Stanley *Poems*." The idea apparently persisted at least into the eighteenth century, for the *OED* also cites Swift (B.4) as using the word in this way.

God creates, he can also reduce his creations to Chaos. To Satan's dismay, God can uncreate. Consequently, as a counterpart of God's "uncreating" act, Satan must indulge in "creative" activity. If Chaos becomes a "Grave" for God, it must become a "Womb" for Satan.[12] The roles are reversed as Satan assumes God's attitude toward Chaos: Satan makes of Chaos a "Womb" through which he "ascends" in the manner of God's creations. Ironically, like God, Satan resorts to the Abyss in order to create, and what he creates is the illusion of his own delivery from Hell. Dialectically, he pretends to give birth to himself.[13]

Satan's journey through Chaos, however, has not merely creational overtones; its dimensions are also scatological. If we are willing to accept the inevitable idea that Milton was polemically bound to debase the arch-exponent of evil, the scatology of Satan's voyage will assert itself logically. Satan, for example, enters Chaos' "Furnace mouth," which "Cast forth redounding smoak and ruddy flame" (II, 888–889).[14] The mouth that belches forth its inwards opens into the "hollow dark" of its "intestine broils" (II, 1001). From the point of view of a personified Chaos, "intestine broils" denotes internal disorders, characterized by the warring of the elements, but such disorders from the point of view of Satan's journey may have debased overtones relating to the digestive process. I am not suggesting

[12] Inherent in the reversal of attitude is the transcendent paradox of the poem. Chaos becomes a "Grave" for God only insofar as it affords a way of re-creation: by uncreating Satan, God provides the means of glorious re-creation for others through the Son as Savior. The full implications of the concept will be discussed in the course of the study.

[13] In reality, of course, Satan's "ascent" is self-destructive (cf. the "Pyramid"— "pyre" derivation). Since the hole cannot possibly be a means of egress for the fallen mind, Satan cannot "deliver" himself from the "Grave" (now ironically become "Womb") of his damnation. A "lower deep," one must remember, is forever threatening to devour him. The "shore" that borders Satan's "sea" is as deceptive as his own conception of godhead.

[14] The oral associations of Chaos' "opening" are fused with the sexual: Satan enters the "wide *womb* of uncreated Night," where he might possibly be "swallowed up" (II, 149–150; italics mine).

that Milton is using "intestine" in any directly anatomical sense (although he does so later in the epic [XI, 484]); I do think, however, that Milton invites us to view Satan's travels as one aspect of a metaphor having to do with digestion. To see Satan's voyage as intestinal, we need only be reminded of the various references to devouring and swallowing associated with the Abyss. Indeed, the nature of Chaos' "broils" may be properly appreciated if we refer once again to Raphael's warning about the effects of "Surfet" (or "waste") on the digestive system: "Nourishment" when abused turns to "Wind" (VII, 129–130). Chaos is certainly "waste" matter from the Satanic point of view, and the "Wind" that Satan encounters in Chaos is produced as the result of his own "Folly."

Pursuing the journey further, we see that Satan's attempts to fly within the "surging smoak" of the vacuity meet with little success. He begins to "ascend" upon the gaseous currents but then falls and is saved only by "ill chance" when "The strong rebuff of some tumultuous cloud / Instinct with Fire and Nitre hurried him / As many miles aloft" (II, 936–938). Satan's journey, then, results in his becoming part of the digestive process that comprises Chaos' internal disorders.

He participates in the process of decomposition or the giving off of "waste" material in the form of "Wind." Ironically, the particular cloud or "furie" that rebuffs Satan is "Quencht in a Boggie *Syrtis*" (II, 938–939). Its explosive nature is extinguished within a mire that has all the characteristics of residual decay. Consequently, what Satan is giving birth to in his "ascent" may be related to what Chaos is excreting as Satan travels through the "crude consistence" (II, 941) of the Abyss. I am implying that Satan's "successful" egress out of the hole of Chaos fuses the oral-anal-sexual imagery previously discussed and that through such a fusion Satan becomes triumphantly debased.[15]

[15] The fusion of degenerate imagery represented by Satan's voyage occurs even earlier. What may be called the Satanic mode of birth is found in a simile that characterizes the hellish soil and relates directly to the combustible winds

The debased connotations of Chaos are further reinforced by the realm that Satan encounters immediately beyond the Abyss. In close proximity to the opening or "inroad" of Chaos and Darkness, Satan alights upon what "seems a boundless Continent" (III, 421–423). Like Chaos it is a tempestuous place; yet unlike Chaos it is no longer within the hole but is "expos'd." Indeed, the realm into which Satan forcibly exits from the hole of Chaos Milton calls at one point the "bare outside of this World" (III, 74) and then later the "backside of the World" (III, 494). There is little reason to think that Milton would employ such language in his description unless there were an underlying meaning clearly derivable from Raphael's statement about the relationship of "Folly" and "Wind" as the result of over-indulgence. The Paradise of Fools (III, 495–496), whose "blustring" storms and devious winds are caused by the tumultuous clouds engendered in Chaos, is the veritable incarnation of Raphael's analogy.

---

of Chaos. Satan in Hell alights "on dry Land" that burns with solid fire and that is described by Milton in the following manner:

> And such appear'd in hue, as when the force
> Of subterranean wind transports a Hill
> Torn from *Pelorus*, or the shatter'd side
> Of thundering *Aetna*, whose combustible
> And fewel'd entrails thence conceiving Fire
> Sublim'd with Mineral fury, aid the Winds,
> And leave a singed bottom all involv'd
> With stench and smoak: Such resting found the sole
> Of unblest feet.
>
> (I, 230–238)

The vehicle of the comparison is quite involved (for a discussion of the mineralogical processes, see Frank Templeton Prince, ed., *Paradise Lost: Books I and II* [London, 1962], pp. 37n., 113; and Balachandra Rajan, ed., *Paradise Lost: Books I and II* [Bombay, 1964], pp. 19–20; and E. M. W. and P. B. Tillyard, eds., *Paradise Lost: Books I and II* [London, 1956], p. 116n.), and it is made even more complex in its relation to the birth process. The anal and generative characteristics of the figure reinforce each other and relate ultimately to the "intestine" quality of Chaos. The vehicle concerns the forced tearing up of a hill from the promontory Pelorus and the volcanic eruption of Mt. Etna. The means of eruption are of most immediate importance. The hill is torn forcibly because of a "subterranean wind," and Etna erupts because its "combustible"

Like a "Vultur on Imaus bred" (III, 431) consumed with
the need to devour and "gorge" itself on the "flesh of
Lambs or Yeanling Kids" (III, 430–435), Satan "Walk'd up
and down alone bent on his prey" within that "windie
Sea of Land" (III, 440–441).[16] The innocence of the lambs
and the newborn quality of the "Yeanling Kids" fore-
shadow the characteristics of Adam and Eve, upon whom
Satan is prepared to "gorge" himself metaphorically.
Joseph H. Summers says of the image: "The vulture is not
only the type of the bird of prey (and carrion), but also . . .
[has the] remarkable ability to 'engender' from the wind."[17]

The association of the vulture as a bird of prey with the
vulture as a creature who engenders from the wind is implicit
in the remainder of the analogy. For the vulture never
reaches the region of prey but alights on a "barren" and

---

[16] For a similar image of feeding and devouring, cf. "Lycidas":

> The hungry sheep look up and are not fed,
> But swoln with wind, the rank mist they draw,
> Rot inwardly, and foul contagion spred:
> Besides what the grim wolf with privy paw
> Dayly devours apace, and little sed.
>
> (ll. 125–129)

The preoccupation with eating is also associated with the connotations of
swallowing, which becomes a mockery of the birth process. Impregnation
here is the result of starvation: the swelling caused by the "wind" and the "rank
mist" results in inward decay, and the offspring of such a pregnancy is the
spreading of "foul" disease. This, moreover, is combined with the image of
being devoured by an animal of prey. Such motifs are of central importance
in the generative conception of *Paradise Lost*.

[17] *The Muse's Method* (Cambridge, Mass., 1962), p. 55.

---

and "fewel'd entrails" undergo a process of pregnancy and birth: the "entrails,"
whose normal function is excretory, now perform a generative function in their
conceiving of fire. The combustible birth is certainly of an anal nature, for the
eruption of the entrails "leave[s] a singed bottom all involv'd/With stench and
smoak." Finally, the implicit allusion to Typhoeus provides an oral dimension
to the eruption, since Typhoeus (here, the type of Satan [cf. Rev. 20:2–3])
was defeated by Zeus and buried under Mt. Etna. The creation of an opening
thereby results in something unpleasant, unhealthy, and absurdly excretory.

Milton is not alone, however, in associating his subject with an imagery of
degeneration. Specifically, the technique of relating digestion to creation for

"windie" plain (III, 437–439). The connotations of "barren" and "windie" indicate birth as well as appetite. The Satanic mode of generation involves the element of sterility: the process of engendering is ultimately fruitless. The Satanic mode of eating involves the element of devouring: the desire to gorge oneself remains ultimately unfulfilled. Consequently, within the immediate context of the description of Chaos and the realm beyond Chaos, we find the motifs of birth, excreting, and eating as they are related to the diabolic consciousness.

The anality of the Paradise of Fools with its gaseous excretions is complemented by its associations with abortive births. The "fruits" or offspring that will inhabit the region in the future will be deformed and monstrous: "All th'unaccomplisht works of Natures hand, / Abortive, monstrous, or unkindly mixt" (III, 455–456). Birth will be an unnatural process which will never reach healthy fruition but will always be frustrated or "unaccomplisht" in its productivity. "Giants" born of "ill-joynd Sons and Daughters" (III, 463–464) and "Embryo's and Idiots" (III, 474) will crowd this world. Here, creativity will be characterized by the barren and "transitorie" aspects of vanity,

satiric purposes may be seen later in Pope and Swift. We might, for example, consider Cibber's manner of creation in *The Dunciad*:

> One Cell there is, conceal'd from vulgar eye,
> The Cave of Poverty and Poetry.
> Keen, hollow winds howl thro'the bleak recess,
> Emblem of Music caus'd by Emptiness.
>
> (I, 33–36)

Stomach gas as the result of hunger (in *Paradise Lost* such gas is the result of "Surfet") is the medium through which Cibber creates, and the offspring of that creative process are "Monsters" (I, 38); or stated differently, out of Cibber's "chaos dark and deep" comes "new-born" nonsense (I, 55–56). Also the "projector" of Swift's *Tale of a Tub* (*Selected Prose and Poetry*, ed. Edward Rosenheim [New York, 1959], p. 37) indulges in similar creative practices. He informs the reader: "I thought fit to sharpen my Invention with Hunger; and in general, the whole Work was begun, continued, and ended, under a long Course of Physick."

whose "Aereal vapours" will produce nothing but emptiness and illusion (III, 445–447).

Here will come such vain creators as the "builders" of Babel (III, 466–468) and those religious orders impregnated with the illusory desire to attain the height of Heaven. Because the worlds that they have created for themselves are unreal, they will become in their ambition the "sport of Winds" (III, 493). The grandiosity of their illusions will transport them almost to the threshold of Heaven, where

> Saint *Peter* at Heav'ns Wicket seems
> To wait them with his Keys, and now at foot
> Of Heav'ns ascent they lift thir Feet, when loe
> A violent cross wind from either Coast
> Blows them transverse ten thousand Leagues awry
> Into the devious Air.
>
> (III, 484–489)

The pattern of flight and illusory transcendence followed by a sudden unexpected drop suggests Satan's own pretensions to godhead.[18]

These vain and ambitious creators who are frustrated in the birth process because their mode of generation is only an illusion find their prototype in the vanity of Satan. The excremental winds that fly out of Chaos and that transport Satan in his illusory belief that he can find a way out of the hole are the same vapors that will inspire those people who are to inhabit the Paradise of Fools. Such people will attain the heights of transcendence and then be plunged into the depths of absurdity with the result that their creations will be unnatural, abortive, and monstrous.

The most ironic implication of frustrated creativity is that it lies in such dangerous proximity to the divine. That is,

---

[18] Satan's aspirations to godhead have a definite anality about them. According to Norman O Brown (*Life Against Death* [New York, 1959], p. 192), "defiance, mastery, will to power are attributes of human reason first developed in the symbolic manipulation of excrement."

the fool's paradise is "not farr off Heav'n" (III, 888), at whose "dores of Bliss" (III, 525) Saint Peter waits with his "Keys" to reveal that opening from which Satan is now excluded. The fallen angel is bereft of the blissful security he once knew, and his only recourse is uncreative: in his despair he will violate the wide aperture that leads down into the unfallen world (III, 526–529). Bent on his voyage of perversion, he will plummet "down right into the Worlds first Region" (III, 562), which he will attempt to transform into a grave.

With Satan's descent, we have returned to the treatment of the hole and its relation to the Abyss. Satan has emerged from Chaos and has re-entered another hole in his monumental voyage. What his encounter with the Abyss implies and the way it contrasts generatively with God's manner of confronting Chaos are indeed complex. I have in no way attempted to deal fully with the matter here; rather, by considering briefly the contrasting attitudes toward generation, I have merely stressed the dialectical framework of Milton's epic. Because of its complexity, the opposition of glorious and debased creativity will certainly necessitate further analysis. Consequently, in the remainder of my study I shall explore creativity as it manifests itself both in a positive and in a negative manner. My first concern will be with the poet, God, and unfallen man as creators.

The Process of Creation

Chapter 1

The Poet as Creator

WHEN CONSIDERING Milton's handling of creation, one must examine the dialectics as they reveal themselves positively. Creativity is a glorious activity as opposed to the inglorious activity associated with the uncreative process. That is not to say that the process of creation has nothing to do with its antithesis; on the contrary, a consideration of the poet as fallen individual reveals that the positive or glorious aspects of creativity manifest themselves only after the negative aspects have been overcome. That is, the poet must confront the uncreative aspects of the fall in order to create positively. And, as I have noted, even God must confront the chaotic realm from which he has withdrawn his influence before he can create gloriously. In that sense, the process of creation asserts itself poetically and cosmically, and my discussion of the creative process will take into account both the experience of the poet as creator and the experience of God as Creator.

The same basic metaphor controls both experiences: poetically, the metaphor operates on the human or psychological level; cosmically, it operates on the deific level. Thus the process of creation, both in relation to man and to God, depends for its full expression upon the process of uncreation. The only aspect of the creative process that operates without its opposite is creativity in the unfallen world. In contrast to the poet as fallen creator, we shall see the unfallen Adam and Eve as creators in an unfallen environment. The process of creation, then, must finally take into account unfallen creativity, as well as fallen and deific creativity, and all three activities will be explored as they indicate creativity in a positive light.

An examination of the creative process may begin with the poet, as that process becomes apparent in the proems to Books I, III, VII, and IX. The poet immediately reveals a self-consciousness about his craft and what he must do as fallen creator to fulfill the exigencies of his craft. He is aware of his limitations as a human being, yet equally aware of his divine obligations as a poet. In order to meet those obligations, he invokes the aid of the "Heav'nly Muse" (I, 7),[1] through whom he would create a work of the first magnitude, a work that might lead to salvation both in himself and in his audience. With no reservations about the exalted nature of the poet's role, Milton invokes the Muse in a manner that reveals the essential mediatorial function the poet must perform through his poem. Indeed, I shall attempt to show that Milton allusively associates the poet of *Paradise Lost* with those very mediatorial offices that are so important to the theological discussions in Book I, Chapter 15 of the *Christian Doctrine*: I refer to the offices of prophet, king, and priest.[2]

To suggest the nature of his prophetic role, the poet associates himself with Moses first on Horeb and then on Sinai (I, 7). Like Moses the Shepherd (I, 8), who received inspiration from the burning bush on Horeb (Ex. 3), the poet is inspired by the divine light of God. That inspirational source is clearly the same light that Milton apostrophizes in the proem to Book III (ll. 1–6). Here, the poet in complete humility confronts the absolute center of his creative world, the complete antithesis of the darkness which characterizes

---

[1] It is not my purpose to discuss the possible analogues and sources of Milton's Muse. See Merritt Y. Hughes' "Milton and the Symbol of Light," *SEL*, IV (1964), 1–33. The most meaningful ascription has been that of William B. Hunter, Jr., who associates the Muse with the Son ("The Meaning of 'Holy Light' in *Paradise Lost* III," *MLN*, LXXIV [1959], 589–592, and "Milton's Urania," *SEL*, IV [1964], 35–42).

[2] See the Columbia Edition of *The Works of John Milton*, gen. ed. Frank Allen Patterson (1933), XV, 285–303. My interpretation of the poet's role as prophet, king, and priest is drawn from and expands John T. Shawcross' account in "The Metaphor of Inspiration in *Paradise Lost*," *Th'Upright Heart and Pure*, pp. 76–78. The pattern is basic to Milton's thought, as may be seen in Barbara Lewalski's discussion of Christ's role as prophet, king, and priest in *Paradise Regain'd* (*Milton's Brief Epic* [Providence, Rhode Island, 1966], esp. pp. 164–321).

the fallen environment. By means of this light, he will be able to transcend the darkness of his fall in what will amount to the "creation of a new nature."[3] That is, as light is brought out of darkness in the process of creation, he will be inwardly illuminated (I, 22–23; III, 51–53) and will be able to "see and tell / Of things invisible to mortal sight" (III, 54–55). Both the ideas of inward illumination and of revealing what others cannot see, Milton specifically associates with the prophetic role.[4]

But Milton's address to light has still further connotations when viewed within the Mosaic context. As the burning bush was unconsumed, so God's light or "bright essence" is "increate," that is, not only eternal but existing totally by and through itself and creating its "bright effluence" out of itself. In that way, it becomes the unceasing and self-perpetuating source not only of wisdom and protection but of eloquence; for as Moses was "slow of speech" and then through God was inspired to speak eloquently (Ex. 4:10), so is the poet given the power to voice God's Word in order to deliver man from the bondage of his fall. In the allusion to the burning bush of Horeb, moreover, one is inclined to recall Milton's reference to "hallow'd fire" (Isa. 6:6–7) both in the "Nativity Ode" (l. 28) and in *The Reason of Church-Government*. Indeed, Milton achieves something like a prophetic strain when in his tract he conceives of "that eternall Spirit who can enrich with all utterance and knowledge, and sends out his Seraphim, with the hallow'd fire of his Altar, to touch and purify the lips of whom he pleases" (I, 820–821).

If Horeb represents the announcement of delivery, Sinai represents the fulfillment of delivery, at least as it typifies the final salvation through Christ. The prophetic overtones are obvious. As Milton informs us, God spoke through Moses to prophesy "by types / And shadows" the coming of the "destind Seed" (XII, 233). The poet likewise interprets

---

[3] Anne Davidson Ferry, *Milton's Epic Voice* (Cambridge, Mass., 1963), p. 33.
[4] *Christian Doctrine*, XV, 289.

God's will prophetically by revealing through types and shadows the entire course of human history. But Sinai also anticipates the poet's other roles. The poet's priestly function, for example, is discernible in Moses' character as intercessor, an office Milton pointedly associates with the priest, both in *Paradise Lost* (XI, 20–25) and in the *Christian Doctrine*.[5] Indeed, like Moses, who received the law on Sinai, the poet becomes an inspired mediator between God and man, for man can neither gaze upon God (Ex. 19:21) nor hear his voice (Ex. 20:19) without dying.

Furthermore, in the *Christian Doctrine*, Milton associates the experience on Sinai with the kingly function;[6] and *Paradise Lost* with its reference to the ordaining of laws on Sinai (XII, 230) implies no less. In his kingly role, the poet acts as earthly guide by instructing man how to prepare himself in this kingdom for his existence in the next. Michael's precepts to Adam (for example, "add Faith, / Add Vertue, Patience, Temperance, add Love" [XII, 582–583]) are relevant here. In accordance with this idea, the allusion to Sinai may be associated with the allusion to Sion (I, 10). Like David, who wished to construct a temple for God's laws after Nathan was inspired at Sion (2 Sam. 7), the poet wishes his poem to reveal how man should arrange his temporal affairs (compare Isa. 2:3, "for out of Sion shall go forth the law"). Such also was Christ's purpose when he informed man about the conduct of his immediate existence (Mat. 5–7), and in the kingly sense, David is a type of Christ.[7]

Milton goes even further, however, in defining the kingly role, for in the *Christian Doctrine*, he associates that role, not so much with outward, as with inward law and cites Heb. 10:16 ("I will put my laws into their hearts") and Luke 17:21 ("behold the kingdom of God is within you") as substantiation.[8] The parallel in *Paradise Lost* may be

[5] Ibid., xv, 291, 295, 297.
[6] Ibid., xv, 299.
[7] Ibid., xv, 297.
[8] Ibid., xv, 299.

found immediately in Milton's preference as poet for "th'upright heart and pure" over "all Temples" (I, 18), a preference that has a direct bearing upon the way in which Christ as king will rehabilitate God's "Umpire Conscience" (III, 195) by destroying Satan's works in man (XII, 394–395). The poet's kingly function, then, is very important to our understanding of Milton's allusions to Sinai and Sion. As I shall attempt to show, his allusions to Siloam are of equal importance in defining the poet's priestly function.

Through the waters of Siloam, the poet will be inspired to sing of re-creation and the eternal life. While, on the one hand, the spiritual effluence of God allows the physically blind poet to be prophetically inspired, the waters of Siloam purify the poet for his sacerdotal office. By associating himself with "*Siloa's* Brook" (I, 11 and III, 30), the poet deliberately causes his "sacred Song" (III, 29) to suggest the character of one inspired by the "Oracle of God" (I, 12), the place of divine revelation. Despite his blindness, his song concerns renewed sight and the healing of blindness through Christ (I, 11–12).[9] In the same manner that Michael cleansed the vision of fallen Adam so that Adam could experience the rebirth process culminating in the Savior, Jesus' baptismal cleansing of the blind man's eyes with the holy waters of Siloam (Jn. 9:7) symbolizes the sacerdotal vision of rebirth the poet receives.

The idea of lustration, furthermore, continues in Siloam's "flowrie Brooks" that "wash" the "hallowd feet" of Sion (III, 30–31). Replete with overtones of anointing in order to make sacred, the imagery suggests both the anointing of Christ's feet (Luke 7:38) and Christ's anointing of his

---

[9] For similar readings see David Daiches, "The Opening of *Paradise Lost*," *The Living Milton: Essays by Various Hands,* ed. Frank Kermode (London, 1960), pp. 62–63; and Harry F. Robins, *If This Be Heresy: A Study of Milton and Origen* (Urbana, Illinois, 1963), p. 161. Jackson I. Cope, *The Metaphoric Structure of Paradise Lost* (Baltimore, 1962), pp. 152–154, also views the transition from Sinai to Siloam as a movement that takes into account the differences between Moses and Christ. Neither Daiches nor Cope, however, considers the allusion to Sion in its kingly context.

disciples' feet (Jn. 13:5). Milton's attitude toward such lustration is revealed quite clearly in the "Sixth Elegy," in which he views the poet as a "priest" "shining with sacred vestment and lustral waters" (ll. 65–66). As priest, then, the poet reflects Christ's Messianic role (and, as we have seen, Christ's office as intercessor).[10] Consequently, we might say that with the allusion to Siloam, the poet's role has moved from the personal (prophet) to the worldly (king) to the divine (priest).

As a counterpart of the threefold function, the purpose of the Muse is first to inspire the poet to sing of creation, since the Muse is intimately associated with that act by which the Spirit of God "with mighty wings outspread / Dove-like satst brooding on the vast Abyss / And mad'st it pregnant" (I, 20–22). Because the poet's desire is to be initiated into the ways of cosmogony, he says, "Instruct me, for Thou know'st" (I, 19). Desiring that knowledge given to prophets on the secret tops of mountains, he hopes in turn to educate his people in the ways of creation. Indeed, through such means, Moses sang of the "Beginning," of the way in which the "Heav'ns and Earth / Rose out of *Chaos*" (I, 6–10). But the poet goes even further: he wishes to become imbued with the divine omniscience which allowed the Spirit to be an actual part of the grand creative event. Such firsthand knowledge antedates the creative act itself, for the poet's source of inspiration existed "before the Sun / Before the Heav'ns" (III, 9–10), "Before the Hills appeerd, or Fountain flow'd" (VII, 8). In defining the purpose of the Muse, therefore, the poet reveals to us not only that the force is of "Heav'nlie" origin (VII, 7), but that it existed before all creation, that it was present at the creation, and that it imparts through revelation an intimate knowledge of the creative process.

[10] The office of priest is still further defined in the *Christian Doctrine* (XV, 291) as one embodying the voluntary sacrificing of oneself to God. As I shall attempt to discuss in much greater detail, the poet heroically fulfills this aspect in his willing descent to Chaos and reascent to light.

Such revelation is further enhanced by the image of the Muse in the precosmogonal state. In this "time" before all time, the poet's Muse "conversed" with her sister "Eternal Wisdom," "and with her didst play / In the presence of th'Almightie Father, pleas'd / With [her] Celestial Song" (VII, 9–12). These lines suggest, I think, some kind of relationship between "play" and creativity. Certainly, a "Celestial Song" arises implicitly out of the Muse's conversing with and playing with her sister. What exactly the word "play" implies in this context becomes clear when we consider that Wisdom and inspiration are the objectified aspects of God's own creativity playing delightfully before him. Although in Freudian terminology "play" is an act central to all artistic creation,[11] in Christian terminology only God may engage in and take pleasure in such "play." Indeed, one might say that the pleasure God takes in viewing the Muse and her sister is similar to the pleasure he receives in his ability to inspire through the Word. Perhaps the deific sense of "enjoyment" in beholding the "play" or manipulation of one's animating powers as they are objectified in one's presence relates to the joy the Father experiences in beholding his manifested reflection in the Son (III, 384–389). Specifically, as the Father inspires through the Muse as a manifestation of his own powers, he creates through the Son as the effectual embodiment of his own creativity. Although he is alone in secret from all eternity (VIII, 405–406), he engages in a dialogue with himself, communicates with himself in order to create. Were man to assume that he could please himself with such "play," the result would be pride: he would view his reflection in the water and love it.[12] If he is to be so inspired, man must avoid all possi-

---

[11] See Sigmund Freud, "The Relation of the Poet to Day-Dreaming," *On Creativity and the Unconscious*, ed. Benjamin Nelson (New York, 1958), pp. 44–54.

[12] In contrast to God's self-sustenance, to his ability to be "entertained" or satisfied with these aspects of self playing and thus creating before him, is Adam's incomplete nature. Although Adam has at his command all living creatures "To come and play before [him]" (VIII, 372), he requires an external

bilities of narcissism. Unlike God, who is the source of inspiration rather than the recipient of it, man must be inspired from without, and both the means by which he is inspired and his reaction to being inspired are essential constituents of the full creative process.

As John T. Shawcross has demonstrated, inspiration in *Paradise Lost* takes on decidedly sexual overtones.[13] The "passive, dormant, cold female factor" representative of the poet's psyche receives God's Spirit as the "dynamic, creative, fiery male force."[14] The metaphor is one of a generative union in which the roles of male (poet) and female (Muse) are reversed.[15] As Satan inspired Eve by whispering in her ear while she was asleep, the Muse inspires the poet by bringing her message "nightly to [his] ear" (IX, 47). Involved is the idea of impregnation in sleep, a phenomenon repeated throughout the poem in the figures of both Adam and Eve. Adam sleeps and then awakes

---

force in Eve as a counterpart of himself to unite with him in creativity. After the fall, the idea of "play" comes to have debased associations. According to Harold Fisch ("Hebraic Style and Motifs in *Paradise Lost*," in *Language and Style in Milton*, ed. Ronald David Emma and John T. Shawcross [New York, 1967], pp. 49–50): "The Jewish commentators had glossed the word *play* (*saheq*) as a reference to sexual orgies following the violation of the divine command. This again serves to relate the corruption of Adam and Eve to the archetypal frame of the Exodus." (Cf. IX, 1027–1028, and Ex. 32:6.)

[13] "The Metaphor of Inspiration," p. 76.

[14] Ibid.

[15] Ibid. Beatrice M. Hinkle (*The Re-Creating of the Individual* [New York, 1923], pp. 344–353) characterizes the sexual connotations of the creative process. The soul is the feminine element, and there is a union of the masculine elemental self with the feminine counterpart. According to Dr. Hinkle, a sort of "psychic coitus" ensues. "It is this play with himself, which is at one and the same time a sort of symbolic incest relation and autoerotic process" (cf. Milton's use of the "play" idea discussed above). As previously stressed, with respect to Milton as a Christian poet, it is extremely important to note the belief that the masculine inspirational force is not a product of the self or of the imagination but proceeds *externally* from God. The consequences of such a creative act, as Dr. Hinkle describes it, are iterated in the poem: Satan's masculine counterpart copulates with his feminine counterpart and produces Death in a sinful act. As explained above, however, God's "play" with his own faculties is glorious and results in divine creation. The Christian poet, finally, copulates with the masculine force and begets the work of art.

to find Eve created out of him; Eve sleeps and then awakes
to find a paradise created within her because of the grace of
God. Paradoxically, however, each figure is "wakeful"
while he sleeps: Adam, for instance, visually experiences
the creation of Eve despite the fact that he is asleep. Adam
relates how he "sought repair / Of sleep," which, he says,

> instantly fell on me, call'd
> By Nature as in aid, and clos'd mine eyes.
> Mine eyes [God] clos'd, but op'n left the Cell
> Of Fancie my internal sight.
>
> (VIII, 458–461)

The poet likewise is "awake," that is, aware of the inspirational process while he is asleep. As a metaphor for the poet,
the "wakeful Bird" (III, 38) is always ready for flight, always
ready for inspiration. The internal "Cell" of vision is always
"op'n" despite the physical posture.

Appropriately, the blind poet as bird[16] "Sings darkling"
(III, 39), that is, sings within the confines of his own darkness,
"and in shadiest Covert hid / Tunes [his] nocturnal Note"
(III, 39–40). The emphasis here is upon the secrecy of the
creative act (compare Moses' being inspired on the "secret
top" of Horeb and Sinai [I, 6–7]): it is an act which cannot
be violated or intruded upon but must occur in the silence
of hidden recesses away from the disturbance of prying
eyes. Within the hidden "Covert" the bird, like God, who
in his secrecy (VIII, 427) never sleeps but is always watchful
and who creates in the likeness of a bird, is "wakeful" the
night long (IV, 602–603).

The poet's wakefulness, then, involves his receiving the
"Word" from the Muse, who "Visit'st [his] slumbers
Nightly" (VII, 29) and who in her "nightly visitation"
"dictates to [him] slumbring, or inspires / Easie [his] unpremeditated Verse" (IX, 22–24). It is very easy to mistake
exactly what the poet experiences if these lines are read
solely as an indication that the poet's process of creation is

---

[16] This image is fully explored by Ferry, pp. 25–33.

spontaneous. We would thus see the poet's work "rise" effortlessly out of himself without the least hint of industry involved. That, of course, is not the case at all. We know that Milton expended a great deal of labor and energy in the composition of his poem,[17] and, as I shall discuss, such an idea is inherent in the work itself. So how, then, should we respond to Milton's use of the word "unpremeditated"?

Perhaps something of an answer can be found in W. B. C. Watkins' idea that the creative process in *Paradise Lost* is paradoxical, that it takes on both a sense of spontaneity and a sense of preparation and consideration.[18] Paradoxically, Milton uses "two distinct methods in dramatizing Creation . . . the spontaneous existence as if by magic with the spoken word and natural . . . evolution through time."[19] This approach, as Watkins applies it to the creation of the world, might also be applicable to the poet's own creative process. According to Watkins,

> both metaphors are in the opening paragraph of the poem, where, as if by a power inherent in the words as they are voiced, "Heav'ns and Earth / Rose out of Chaos" (I, 9–10); whereas a moment later we find that the heavenly spirit for an indeterminate period "Dove-like satst brooding on the vast Abyss / And mad'st it pregnant" (I, 21–22).[20]

Perhaps, then, through the possible application of these metaphors to his own creative act, the poet desires to give the illusion of spontaneity. As interesting as such an idea might be, "unpremeditated," I think, means something entirely different from what we would ordinarily expect.

[17] Ida Langdon, *Milton's Theory of Poetry and Fine Art* (New Haven, 1924), pp. 62, 162. See also Northrop Frye, *The Return of Eden* (Toronto, 1965), pp. 7–9; and Allan H. Gilbert, *On the Composition of Paradise Lost* (Chapel Hill, North Carolina, 1947), pp. 163–171.

[18] *An Anatomy of Milton's Verse*, p. 62.

[19] Ibid.

[20] Ibid., pp. 62–63. Cf. also the construction of Pandaemonium, which is first worked over and then rises suddenly as if by magic.

To understand its true meaning within the framework of the full creative process, let us consider the second metaphor that Watkins mentions, the Spirit of God "brooding on the vast Abyss."

In *Paradise Lost*, "brooding" becomes a metaphor for the act of causing birth and for the act of meditating. Thus, the Spirit's "brooding" over Chaos is simultaneously impregnation and cognition. As it represents the creative process, the meditative act applies to the poet also. For example, the poet, as part of the creative process, must "feed on thoughts, that voluntarie move / Harmonious numbers" (III, 37–38). After inspiration, the poet must *digest* what he has been given: there is a fusion of the ideas of meditating or brooding and chewing or feeding as means of creativity.[21] The result of feeding or meditating is the willful or "voluntarie" "moving" of "Harmonious numbers." "Voluntarie" thus implies that which is deliberate or deliberative, an assertion of the will. And "move" is synonymous with the creative act of God's "moving" upon the face of the waters or "brooding" upon the Abyss in order to create.[22] "Move" and "brood" or "move" and the meditative process thereby also become synonymous.

When at last we reconsider the lines, "And dictates to me slumbring, or inspires / Easie my unpremeditated Verse" (IX, 23–24), we can see the meaning in a new light. "Unpremeditated" does not suggest a form of creation completely devoid of meditation; rather, it characterizes a stage in the creative process that precedes meditation and that by extension has nothing to do with the act of thinking. As a Christian poet, Milton is saying that his verse cannot be self-initiated (to say otherwise would, of course, result

[21] The idea of mental and physical digestion and rumination as that aspect of the creative process which is preceded by inspiration appears, among other places, in Bede's account of Caedmon, which Milton knew. (See Milton's *Commonplace Book*, I, 381.)

[22] See Daiches, p. 66. "One patristic rendering of the biblical word 'moved' is actually incubabat." See also Donald Davie, "Syntax and Music in *Paradise Lost*," *The Living Milton*, p. 73.

in pride): he must wait patiently until after he is inspired to "brood" upon what he has received. That "unpremeditated" aspect of the creative process thus is "easie" because it does not require labor as the meditative aspect does and because it comes from the Celestial Patroness. The poet receives his inspiration passively and then works or meditates upon his previously unthought of (or "unpremeditated") ideas "dictated" to him during slumber. Helen Gardner defines the creative process when she talks of Milton's having "conceived, meditated, and finally brought to completion, his poem."[23] Conception results from inspiration, which is followed by meditation (or gestation) as a prelude to birth.[24] The full import of "unpremeditated" makes itself felt when we consider the decidedly contrasting manner in which unfallen man engages in song.

Spontaneous and instantaneous, the song of unfallen man requires no meditation and is therefore not "unpremeditated" but "unmeditated" (v, 149). The distinction is obviously significant. Meditation involves labor, and labor is God's punishment upon fallen man. Since Adam and Eve are not fallen, they are not required to labor at their song (v, 145–150), to "meditate" or "brood" as the fallen poet must.[25] Their "eloquence" is "prompt" and immediate like the

[23] *A Reading of Paradise Lost* (London, 1965), p. 16.

[24] See also Daiches, p. 67: "Milton is thus taking an established tradition of the Spirit of God brooding over the waters at the creation and associating it with the poet brooding over his material in the process of poetic creation." For the idea of the poet as a laborer, see E. M. W. Tillyard, *The Miltonic Setting, Past and Present* (London, 1938), p. 63. In light of this bipartite process of inspiration and then meditation as preludes to birth, Harris Francis Fletcher's statement in *Milton's Rabbinical Readings* (Urbana, Illinois, 1930), p. 127, that "brooding" is the "first step in the process of Creation" may prove somewhat misleading when applied to the poet. Fletcher views the paradox of instantaneous creation as opposed to "mediated" creation in terms of the theory of accommodation. He says that "Milton conceived of the Creation as having actually occurred instantaneously, but to angels or men, it can only appear as a process" (p. 123).

[25] Thus, as Arnold Stein (*Answerable Style* [Minneapolis, 1953], p. 87) says, the poetry of the fallen world is "labored." Cf. the "love-labor'd song" that the "night-warbling Bird" sings (v, 40–41) in Eve's Satan-inspired dream. Satan inspires dreams which are characteristic of the fallen world he will inhabit.

offspring of unfallen Nature. Their music is that "perfect Diapason" which Milton celebrates in "At a Solemn Musick." The fallen poet, on the other hand, has been initiated into that realm which unfallen Adam and Eve, for the present, know nothing about. I refer, of course, to the chaotic Abyss that resides within the poet and that fallen man must confront in order to create. The two halves of the cosmic metaphor operate significantly: the Spirit of God's "brooding" becomes the fallen poet's laborious meditation, and the Spirit of God's confrontation with the Abyss while in the act of "brooding" becomes the fallen poet's confrontation with the Chaos within him as a concomitant of creation.

It is that aspect of the creative process which is so fascinating and so heroic. Now we can more fully understand what Milton means when he talks about his "adventrous Song" (I, 13) upon which he stakes all and through which he "attempts" what has never been attempted (I, 16). His journey to the nether world risks all the dangers and horrors of the descent, and it is only by means of the divine creative power that he is able to "escape" the "*Stygian* pool" (III, 14),

> Taught by the Heav'nly Muse to venture down
> The dark descent, and up to reascend.
>
> (III, 19–20)

He must resort to Chaos and create himself out of that Chaos; he must resort to that part of him which has been uncreated in the fall and attempt to issue out newly created. (The uncreated Satan, we remember, attempted the same act in Book II, but his "birth," although apparently successful, was really not so because it was performed without God's aid.) Because it is successful, the poet's dangerous journey associates him with what Joseph Campbell calls the fate of the hero:

> The disciple has been blessed with a vision transcending the scope of natural human destiny, and amounting to a glimpse of the essential human nature of the cosmos.

Not his personal fate, but the fate of mankind, of life as a whole, the atom and all the solar systems, have been opened to him;

he becomes the "Cosmic Man."[26] He "delivers" his race out of bondage through the archetypal pattern of descent and reascent, and his performance of such a task becomes certainly heroic in its demands. Involving a lifetime of preparation, the task associates the poet immediately with the complete heroic experience.

In mythic thinking, the experience of the hero is generally referred to as the "nuclear unit of the monomyth," and it involves three stages: "separation," "initiation," and "return."[27] Northrop Frye characterizes the idea of the "separation" by referring to the "Sixth Elegy," in which Milton "distinguishes the relaxed life permitted the minor poet who writes of love and pleasure from the austerity and rigorous discipline imposed by major powers."[28] The poet must purify himself so that he can become a "fit vessel of inspiration."[29] He sets himself apart from the common indulgences of man and prepares himself for his great task, and only when he is ready, fully mature, does he begin. Thus the poet himself refers to the rigorous nature of that heroism, which becomes the "better fortitude / Of Patience and Heroic Martyrdom" (IX, 31–32).

Such fortitude and patience the poet exhibits by the trial of waiting, of "long choosing, and beginning late" (IX, 26), until he can forge an "Heroic name" for "Person" and for "Poem" (IX, 40–41). According to Frye, the "simultaneous pull in Milton's life between the impulse to get at his poem and finish it and the impulse to leave it until it ripened sufficiently . . . must have accounted for an emotional tension in Milton of a kind that we can hardly imagine."[30] That the

---

[26] *The Hero with a Thousand Faces* (New York, 1949), p. 234.
[27] Ibid., p. 30.
[28] *The Return of Eden*, p. 8.
[29] Ibid.
[30] Ibid., p. 9.

poet dramatically imagines it for us, however, may be seen when he wonders if the self-imposed trial of years will dampen his "intended Wing" (IX, 44–45), thus "Deprest"; and well it may, he maintains, if he alone be responsible for the inspiration. But such, we recall, is not the case, since the initial impetus of the poem derives from the exterior power, the "Celestial Patroness" (IX, 21). Consequently, even after the personal trial of "separation" has been withstood, God rather than the Christian poet receives the glory. "A Christian has to work hard at living a Christian life; yet the essential act of that life," says Frye, "is the surrender of the will; a poet must work hard at his craft; yet his greatest achievements are not his but inspired."[31]

The second or initiatory stage of the monomyth involves the attempt at a conquest to be "Won from the void and formless infinite" (III, 12), the "*horror vacui*," as C. G. Jung calls it,[32] of oneself. The poet becomes a Redeemer who must destroy himself, uncreate himself, so that he may conquer himself in birth. After being impregnated by the divine exterior power, the poet withdraws into himself to "brood" or meditate in introversion.[33] "Initiation," then, is the paradoxical act of destroying and creating through meditation (a feeding on thought or a symbolic digesting) as a means to rebirth.

Exactly what the psychological experience of descent involves may be ascertained in two ways: from what Milton describes in his poetry and from the way in which Milton's description becomes typical of other cultural and mythical patterns. The second way is helpful in illuminating the first, especially since Milton so often works with similar patterns as a means of enriching his own work. That is, in dealing with a motif such as "initiation," we are invited by Milton's own practices to consider the familiar idea of the hero's willingness to undergo hardship (here, psychological and

[31] Ibid., p. 7.
[32] *Psyche and Symbol*, ed. Violet S. de Laszlo (New York, 1958), p. 133.
[33] Jung, *The Psychology of the Unconscious*, p. 415.

spiritual) in order to restore health to a world of corruption. Familiar patterns present themselves at every turn. The plight of the Redcross Knight to attain holiness in *The Faerie Queene* comes immediately to mind, but for Milton's purposes the experience of Jesus in *Paradise Regain'd* is even more to the point. Like the Savior's pilgrimage in the wilderness, the poet's "pilgrimage" into Chaos is sacrificial: it serves to show fallen man how to regain paradise. Culturally, the pattern finds compelling relationships in the figure of the shaman.

To my knowledge, Maud Bodkin first saw the shamanistic elements in Milton's concept of the poet.[34] Like the shaman, the poet cures his people by first undergoing corruption himself. The initiation of the shaman is one of returning to the womb to be digested, to be taken into the monster's jaws (the *vagina denta*) and then of finding one's way out.[35] In Milton's poem, one finds egress from Death's maw through Christ, of whom the Christian poet as Redeemer becomes the type. Digestion is a prelude to rebirth in the process of creation. The poet conforms to Mircea Eliade's definition of a shaman as one who

> reproduces a traditional mystical pattern. The total crisis of the future shaman [that man who attempts to become a shaman], sometimes leading to . . . madness, can be evaluated not only as an initiatory death but also as a symbolic return to the precosmogonic Chaos, to the amorphous and indescribable state that precedes any cosmogony . . . It follows that we may interpret the psychic Chaos of the future shaman as a sign that the profane man is being "dissolved" and a new personality being prepared for birth.[36]

A further phase of the initiatory ritual is that of dismember-

[34] *Archetypal Patterns in Poetry* (New York, 1958), p. 225.
[35] Mircea Eliade, *Rites and Symbols of Initiation*, trans. Willard Trask (New York, 1958), pp. 14, 51.
[36] Ibid., p. 89.

ment, in which the bodies of the shamans are dismembered before rebirth.[37] In Christian terminology, such a dismemberment has apocalyptic overtones. Thus we have the bodily dismemberment of Lycidas before he is reborn. "Ay me!" laments the shepherd,

> whilst [Lycidas] the shoars and sounding seas
> Wash far away, where ere thy bones are hurl'd,
> Whether beyond the stormy *Hebrides*
> Where thou perhaps under the whelming tide
> Visit'st the bottom of the monstrous world.
> ("Lycidas," ll. 154–158)

Milton is indeed fearful of such dismemberment, and as a Christian poet he implores his Muse to save him from the fate of Orpheus, who was totally dismembered by the bachanalian revelers (compare "Lycidas," ll. 58–63):

> drive farr off the barbarous dissonance
> Of *Bacchus* and his revellers, the Race
> Of that wild Rout that tore the *Thracian* Bard
> . . . .
> nor could the Muse defend
> Her Son. So fail not thou, who thee implores:
> For thou are Heav'nlie, she an empty dream.
> (*PL*, vii, 32–39)

In his symbolic return to the chaotic state, the poet desires to have the protection of the Christian Muse, and like Lycidas and Arion ("Lycidas," l. 164) to be saved from complete destruction. For, as Jung maintains, the "psychic substratum . . . that dark realm of the unknown . . . threatens to become the more overpowering the further [one] penetrates into it. The psychological danger that arises here is the disintegration of the personality into its functional components."[38] Through God, therefore, the poet wishes to

---

[37] Ibid., pp. 91–92.
[38] *Psychology and Alchemy*, trans. R. F. C. Hull (New York, 1953), pp. 322–323.

be able to withstand his own dismembering and annihilating energies and be reborn in his return to light. After experiencing "all that pain" (IV, 271)—to borrow Milton's reference to Ceres—in his underworld journey, the poet desires to "revisit now with bolder wing" (III, 13) that light which is the source of all creativity. Like Lycidas, he wishes to "mount high" ("Lycidas," ll. 172–173) and become a Redeemer who guards "all that wander in that perilous flood" ("Lycidas," l. 185).[39]

The poet's mounting high leads to the final stage of the monomyth—the "return." "Everywhere there is this spiritual regeneration, a palingenesis, which [finds] its expression in the radical change in the mystes' existential status."[40] Paradoxically, the entire journey of descent and reascent is both agonizing and ecstatic (compare "At a Vacation Exercise," ll. 33–36). In his journey downward and then upward again to light, the poet experiences the "anguish" and "ecstatick fit" that accompany "holy vision" and "pensive trance" ("The Passion," ll. 41–42).

For the Christian poet, the reascent is not to the realm of earth but to the realm of Heaven, as equally dangerous a venture as the descent.[41] Thus, after the poet has, through

---

[39] For further instances of the dismemberment motif, see *Areopagitica*. I quote the passage to point out the associations here of dismemberment and the apocalypse: "Truth indeed came into the world with her divine Master, and was a perfect shape most glorious to look on: but when he ascended, and his Apostles after him were laid to sleep, then strait arose a wicked race of deceivers, who as that story goes of the *Aegyptian Typhon* with his conspirators, how they dealt with the good *Osiris*, took the Virgin Truth, hewed her lovely form into a thousand peeces, and scatter'd them to the four winds. From that time ever since, the sad friends of truth, such as durst appear, imitating the carefull search that *Isis* made for the mangled body of *Osiris*, went up and down gathering up limb by limb still as they could find them. We have not yet found them all . . . nor ever shall doe, till her Masters second comming; he shall bring together every joynt and member, and shall mould them into an immortal feature of loveliness and perfection" (II, 549). Here we have a further dismemberment by the representatives of Chaos and the reuniting of those members by an apocalyptic event. The poet as shaman psychologically undergoes the same process.

[40] Eliade, *Rites and Symbols*, pp. 112–113.

[41] According to Eliade (*Rites and Symbols*, p. 78), the "initiatory theme of

Raphael, described the War in Heaven, he addresses the Muse:

> Up led by thee
> Into the Heav'n of Heav'ns I have presum'd
> An Earthlie Guest, and drawn Empyreal Air,
> Thy tempring; with like safetie guided down
> Return me to my Native Element.
>
> (VII, 12–16)

In recounting the War in Heaven, the poet has been permitted to view the timeless workings of a transcendent world, a world "above th'*Olympian* Hill . . . Above the flight of *Pegasean* wing" (VII, 3–4). He has beheld in ecstatic vision the symbolic warring of good and evil and the overcoming of evil by good.[42] Through his Muse, he has been able to breathe the air of Heaven, that is, be heavenly inspired despite his earthly limitations. And after the experience of such a vision, he has been able to descend to his own limited environment, because again he has been guided in safety by his Muse.

Consequently, the poet has traversed the gamut of the poetic experience. He has undergone destruction and creation, and with the help of his Muse he has symbolically overcome his fallen condition and given birth in that triumph to a work of art, an exemplar by which a fit audience may also find a way to undergo a similar process of creation. Man, then, will be able to enact his salvation through the work of the poet, whose personal experiences have the mediatory function of revealing to the chosen few the secret workings of the creative process on a poetic plane. In its various aspects, however, that process is reflected not only on the poetic level but on the cosmic level also.

---

ascent to Heaven differs radically from that of the swallowing monster; but, although in all possibility, they originally belonged to different types of culture, we today often find them together in the same religion; even more, the two themes sometimes meet during the initiation of a single individual."

[42] See J. H. Adamson's "The War in Heaven: Milton's Version of the *Merkabah*," *JEGP*, LVII (1958), 690–703, for an interesting account of the poet's ecstatic experience as a "Merkabah rider."

Chapter 2

Glorious Creativity

GOD AND UNFALLEN MAN

P ROBABLY THE MOST glorious and celebrative aspects
of the creative process concern God as Creator[1] and
unfallen man as creator. The two aspects, divine and
human (before the fall), complement each other in fulfilling
the idea of a creativity that is entirely unpolluted. Indeed,
the second aspect, characteristic of Adam and Eve in Eden,
follows naturally from the first, characteristic of God's
cosmogonal act. And a discussion of glorious creativity
might logically move from the cosmic dimension to the
unfallen human dimension, being constantly aware that each
dimension represents a type of celebration that we as fallen
individuals can experience only through Milton's powers as
mediator.

In considering God's creation of the universe, one
immediately recognizes an exuberance of detail that is
reinforced by a verse symphonic and bounteous in its
effects.[2] The entire account reverberates with a sense of

[1] My purpose here will not be to discuss the sources of Milton's account of
cosmic creation. Aside from those studies mentioned in the Introduction, n. 10,
the following offers a brief list of those who have explored the hexaemeral
tradition both generally and with particular reference to Milton: Arnold
Williams, *The Common Expositor* (Chapel Hill, North Carolina, 1948); George
Wesley Whiting, *Milton's Literary Milieu* (Chapel Hill, North Carolina, 1939);
Frank Egleston Robbins, *The Hexaemeral Literature* (Chicago, 1912); George
Coffin Taylor, *Milton's Use of Du Bartas* (Cambridge, Mass., 1934); and Sister
Mary Irma Corcoran, *Milton's Paradise with Reference to the Hexameral Background*
(Washington, 1945). For a discussion of Milton's cosmogony, see Curry,
Milton's Ontology, Cosmogony, and Physics; for rabbinical analogues, see Fletcher,
Milton's Rabbinical Readings. Still interesting, if erroneous, is Saurat's relating
of Milton's concept of creation to the Zohar in *Milton, Man and Thinker* (New
York, 1925).

[2] E. M. W. Tillyard (*The Miltonic Setting, Past and Present*, pp. 70–71) notes
that the feeling of fertility pervades the "very verse-technique of *Paradise Lost* . . .

excitement, a sense of energy being released and exulting in its own volition. All creatures glory in the creation; all creatures instinctively celebrate the creative act, from Uriel, who ironically and unsuspectingly instructs the disguised Satan in the ways of creation, to Raphael, who instructs Adam in his Maker's works. In Raphael's narration, creation immediately follows upon destruction: the "detriment" caused by the fall of the angels is "repaired" by God's creation of "Another world" (VII, 152–155).[3] And that world, to be inhabited by the race of man, is created through the agency of the Son, God's effectual might, accompanied by God's "overshadowing Spirit" (VII, 165). The Son is to "ride forth, and bid the Deep / Within appointed bounds be Heav'n and Earth" (VII, 166–167).

As the manifestation of God's creative power, the Son becomes the Word whose utterance results in life: "speak thou," God says to the Son, "and be it don" (VII, 164). The verb "be" in its various forms becomes the predicate of creation: to utter the imperative of life is to cause life, and the entire account of the cosmic creation reflects that vocal act. Book VII is the narrative of the spoken word: instantaneous with the utterance is the creation, for "Immediate are the Acts of God, more swift / Then time or motion" (VII, 176–177). But so that those acts can be comprehended by man, they are placed within the context of temporal and spatial measurement.

The Son issues from Heaven's gates bent on his glorious and creative mission as Satan in Book II issued from Hell's gates bent on his inglorious and uncreative mission. The divine agent of creation, as an issue of his world, Heaven, finds his counterpart in the debased agent of uncreation, as an issue of his world, Hell. Both are "born" out of their respective worlds, and both confront the chaotic element which

Milton's verse paragraph was dictated by his inner needs . . . [and] one of them was precisely this feeling for fertility . . . He must prolong his sentences . . . till they are ripe to dropping."

[3] Such, of course, is the major pattern of the poem: creation springs from destruction as good springs from evil.

will become the medium of their respective creative and uncreative ends. In the process of creation, "Heav'n op'n'd wide / Her ever during Gates . . . to let forth / The King of Glorie in his powerful Word / And Spirit coming to create new Worlds" (VII, 205–209).

Chaos must be tempered in order that creation may ensue, and that tempering implies the making of boundaries (VII, 167) and the regulating and ordering of that which was previously unregulated and disordered. As Uriel had said to Satan, when Chaos heard the voice of the Son, "wild uproar / Stood rul'd, stood vast infinitude confin'd" (III, 710–711). Creation, then, becomes the imposition of finitude upon wasteful infinitude, and uncreation becomes the intemperate return of finitude to infinitude.[4]

After quelling the waves of the Abyss and causing the "Deep" to be peaceful, thereby ending "discord" (VII, 216–217), the Son rides into Chaos in the type of that "Chariot of Paternal Deitie" (VI, 750) that carried him on his mission to destroy the angels. Now the Chariot of God will be used to transport the Son in his mission to create the world. With his "golden Compasses"[5] the Son proceeds "to circumscribe / This Universe, and all created things" (VII, 225–227). As the counterpart of the all-creating voice that tempers, the compass is that which describes precise and discernible boundaries:

> One foot he center'd, and the other turn'd
> Round through the vast profunditie obscure,
> And said, thus farr extend, thus farr thy bounds,
> This be thy just Circumference, O World.
>
> (VII, 228–231)

---

[4] It is the attempt of finite creatures to attain the infinite that results in the process of uncreation.

[5] For the rabbinical analogues of this idea, see Fletcher, *Milton's Rabbinical Readings*, p. 106; and for a full discussion of Milton's use of the "Golden Compasses," see George Wesley Whiting, *Milton and This Pendant World* (Austin, Texas, 1958).

The shape of perfection is revealed in that which is shapeless: obscurity gives way to that which is rationally perceivable. In a realm where extension was previously meaningless, it now has geometrical significance. Circumference becomes an emblem of order in a world of anarchy: man is soon to have his own circumference, his own just boundaries beyond which he cannot go without disobeying. The conscious mind as a rational entity will be sustained in this emblematic circle until it overreaches itself and its boundaries, and encounters the Abyss beyond. The Son in his geometrical act has circumscribed the "O" or round "World," thereby differentiating it symbolically from the square of Heaven (x, 381), and the uniting of the two realms results in impregnation and birth.[6]

The initial process is completed in the image of the Spirit of God's spreading out his "brooding Wings" on the "watrie calm," in which he "infus'd" "vital vertue" and "vital warmth / Throughout the fluid Mass, but downward purg'd / The black tartareous cold infernal dregs / Adverse to life" (vii, 234–239). After the calming and ordering, there is the impregnating, the imbuing with vitality that which is passive and dormant, followed by the purging of the impure and the molding and globular collecting of the pure (vii, 239–240) into similar masses. Those which are not similar are "disparted" to their respective places (vii, 240–241). Inherent in the description is the sexual metaphor of the male (God) impregnating the female (matter).[7] That same basic pattern characterizes the inspiring of the poet and, in its degenerate form, Satan's infusing of his poison into all those he successfully tempts.

The impregnation activates those seminal or latent powers within the mass to undergo the birth process within itself, so that when God's voice calls for forms to appear from the

---

[6] See John F. Huntley, "Aristotle's Physics as a Gloss on *PL* viii. 152," *PQ*, xliv (1965), 131.

[7] Ibid.; and Fletcher, pp. 126, 148; Watkins, *An Anatomy of Milton's Verse*, p. 63; Curry, *Milton's Ontology, Cosmogony, and Physics*, pp. 105–106.

mass, such forms will yield themselves almost as a result of their own energy and volition. Those elements adverse to impregnation are purged downward and become characteristic of Hell because of their infernal quality. Consequently, all that is produced, all that comes forth as the result of responding obediently to God's beckoning, is pure, healthy, and unfallen.

After the "fluid Mass" has been prepared, God's voice articulates the world into existence. Light is first created as it springs from the "Deep," "Sphear'd in a radiant Cloud" (VII, 243–247), thereby dividing Night from Day. Symbolically, the physical "exhaling" of light from darkness reiterates the creative pattern of good springing from evil. The act, as is each of God's acts, is celebrated symphonically by the angels. The first dividing leads to a second dividing, so that the "Firmament" divides the "Waters from the Waters" (VII, 263) in order to contain the "loud misrule / Of Chaos" (VII, 271–272).

The third act involves the completion of the partially formed earth. Before it is fully created, the earth is like the fertilized ovum floating in the "genial moisture" (VII, 282), comprising the "Womb . . . / Of Waters" (VII, 276–277).[8] The earth, then, as it is described in this decidedly generative language, is in the embryonic or prefetal state of development (VII, 277), surrounded by the fertilizing waters and ready at God's call to bring forth life. Paradoxically, the earth is also the mother, as well as the embryo; the dual roles complement each other:

> over all the face of the Earth
> Main Ocean flow'd, not idle, but with warm
> Prolific humour soft'ning all her Globe,
> Fermented the great Mother to conceave,
> Satiate with genial moisture.
> (VII, 278–282)

---

[8] Huntley, p. 131.

The earth, both as mother and as that which is to be born, is penetrated by that life-giving power which God had infused into quieted Chaos.

And at God's word, the huge Mountains emerge, "and thir broad bare backs upheave / Into the Clouds" (VII, 285–287).[9] The great mother gives birth to her offspring the "tumid Hills" (VII, 288): their tumescence implies their fertility. After the gathering of the seas as the result of an even further process of dividing (land from water), God commands the earth to "Put forth the verdant Grass, Herb yeilding Seed, / And the Fruit Tree yeilding Fruit after her kind; / Whose Seed is in her self upon the Earth" (VII, 310–312). The life cycle of birth and regeneration from earth to plant to seed is begun. The entire process resembles a dance, an immediate springing to life of organisms: scarcely have the flowers bloomed when "Forth flourish't thick the clustring Vine, forth crept / The smelling Gourd, up stood the cornie Reed" until at last "Rose as in a Dance the stately Trees" (VII, 317–324). All Nature responds to God's omnific voice as in a celebration of organic birth. "God saw that it was good. / So Eev'n and Morn recorded the Third Day" (VII, 337–338).

The fourth day represents a continuation of the process of division: "Lights" are created "to divide / The Day from Night" (VII, 339–341). These luminary spheres, such as the sun, the moon, and the stars, become signs of cyclical rebirth within time: they record the "Seasons," the "Dayes," and the "circling Years" (VII, 341–342), all of which incidentally the poet in his blindness cannot experience (III, 40–43). (Rather, he must undergo an internal sense of rebirth whose characteristics are those of a world without time.) After the creation of the sun and the moon and after the heavens have been "sowd with Starrs . . . thick as a field" (VII, 358), God generates new offspring on the fifth day.

Thus from the "Waters" spring "Reptil" with their

[9] Cf. Milton's "A Paraphrase on Psalm 114": "The high, hugh-bellied Mountains skip like Rams."

"abundant" "Spawn" (VII, 387–388). The waters generate the creeping animals, which create more offspring out of themselves. Likewise, birds are created to fly in the firmament, whales to inhabit the seas (VII, 389–394), and God blesses his offspring by saying: "Be fruitful, multiply, and in the Seas / And Lakes and running Streams the waters fill; / And let the Fowl be multiply'd on th'Earth" (VII, 396–398). After the initial creative or energizing impulse, Nature becomes self-perpetuating and abounds in healthy and prolific birth. Following the creation of plants and seeds, the life cycle of plants begins; following the creation of fish, the fish perpetuate themselves instinctively; following the creation of birds, the birds perpetuate themselves instinctively; even the celestial spheres, the stars, the moon, and the sun, once created, move cyclically of their own volition. The creative urge fosters itself through further re-creation and procreation. It expresses itself by the perpetual repetition of its own act.

In a magnificent passage, the sixth and final day of creation is recounted. The earth literally becomes the all-bearing mother out of whose womb the animals are born. Triumphantly the animals rise or spring up from the womb that bred them, so that their upward motion itself symbolically enacts the creative or rising motion of birth as opposed to the uncreative motion of the fall. As an obedient mother, at God's command, the earth "obey'd, and strait / Op'ning her fertil Woomb teem'd at a Birth / Innumerous living Creatures" that "out of the ground up rose" (VII, 453–456). The rising motion is reiterated throughout the passage: the cattle are "upsprung" (VII, 462); the stag "Bore up" his head (VII, 469–470); the Behemoth "upheav'd / His vastness" (VII, 471–472). And all these creatures become part of God's perfection because they are born in the environment of the unfallen world.

The *obedience* of Nature to God results in abundant and healthy birth. We are presented with an imagistic celebration of the very process of generation:

The Tawnie Lion, pawing to get free
His hinder parts then springs as broke from Bonds,
And Rampant shakes his Brinded main.

(VII, 464–466)

Struggling to free itself from its womb, energy is symbolically
emancipated by form.[10] The earth yields its offspring as a
mother yields her child. Forms from the underground world
of gestation assert their own strength and their own exuberance. They throw the crumbled earth above them (VII, 468)
in a revelation of their generated state. As a result, "Air,
Water, Earth / By Fowl, Fish, Beast, was flown, was swum,
was walkt / Frequent" (VII, 502–504). This summary exhibits
the procreative urge and the liberating motion of birth.
The energy contained in the stressed monosyllabic reiteration
of "Fowl, Fish, Beast" suddenly breaks forth in the respective
physical movements implied by the nouns. Form releases
energy that results in motion: birds fly, fish swim, beasts
walk.

The great creative hierarchy, however, has yet to be
completed: "There wanted yet the Master work the end / Of
all yet don" (VII, 505–507). The upward motion of birth
must be completed in man, who "might erect / His Stature,
and upright with Front serene / Govern the rest" (VII, 508–
510). Raphael's account of God's creating man is expanded
by Adam. The first account is related from an objective point
of view: God, according to Raphael, formed Adam from
the dust and then "inspired" Adam by breathing the "breath
of Life" into his "nostrils" (VII, 524–526). The second (and
fuller) account is related from a personal point of view,
thereby greatly expanding the biblical narrative. Adam's
relating of his own experience of birth is an implicit glorification of the Creator and an exultation in the opportunity to
relate that process: we have, then, not only the poet's account

---

[10] Frye, *The Return of Eden*, pp. 49–50; and Helen Gardner, *A Reading of Paradise Lost*, p. 73. Cf. W. H. Auden's "Mundus et Infans" (ll. 1–2) and Blake's "The Tyger" for the idea of "form" emancipating "energy."

of poetic creation, Uriel and Raphael's account of cosmic creation, but also man's account of personal creation.

Adam's task is difficult, "for who himself beginning knew?" (VIII, 251), and yet Adam proceeds:

> As new wak't from soundest sleep
> Soft on the flowrie herb I found me laid
> In Balmie Sweat, which with his Beames the Sun
> Soon dri'd, and on the reaking moisture fed.
> Strait toward Heav'n my wandring Eyes I turnd,
> And gaz'd a while the ample Skie, till rais'd
> By quick instinctive motion up I sprung,
> As thitherward endevoring, and upright
> Stood on my feet.
>
> (VIII, 253–261)

The metaphor asserts itself in the sleeping and waking pattern central to the idea of birth in *Paradise Lost*. Sleeping is the prebirth state of pregnancy and gestation, and waking is the birth state of coming to awareness. The "Balmie Sweat" recalls in its fluidity the waters of life from which the world is born. The cosmic image associated with the earth floating in its "genial moisture" (VII, 282) is suddenly transferred to the human level in the figure of the newborn Adam.

Adam instinctively looks "toward Heav'n" as the place of his spiritual origin and the dwelling place of his Creator. His visual motion is directly accompanied by a physical motion: Adam symbolically re-enacts the birth process of rising upward. He is suddenly quickened by a sense of his own limited omnipotence, which reflects God's total omnipotence. His looking toward Heaven inspires him in that direction, since all God's creatures tend upward toward God. Man will be able to attain that height only through obedience to his Maker.

Adam, like Satan in Hell, surveys his new environment; unlike Satan, however, he does not see a torturous place but a temperate and beautiful place, a place of birth, of living and moving and walking and flying, rather than a place of death. After examining his environment, the newly created being examines himself, and discovers that he can walk and run, speak and "name" or identify the objects around him. And yet he still feels unsatisfied, because, as he says: "But who I was, or where, or from what cause, / Knew not" (VIII, 270–271). He recognizes objects outside himself but does not know who he is himself, and like Eve who had to be told by the voice who she was (IV, 467–469), Adam must also receive such knowledge from his Creator. He instinctively knows that he did not cause himself to be created but that he is the work of an exterior force greater than he, the work of a "Maker" "in goodness and in power præeminent" (VIII, 277–279). And, like all unfallen creatures, he instinctively wishes to "adore" his Creator (VIII, 280).

His reaction to his inability to ascertain the nature of his birth and of the force that generated him is to sit down "pensively" and to "brood" upon his state. With the help of the creative force, his pensiveness will be fruitful; inspired thought will cause birth. First, however, he must sleep again, return mentally to the gestation stage as a prelude to the birth of a new awareness (VII, 286–290). He is afraid that he is about to return entirely to the precreative environment of dissolution, "When," as Adam says,

> suddenly stood at my Head a dream,
> Whose inward apparition gently mov'd
> My fancy to believe I yet had being,
> And liv'd.
>
> (VIII, 292–295)

Adam is far from being uncreated; he is, rather, undergoing a new creation, whereby he will become a human being responsible for his actions, for he will know that his actions concern not only himself but his offspring. In sleep he is inspired by an "apparition" that will guide him to his paradisiacal state, the "Garden of Bliss" (VIII, 295–299). And as Michael is to lead fallen man by the hand out of

Eden, this divine shape guides Adam "by the hand" into Eden, into the blissful environment of the unfallen consciousness.

The trip represents a flying dream: as the poet is led upward in his flight to paradise, as Eve is borne upward in her ecstatic flight after she has dreamed that she has eaten the Fruit (v, 86–92), Adam experiences this sense of paradisiacal climax. Yet, unlike Eve, whose dream results in a postclimactic depression (and even unlike the poet, who must also descend), Adam remains in a world of complete fulfillment, of complete fertility (VIII, 300–306). The trees are bursting with birth, with "fairest Fruit," and even then Adam is tempted to "pluck and eat" as Eve was immediately tempted when she saw her form in the water (VIII, 306–309).

In the unfallen realm, the dream becomes the reality: transcendence is not illusory as it is in the Satanic world, but that which is experienced in dream is a prefiguration of the actual world. Sleep merely typifies what will be experienced outside sleep rather than providing an escape from the oppressions of reality. Thus Adam "wak'd, and found / Before [his] Eyes all real, as the dream / Had lively shadowd" (VIII, 309–311). That same pattern is repeated in the creation of Eve: Adam sleeps while the process of creation ensues and awakes to find it true. God will bring to Adam his "other self / [His] wish exactly to [his] hearts desire" (VIII, 450–451). In the unfallen world, wish becomes reality.

Sleep instantly falls on Adam as God creates Eve from Adam's rib, and as Adam had beheld paradise in his dream as a prefiguration of reality, he beholds woman in his dream before he awakes. But, as Adam says, "She disappeared, and left me dark, I wak'd / To find her . . . When out of hope, behold her, nor farr off, / Such as I saw her in my dream" (VIII, 478–482). Both in the instance of paradise and Eve, the dream-wish is realized through God's willingness to provide for his unfallen creatures. (Only in the fallen world where God's Providence is renounced does the fulfillment of the dream-wish become self-deluding, an insubstantial projection of the self.) In the unfallen world, God's Providence is everywhere, expressing itself as an essential aspect of his creativity from his first act of generation to his creation of man on the sixth day.

After that creative act, God ascends "unwearied" to Heaven to behold the "new created World" and to see "how good" and "how fair" it is, "Answering his great Idea" (VII, 548–557).[11] Appropriately, the satisfaction he takes in his own work is reflected in the cosmic celebration, the "acclamation and the sound / Symphoneous of ten thousand Harps" (VII, 558–559), that accompanies his return. Just as the creative act was represented by an harmonious dance (VII, 324), God's performance elicits an overwhelming symphonic acclamation. Harmony responds to harmony in musical congratulation, and, as I shall discuss in greater detail, the celebration of the Creator by the created redounds upon the offspring, so that all who participate in the creative event are thereby glorified.[12] The effect is one of complete reverence in response to the new cosmic birth: "The Planets in thir stations list'ning stood, / While the bright Pomp ascended jubilant" (VII, 563–564). (Indeed, such reverence looks forward to the second great nativity—the birth of Christ. Then, too, the stars will "stand fixt in stedfast gaze" as part of the symphonic celebration in "On the Morning of Christs Nativity," [ll. 69–70 and 93–132].)

On the seventh day God rests and causes the Sabbath to become holy (VII, 591–593), and the Sabbath is kept with "*Halleluiahs*" celebrating the Creator:

---

[11] God from his infinite Wisdom has produced an ideational construct resulting from some ideal and transcendent cognitive formulation. See Prov. 8:30 and Fletcher, pp. 109, 119–120; and Harry F. Robins, *If This Be Heresy*, p. 170. There is, in addition, apparently an association of the "answering" of an "Idea" with the Demiurge's fulfilling of the ideal represented by the Platonic Forms in the *Timaeus*. Such an idea is related to the concept of God's foreknowledge (Merritt Y. Hughes, ed., *Paradise Lost* [New York, 1962], p. 181n).

[12] For an interesting variation of the symphonic idea fused with the creative, cf. Dryden's "A Song for St. Cecilia's Day."

Creation and the Six dayes acts they sung,
Great are thy works, *Jehovah*,

. . . .

greater now in thy return
Then from the Giant Angels; thee that day
Thy Thunders magnifi'd; but to create
Is greater then created to destroy.

(VII, 601–607)

The consummation of God's act, as well as the consummation
of Book VII, is a prayer to God in his creative capacity.
Inherent in the celebration is the awareness of the event
that preceded the creation: the destruction of the rebel
angels. In both instances God returned through his Son in
triumph to his native seat. The second return is now celebrated as a more glorious occurrence than the first because
the creation of good is a greater act than the uncreation of
evil.

A discussion of glorious creativity, however, is incomplete
without a consideration of Adam and Eve's creative practices.
And the extended result of God's creative act is nowhere
more fully expressed than in the account of prelapsarian
man. To appreciate Adam and Eve as creators, we must
move from the cosmic to the human dimension; the best
way of effecting that movement is through Satan. For
through Satan we will be able to understand more clearly
what Eden represents.

With the Arch-Demon, then, let us first approach the
garden from the outside and come "to the border"

Of *Eden*, where delicious Paradise
Now nearer, Crowns with her enclosure green,
As with a rural mound the champain head
Of a steep wilderness, whose hairie sides
With thicket overgrown, grotesque and wild,
Access deni'd.

(IV, 132–137)

The insulated world (compare the *hortus conclusus* of the Song of Solomon) that Satan approaches becomes in itself a living organism that takes on characteristics of bodily functions. The deliberate use of "hairie sides" that are "grotesque and wild" in order to describe the "steep wilderness" leading up to Eden places the whole description within the human context. And such an anatomical reorientation would be by no means unusual for a poet who was familiar with the metaphoric technique of *The Purple Island.*

The bodily image operates in at least two ways: sexually and psychologically. Sexually, Satan assumes the posture of an assault: he is about to attempt to penetrate and thereby defile a pure, unfallen, womb-like area that shelters and sustains what exists within. Psychologically, Satan represents the upsurge of the subconscious or chaotic forces that are attempting to overwhelm the bliss of the innocent personality. Indeed, the implication of Chaos is in the very description: the "overgrown" or untempered "thicket," the "grotesque and wild" "wilderness" are integral parts of the scenery. Finally, that wilderness will become the fallen or chaotic environment into which Adam and Eve will be forced to descend after they fall. Then, the "delicious Paradise," which is now the reality of Adam's flying dream, will deny access to all corrupt creatures who inhabit the world of the "steep wilderness."

Once inside its confines, Satan views the womb world he is about to corrupt. He surveys "In narrow room Natures whole wealth," a veritable "Heav'n on Earth," a "blissful Paradise" (IV, 207–208). The self-enclosed area becomes an insular retreat which gives life to those who live off its abundance. The garden is itself "a living body," as Isabel MacCaffrey says, "a being with its own metabolism."[13] Indeed, underlying Milton's description of Eden is a "physiological vocabulary" reinforcing the idea that Eden is an organism.[14] Supplying life-giving water to the organism,

[13] *Paradise Lost as "Myth,"* p. 149.
[14] Ibid. See also Svendsen *Milton and Science*, p. 134.

"Southward through *Eden* went a River large" that passes underneath the ground and travels in currents: "through veins / Of porous Earth with kindly thirst up drawn, / Rose a fresh Fountain, and with many a rill / Waterd the Garden" (IV, 223–230). "Veins" and "thirst" are, of course, human characteristics, so that the substance that quenches is also the substance that becomes the lifeblood of the garden. Such a river recalls the life-giving waters of Heaven, for, as Don Cameron Allen reminds us, "here is life without end, the eventual awakening to life"[15] that sustains not only the womb world itself but the inhabitants of the womb as well. Moreover, the organism is further sustained in its union with the sun, whose "fervid Raies . . . warm / Earths inmost womb" (V, 301–302). Even in Nature, male (sun) and female (earth) join as a representation of the "two great Sexes [which] animate the World" (VIII, 151).[16] A process of sexual union ensues between the elements, and the result of such a union in the unfallen world is immediate and glorious impregnation.

Indeed, the ever-present generative awareness asserts itself in every phase of the unfallen relationship between Adam and Eve:

> he in delight
> Both of her Beauty and submissive Charms
> Smil'd with superior Love, as *Jupiter*
> On *Juno* smiles, when he impregns the Clouds
> That shed *May* Flowers; and press'd her Matron lip
> With kisses pure.
>
> (IV, 497–502)

The mere act of smiling in Eden results metaphorically in impregnation: as the sun impregnates the womb world of earth, Adam's smiling with love upon Eve is compared with

---

[15] *The Harmonious Vision: Studies in Milton's Poetry* (Baltimore, 1954), p. 99.

[16] See Summers' excellent discussion of this concept in *The Muse's Method*, pp. 87–111. Purvis E. Boyette also considers unfallen sexuality in detail in "Something More About the Erotic Motive in *Paradise Lost*," *Tulane Studies in English*, XV (1967), 19–30.

Jupiter's (sun) smiling upon Juno (air),[17] thereby impregnating the clouds. The sexual union of Nature's elements is
reflected in human sexual union, which is reflected again
in the natural world. And that natural world is embodied
in human, physiological, and biological terms: a direct and
unifying intercourse exists between unfallen man and unfallen Nature, in which the functions of one are reflected
in the functions of the other. Nor is that holy communion
to be broken until man falls and alienates himself from
Nature. As a result, Eden becomes a timeless world of perpetuated bliss, where every action has creative possibilities
"To all delight of human sense expos'd" (IV, 206).

As inhabitants of paradise, Adam and Eve are part of its
grandeur and its magnificence. They reflect in their de-
meanor their unfallen situation void of corruption: they are
"erect" and "clad" with "native Honour," that is, dressed
in the nobility of the nakedness in which they were born.
They reflect in their severity and purity the divine "image
of thir glorious Maker" (IV, 288–292). Since they have no
knowledge of their nakedness, they do not have to conceal
"those mysterious parts," for no shame existed then of any
of Nature's creations, and no hypocrisy defiled the idea of
purity (IV, 312–318). The inequality of male and female adds
to their glorification, for, since the implication of the "two
great Sexes" is that the female play the passive role and the
male play the active role, the second must be superior to the
first. And, ideally, such is exactly the situation between the
unfallen Adam and Eve: the male dominates and the female
obeys with "sweet attractive Grace" (IV, 295–301).

The very description of the unfallen couple has associations
with what may be called their creative occupation (gardening) and their entire sexual relationship. For example, the
way in which Eve "wore" her "tresses" is described as

> Dissheveld, but in wanton ringlets wav'd
> As the Vine curls her tendrils, which impli'd

[17] Shawcross, ed., *The Complete English Poetry*, p. 300n.

> Subjection, but requir'd with gentle sway,
> And by her yeilded, by him best receiv'd,
> Yeilded with coy submission, modest pride,
> And sweet reluctant amorous delay.
>
> (IV, 306–311)

Almost imperceptibly the description of the way in which the tresses are handled evolves into a description of the way in which female yields to male in the union of love. As the "dissheveld" state of the tresses implies the need for "subjection" to the "gentle sway" of some type of support lest the "wanton ringlets" get completely out of hand, so Eve must be sexually dominated by the superior force and thus yield herself, as the hair would yield itself to a higher rule. The mode of that submission would be characterized by the submission of the hair, which would resist order with a "sweet reluctance." Such an implication reveals a good deal about the love relationship itself: sexual union in the unfallen world is not mere dalliance but has the higher and more creative purpose of the submission of disorder or wantonness to the temperance of a higher or superior order. And, remarkably, we shall find that the act of ordering, of subduing wantonness characteristic of the sexual union, is exactly what defines the creative occupation of the unfallen gardeners. In a world in which the properties of Nature correspond physiologically to the attributes of man, we are not surprised to find Milton comparing the state of Eve's tresses to the "Vine" which "curls her tendrils." The comparison is indeed appropriate, for as Eve's tresses imply the need for order, unfallen Nature in her femininity requires the same attention.

As gardeners, Adam and Eve must "reform" Nature's "wanton growth" (IV, 625–629):

> On to thir mornings rural work they haste
> Among sweet dews and flowrs; where any row
> Of Fruit-trees over woodie reach'd too farr
> Thir pamperd boughs, and needed hands to check

Fruitless imbraces: or they led the Vine
To wed her Elm; she spous'd about him twines
Her marriageable arms, and with her brings
Her dowr th'adopted Clusters, to adorn
His barren leaves.

(v, 211–219)

Following the lead of the "sovran Planter" (IV, 691), who
is likewise the Creator, the unfallen gardeners in their own
way perform the creative act of effecting union and of
tempering what is otherwise "wanton" like Eve's ringlets
or like Eve herself without the sexual superiority of Adam.
They support Nature's growth, supply a means by which the
"Vine" may productively curl her "tendrils," "check" the
"Fruitless imbraces" of Nature, so that those "imbraces"
when properly bestowed may cause life to come forth. The
underlying image undeniably relates to the basic sexual
metaphor of propagation. Adam and Eve cause a wedding to
occur between plant and plant, so that barrenness may be
avoided. Consequently, there is a creating of fruitful growth
through sexual union and a creative ordering of what is
disordered as God creates life from Chaos.

Adam and Eve thereby have a very important generative
occupation: they effect on a minor scale what God effects on a
major scale. Even in unfallen Eden, man must channel
growth and maintain a sense of order, so that Nature's
overwhelming abundance does not result in wastefulness,
"for Nature here / Wantoned as in her prime, and plaid at
will / Her Virgin Fancies, pouring forth more sweet, / Wild
above Rule or Art; enormous bliss" (v, 294–297). Before
the fall, Nature's spontaneous fertility must be controlled.
As gardeners, Adam and Eve must deliver Nature of her
"enormous" birth.

If Adam and Eve fulfill their role as gardeners by taking
an active part in that creative occupation, they fulfill their
role as lovers by participating actively in love's delights.
Indeed, love in the unfallen environment is such a glorious

thing, that God deliberately creates for his lovers a "blissful Bower" (IV, 690),[18] whose sanctity remains undisturbed by every other creature: "Beast, Bird, Insect, or Worm durst enter none; / Such was thir awe of Man" (IV, 704–705). This retreat within the retreat of Eden has overtones of God's holy Hill, where the Father dwells alone and unapproached from all eternity. In their own sacred "inmost" place of seclusion, the unfallen couple perform the mysteries of love. They withdraw into the privacy of the enclosed area to create as the poet withdraws into himself to meditate. However, Adam and Eve's withdrawal does not have the same implications as the poet's: their enactment of the introverting pattern does not represent a return to the chaotic state but a return to a womb from which birth issues effortlessly and naturally.

Here they would perpetuate the race of man; here "strait side by side were laid . . . nor *Eve* the Rites / Mysterious of connubial Love refus'd" (IV, 741–743). There is no need to conquer a destructive and annihilating element as the result of this withdrawal. Rather, the process requires the mutual love, both sexual and emotional, of both parties and the fulfillment of that love in the procreative act. Eden is no place of sterility; abstinence is the decree of the Destroyer, the Uncreator, who would frustrate the union of love.[19]

The poet, then, celebrating that union in the same language with which he bids "Hail" to the "holy Light," the source of all creativity, bids "Hail" to "wedded Love, mysterious Law, true sourse / Of human ofspring, sole proprietie, / In Paradise of all things common else" (IV, 750–752).[20] Like the animating "Fountain" (III, 8) of the poet's own inspirational source, the mysterious source of human animation

---

[18] Cf. Arcrasia's bower in *The Faerie Queene*, II. The positive aspects of Milton's "blissful Bower" are made so by the unfallen nature of its inhabitants. When man falls, Eden becomes merely a place subject to destruction.

[19] See Boyette: "in Paradise physical love, because spiritual, was more exquisite than anything we can know in our fallen condition," p. 26.

[20] "Hail," of course, is also Gabriel's greeting to Mary in the annunciation and thereby takes on associations of the promised regeneration.

and human offspring becomes the "Perpetual Fountain of Domestic sweets" (IV, 760). The dialectic views both these sources, poetic and biological, with the highest reverence, for they are both of divine origin; they both inspire; and the miraculous operations of both are one of the mysteries of life.

The same sense of reverence with which the poet views his own inspiration and the inspiration that perpetuates mankind is revealed in Adam and Eve's reverence for their Maker. In their *Te Deum* they praise God and celebrate God, appropriately, as a Creator when they sing their orisons each morning. The prayer is directed both to God and to his creations, or, rather, is directed to God through his creations. The apostrophic structure of the prayer becomes an aspect of the creational idea: Adam and Eve animate apostrophically God's creations to praise their Maker. They first identify the Progenitor with his offspring: "These are thy glorious works, Parent of good" (v, 153), and then they call upon the offspring, all God's creations, from angels to animals to the heavenly bodies, sun, moon, and stars, "to extoll / Him first, him last, him midst, and without end" (v, 164–165) and "resound / His praise, who out of Darkness call'd up Light" (v, 178–179). Praise will perpetuate more praise until there is an endless symphony of praise for the creative Divinity.

Each element animated through invocation by Adam and Eve's initial orison, "Made vocal by [their] Song, and taught his praise" (v, 204), will celebrate God in its own way: a pattern of symbolic motion equivalent to vocal celebration is thereby effected. The planets "move / In mystic Dance not without Song" as a means of praise; the "Elements," which are the "eldest birth / Of Natures Womb," run in "Perpetual Circle" as a means of praise; the "Mist and Exhalations" rise and fall to advance God's praise; the winds breathe "soft or loud," and the pines wave their tops back and forth as a means of praise; birds ascend, fish glide, and beasts walk to sound his praise (v, 177–201). The entire universe is set in motion as at the creation of the universe to celebrate the Creator. Such is Adam and Eve's "various style" (v, 146):

the "ceasless change" of circular motions, rising and falling motions, sound modulations, backward and forward motions, becomes not only a symbolic celebration of God's creativity but paradoxically an expression of the harmonious and patterned changelessness of the eternal world. That eternity of changeless change, of "grateful vicissitude,"[21] evoked by the orison of the unfallen Adam and Eve contrasts with the inharmoniousness and haphazard change of Chaos, into which Adam and Eve will be introduced after their fall.

Adam and Eve's prayer causes "Heav'ns high King" to pity them and to send Raphael the "sociable Spirit" to "advise [Adam] of his happie state" and "warn him to beware / He swerve not too secure" (v, 219–238). When Adam sees Raphael moving toward him, he says to Eve:

> But goe with speed,
> And what thy stores contain, bring forth and pour
> Abundance.
>
> (v, 313–315)

Eve in turn gathers for the dinner "Tribute large, and on the board / Heaps with unsparing hand" (v, 343–344). As established by the words, the meaning of the action here takes on complex overtones. Eve is not merely serving food: the language commits us to view her actions on a larger scale. Bringing forth from one's stores and pouring abundance in *Paradise Lost* is repeatedly associated with the generative activities of Nature (iv, 254–255, 730–731; vii, 451; ix, 620–621). Even in *A Mask*, Nature is seen as a "cateress" whose food or "provision" is related to the birth of offspring (ll. 762–766). I am hardly suggesting that in preparing and serving food Eve is likewise generating offspring. What I am suggesting, however, is that the language describing her activities obliges us to view her within a generative context.

The exact significance of that context will present itself,

[21] Cf. Summers' discussion in *The Muse's Method*, pp. 71–86.

I think, when we see that food in the unfallen environment takes on decidedly spiritual overtones. As the offspring of Nature, food, in fact, becomes the emblem of God's body or the body of the world created in six days through the agency of the Son, and Eve likewise becomes the maternal means by which man may receive the sustenance of God the "Nourisher" (v, 398). Eating represents a spiritual or life-giving act, an assimilation of the food of God for the purposes of spiritual as well as bodily sustenance. At this point, then, the exact creational overtones of Eve's "bringing forth" and "pouring abundance" may be discerned, especially when we consider the nature of Raphael's salutation to Eve.

Raphael addresses Eve in this manner: "Hail Mother of Mankind, whose fruitful Womb/Shall fill the World" (v, 388–389). His greeting reverberates throughout history: for as Eve provides the food of God's body in the form of Nature's offspring, Mary, "second *Eve*" (v, 387), will provide the food of Christ's body, and the place for engaging in such nourishment will be the Communion table. Then man will be "restored" after the fall or provided again through Christ with "store," that is, with the food of unfallen Nature's birth. As the counterpart of that future event, however, the present circumstances assume a definite sacramental dimension. Indeed, the "board" upon which Eve "heaps" her "Tribute large" becomes figuratively the first of Communion tables at which is assimilated the Eucharist (literally, "a giving of thanks" and therefore a "Tribute") in the unfallen world. Adam and Eve are to participate in the Communion with their visitor Raphael, for whom eating is an act of "transubstantiation" (v, 437–438) and whose visit for man signifies not only a social communion but a spiritual Communion as well.[22]

---

[22] For a full discussion of Eucharist symbolism in the Renaissance, see Malcolm Ross, *Poetry and Dogma* (New Brunswick, New Jersey, 1954). I should also like to note that my reading of the breakfast scene merely considers some of the metaphorical aspects of Milton's language. My interpretation must be "placed" within the scene's decidedly comic and domestic framework, which is treated by Kranidas in *The Fierce Equation*, pp. 147–154. But even Kranidas stresses the

With this final reference, the animating occupations of Adam and Eve are even further suggested: as a complement of God's cosmic creativity, Adam and Eve's creativity finds expression not only in gardening, in love-making, and in praying, but also in eating. Through each of these activities, unfallen man enacts in his own limited environment what God has enacted in his grand cosmogony. If man were to continue in such activities obediently, he would eventually ascend to ultimate union with God (VII, 155–161). But man is to fall, and the idea of creativity is to find its counterpart in uncreativity before man is allowed to discover a means of regeneration.

---

fact that the scene does not "exist independent of the epic background" (p. 148), and ultimately the scene in its entirety tends away from the "limited and domestic" (p. 152).

The Process of Uncreation

Chapter 3

The War in Heaven

UNION AND DISUNION

AVING DISCUSSED in some depth the concept of creation in *Paradise Lost*, I shall now consider the idea of uncreation. The fittest place to begin, of course, is with the War in Heaven, where the entire process of uncreation originates. To be properly appreciated, however, that process should be viewed against the background of Milton's dialectical stance. That is, to know what uncreation implies, one should know, at least cursorily, what relation it has to creation and re-creation in Heaven. Consequently, I shall first attempt to establish the conditions and repercussions of Satan's rebellion and then attempt to suggest the significance of Satan's uncreative motives.

The immediate act which motivates Satan to disobey God is the "begetting" of the Son by the Father. God voices his "Decree" before the assembled angels:

> This day have I begot whom I declare
> My onely Son, and on this holy Hill
> Him have anointed, whom ye now behold
> At my right hand; your Head I him appoint.
> (v, 603–606)

Presumably, Milton refers here not to the literal creation of the Son upon that day but to the figurative creation of the Son as king.[1] The generation of the Son is therefore a figurative act. That is, the

> Father can be properly said, in one sense of the word, to beget the Son, because in proclaiming that Son ruler and vicegerent over the angels, he is metaphorically generating a new thing—a king.[2]

[1] See Ps. 2 and its various exegeses.
[2] Maurice Kelley, *This Great Argument* (Princeton, New Jersey, 1941), p. 105.

In this instance, creation becomes intimately associated with the idea of kingship. Indeed, the various aspects of godhead take on overtones of birth.

We might, for example, consider God's statement, "your Head I him appoint." The "Head" refers not only to the hierarchical seat of authority but to the center of ideas, and God's very creation of the universe through the agency of the Son represents the conceptual fulfillment of his "great Idea" (VII, 557). As the center of ideas, then, the head becomes intimately associated with creativity, with the manifestation of the Wisdom (VII, 9–10) that characterizes God as Logos (see Pr. 8:22–31 and Jn. 1:1–5). The dramatic counterpart of such an idea, of course, may be found in Satan's giving birth to Sin through his head (II, 752–758). If that act parodies cosmic creativity, it likewise contrasts with God's fathering of the angels through the Son (appointed as "Head") and with his saving of man. In the last instance, the Son as Savior (and therefore "Head of all mankind") "fathers" man in place of Adam, the original progenitor (III, 285–286). (Here, incidentally, the Son's animating function is further reinforced through images of roots and transplantations. Because of the Son, man "As from a second root shall be restor'd" [III, 288], so that man will "live in [his Savior] transplanted, and from [him]/Receive new life" [III, 293–294].)

Generation is further associated with physical location in the Son's having been consecrated on the "holy Hill." Because of its associations, God's mount takes on the characteristics of the mythopoeic mountain which is the source of life.[3] The "holy Hill" contains a "Cave," and appropriately enough that cave does have an "issue" or offspring: "Light issues forth, and at the other dore / Obsequious darkness enters" (VI, 4–10). The mount also "exhales" the "ambrosial Night," and from it "spring" both "light and shade" (V, 642–644). Exhalation and springing

[3] Mircea Eliade, *Cosmos and History*, trans. Willard R. Trask (New York, 1959), pp. 12–17.

forth are gestures that metaphorically suggest the birth process. The pattern of cyclical return (represented by the "perpetual round" of light and dark), coupled with the obsequiousness or metaphorical obedience of the "offspring," finds its debased counterpart in the periodical return of the hellhounds to devour the womb of the mother Sin (II, 795–802). Here the generative image of return in obedience is perverted from that which is creative and sustaining to that which is destructive and devouring. The way in which the concept of return characterizes the angelic union with God will now become apparent.

According to John T. Shawcross, Milton causes the idea of "union" in *Paradise Lost* to have sexual significance: it represents a sort of "mystic" uniting or joining, as Shawcross says, "in terms of sexual intercourse."[4] And, indeed, this union pervades the entire poem. Consider, for example, the "intercourse" between the Spirit of God and Chaos to create the universe; between the Muse and the poet to create the poem; between God and man to engender offspring (compare VIII, 604); and between angel and angel "Union of Pure with Pure / Desiring" (VIII, 627–628). "Union," continues Shawcross, "will create, the opposites being fused into that which partakes of both . . . ."[5]

Such an idea also extends "creatively" to the Son's position of power and authority at God's "right hand," for through the Son the angels are "united as one individual Soul" (V, 610). In the blissful union of dependency, the angels live by means of God's creative power as it manifests itself in the Son. The one "world" soul receives its sustenance or livelihood from that source. As a debasement of the glorious image, consider once again the figure of Sin, who "shall Reign / At [Satan's] right hand . . . / [His] daughter and [his] darling, without end" (II, 868–870). On the degenerate level, those who seek union with Satan the father will, like Sin's hellhounds, resort to the womb of the mother to be

[4] "The Metaphor of Inspiration in *Paradise Lost*," p. 76.
[5] Ibid.

forever "sustained" by the absolute source of vilification.

Whereas on the debased plane union implies death and damnation, on the divine plane obedience to the life source becomes a natural means of self-glorification and self-livelihood. As Abdiel says:

> And of our good, and of our dignities
> How provident he is, how farr from thought
> To make us less, bent rather to exalt
> Our happie state under one Head more near
> United.
>
> (v, 827–831)

The holy union of "one individual soul" contains an essential paradox: as the angels glorify the source of life and are themselves glorified, the omnipotence of God reduces itself to the equal of that unified soul which is dependent upon God for sustenance. Thus, continues Abdiel, in their obedience to God the angels are not diminished or "obscur'd"

> But more illustrious made, since he the Head
> One of our number thus reduc't becomes,
> His Laws our Laws, all honour to him due
> Returns our own.
>
> (v, 842–845)

As the mother nourishes the child within her womb, the complete dependence of the child upon the mother causes the child to grow stronger through the sustenance it receives, and the omnipotence of the mother as the source of life and bliss is paradoxically reduced to the state of serving the child.

The Son's "begetting" or anointing, then, becomes the means by which God further glorifies the angels, because the Son acts as a mediator between the angels and their source of existence. (To break from the happiness of such unity is, as I shall attempt to show, to abort oneself from the womb of bliss and to be no longer sustained in the paradisiacal world of oneness.) At the center of the entire conception is the womb and the idea of giving birth from the womb. If, for obvious reasons, Milton does not relate the word "womb" directly to the Son, he does so in suggestive terms and in deliberate contrasts with figures such as Sin who does have a womb and whose imagistic "situation" in the poem allows Milton to say a great deal about divine union. The idea of contrasts is always operating and always defining itself dialectically.

Ultimately, behind the whole concept of the union lies the idea that at the end of things God "shall be All in All" (III, 341); then the Son will "resign" his "Scepter and Power" and will reside in God forever, and in the Son will reside all whom God loves (VI, 730–733). That is, there will be a final and total reduction within the union through which all purified offspring will be sustained and in which the "just" who have suffered "tribulation" will behold the "fruits" of their torments in the transcendent vision of a renewed state (III, 334–338). Rebirth will spring from destruction, as a final conflagration foreshadowed by the War in Heaven will yield a new world. The promise of that apocalyptic "moment," the final return to the womb, underlies the basic concept of regeneration that motivates the action of the poem. The central pattern, as I hope to demonstrate, is one of union, followed by fission or forced birth causing destruction, and a final reunion.[6] Or, put in another way, the pattern is one in which union proceeds through destruction to reunion. Destruction thereby becomes the vehicle by which the ultimate state is attained.

The very language in which the War in Heaven is cast serves to point up the various aspects of this idea. The

---

[6] In that pattern, the Son, of course, plays the essential role: through God's efficacy in the Son, the union of birth is sustained, the antiunion is quelled, and the reunion or regeneration is brought about. Furthermore, if the role of the Son within the union is generative, then his role within the reunion is regenerative. As the "Christ" or Redeemer, he is the means by which those who have been "just" may experience a new birth in the glorification of God. "Christ" is the Son's regenerative name: the Son, we recall, will replace Adam as the progenitor of mankind.

anticipation of the final reduction, for example, is evident in what Michael does when he sees the Son coming to defeat the rebel angels: the Arch-Angel "soon reduc'd / His Armie, circumfus'd on either Wing, / Under thir Head imbodied all in one" (VI, 777–779). The description likewise suggests the union of sustenance sublimely represented by the total embodiment of all the angels or sons of God under one "Head." All the members are reduced in a single, sublime, self-sustaining symbol of unity in which one member is united totally and equally with every other member.

If the return to a source has creative overtones, then a breaking away from that source must also relate to the idea of birth. From the point of view of Sin, the debased "union" caused by the return of the hellhounds to the womb (the implications of which will later be explored in more depth) is followed by a "disunion" or birth of the hellhounds from the womb (II, 795–802). Something of the same pattern occurs in Satan's separation from the heavenly union. The description of his fall draws upon a language that strongly suggests a similar idea of birth.

At the point of the fall, the "Chrystal wall of Heav'n, which op'ning wide, / Rowld inward, and a spacious Gap disclos'd" (VI, 860–861), with the result that "confounded Chaos" becomes "incumberd" with the "huge" or prodigious issue (VI, 871–874). Chaos may be "confounded," but "disburd'n'd Heav'n" certainly rejoices, "and soon repaird / Her mural breach, returning whence it rowl'd" (VI, 878–879). If it is not apparent what the opening and closing of the walls and the disburdening process represent, we might profitably examine the word "Disburd'n'd" in another context. (I suggest such an approach because I feel that Milton causes meanings to adhere to words when he uses them in special contexts. That is, as a poet drawing upon specific semantic associations, Milton very often allows one context to define a word with the result that whenever the word appears in a similar context, its associations will also be similar.[7]) For

[7] Among others, Edward S. LeComte, *Yet Once More: Verbal and Psychological*

example, when Eve tells the serpent that more "hands" are needed to "Help . . . *disburden* Nature of her *birth*" (IX, 623–624; italics mine), we are invited to relate the same meaning to a situation in which the idea of giving birth is so strongly suggested. There seems to be little question as to whether at least a metaphorical birth is occurring in the fall of Satan and his crew. What should concern us, rather, is what kind of "birth" is being portrayed and what it means.

As was discussed earlier, Satanic birth always implies its opposite: not a glorious creating out of Chaos but a returning into Chaos. And appropriately enough, through their unnatural birth, Satan and his crew are returned to a chaotic state. Indeed, their encountering of Chaos in their fall becomes a metaphor for the process of uncreation they undergo. They are not, of course, completely annihilated, for the Son "meant / Not to destroy, but root them out of Heav'n" (VI, 854–855). Their experience of uncreation is figurative. According to Arnold Stein, "if they regain their form in Hell, that is because they regain free will"[8] and the ability to wreak destruction on the world according to the divine plan, so that God will be able to create a new birth out of that destruction.

The imagery of uncreation is a reversal of that having to do with re-creation: the Son here does not act as the root through which transplanted man receives new sustenance. Rather, he "roots" the rebel angels out of Heaven as one would root out a harmful organism from the soil and thereby deprive that organism of its means of sustenance. The Son's withholding half his power uncreates the rebel angels to the extent that they become initiates of Chaos but inhabit that world in which all creation is negated, abortive, and unfulfilled—Hell itself. Consequently, the angels undergo a qualified process of uncreation that involves both Hell and Chaos.

Pattern in Milton (New York, 1953), stresses the extreme importance of verbal reiteration not only in *Paradise Lost* but elsewhere in the poetry and prose. Through reiteration, Milton establishes meaning.

[8] *Answerable Style*, p. 26.

Satan and his fellow angels' "uncreative birth" into Chaos has at least two implications, which become clear if we recall a point made in an earlier discussion: Satanic birth is always ludicrous, always associated with what is both degraded and unnatural. That Chaos into which Satan and his crew are reduced is, of course, the "wastful Deep" (VI, 862). "Wasteful," as I have discussed, implies, among other things, that which is unnecessary, residual, or ultimately excremental. In one respect, then, Satan's birth becomes a voiding of defilement downward into a realm of defilement. Heaven must rid itself of all possibilities of corruption in order to remain pure. When the rebels against God have been "voided," "Then shall God's Saints unmixt, and from th'impure / Farr separate" (VI, 742–743).

The second implication concerns the "unnaturalness" of Satan's birth. The image of the unnatural birth by which Satan's fall is expressed is made evident first in the "physical" unnaturalness created in the forced opening in Heaven's wall. The opening in the side of Heaven out of which Satan and his crew are expelled is not the natural opening of Heaven's gates through which the Son and the faithful angels exit and enter.[9] Moreover, the "fallen angels enter Hell not through its gate but through a temporary opening in its fiery vault."[10] Thus both in relation to Heaven and to Hell the birth is unnatural. With that interpretation, the ideas of a "breach" and the "repairing" of a breach (VI, 878–879) after the process of "disburdening" are consistent. As a forced and unnatural opening that must be repaired, "breach" suggests both the abnormality of the birth and the unnaturalness with which Satan causes a "breach" in the holy union.

Further, the "breach" indicates the aberration within Satan's own mind. Satan has forcibly excluded himself from the peaceful bliss and restful security of the holy union. He

[9] Harry F. Robins, "Satan's Journey: Direction in *Paradise Lost*," *Milton Studies in Honor of Harris Francis Fletcher*, ed. G. Blakemore Evans et al. (Urbana, Illinois, 1961), p. 95.

[10] Ibid.

has caused himself to undergo the torment of exile, of never being able to return to his previous state of contentment. Such is the psychological state of uncreation which involves a mental return to that Chaos out of which all creation, peace, and order come (compare IV, 18–23). The aberration or "breach" of the holy union results in a complete loss of security and an enforced subjection to the distraction of "horror and doubt." Satan undergoes the Chaos of a world bound to an utter loss of sublime creativity. His own personal Chaos is conceived of as a Hell. Indeed, through his subjection to the self, he creates his own Hell, and he remains as a result of his "breach" an uncreated personality.

In the remainder of this chapter, I shall discuss the full implications of the "breach" or "disunion." How Satan effects such a "breach," both in himself and in others, what are the motivations and the consequences of the "breach"— in short, the process of uncreation itself—may now be more fully understood in light both of the union and reunion previously discussed.

As stated, Satan's rebellion against the "begetting" of the Son has its basis in the idea of generation. Indeed, the Son's glorification causes Satan to "conceive" malice and disdain within himself (V, 666). And Satan's recourse to action is one of seducing the angels under him into a similar type of rebellion. Assuming what will become the familiar pattern of an assault, the Arch-Tempter begins with Beelzebub, into whose "unwarie brest" Satan "infuses" the poison of his influence (V, 694–696). The vocabulary is essentially one of generation: the process of conception and birth within Satan's mind turns destructively outward as Satan seduces others into undergoing the same process. The imagery of sexual perversion continues in Satan's "alluring" of the angels to swerve from God. As a consequence of his temptations, he is able to draw after him a "third part of Heav'ns Host" (V, 709–710).

In a continuation of the uncreative process, Satan then parodies sublime creativity through the glorification of himself. His "Royal seat" is described as being built

> High on a Hill, far blazing, as a Mount
> Rais'd on a Mount, with Pyramids and Towrs
> From Diamond Quarries hew'n, and Rocks of Gold,
> The Palace of great *Lucifer*
>
> .   .   .   .
>
>   which not long after, he
> Affecting all equality with God,
> In imitation of that Mount whereon
> Messiah was declar'd in sight of Heav'n,
> The Mountain of the Congregation call'd.
>
>   (v, 757–766)

According to Arnold Stein, Satan attempts "to possess the power of spirit by means of matter" and therefore elevates the self to godhead by means of the material.[11] Satan's purpose is to mimic God's "begetting" of the Son by creating as closely as possible the entire accoutrement of that generation. The assumption is that in order to simulate the sublime creativity of the godhead, one must accumulate as much of the apparent glory associated with the godhead as is possible. The mode of accumulation is, of course, entirely physical. Satan would "affect" equality with God by imitating the "Mount" of generation, not through a spiritual attempt at birth but through a physical approximation of the birth process. Thus Satan, incapable of spiritual ascent, undergoes a physical ascent by raising himself literally upon a high seat.

Satan's omnipotence is not spiritually generative but physically impotent. He attempts to express through a physical glorification of the self what God expresses through a spiritual glorification of those who are part of the union. Satan manifests his consummate pride in order to imitate the essentially selfless act of God. The Tempter's absurd exaggeration of the self as a means of glorifying the self is a parody of God's reduction of the self as a means of glorifying

---

[11] *Answerable Style*, p. 36.

others. As Coleridge maintains, Satan's "lust of self" in opposition to the "denial of self" is Satan's "sole motive of action."[12] "Milton," says Coleridge, "has carefully marked in his Satan the intense selfishness, the alcohol of egotism."[13]

Gold and diamonds, pyramids and towers, and piled-up mountains become the equivalent in the Satanic consciousness of the omnipotence and spirituality of deific generation. Satan's material creations are illusory (nonsubstantial), whereas God's spiritual creations are real (substantial). In Satan's mode of thought, wealth becomes the substitute for divinity. As I suggested earlier, Milton's attitude toward such wealth and ostentation may be gathered from *Of Reformation*, in which the prelates' "excessive wast of Treasury," "Idolatrous erection of Temples," "snares of Images, Pictures, rich Coaps, gorgeous Altar-clothes" are associated with a "putrifi'd Masse" from which a "Monster" is spontaneously generated. "What other materials then these," Milton continues, "have built up the *spirituall* Babel to the heighth of her Abominations?" (I, 590). In the prose the material strives to become a substitute for the spiritual. And the exact composition of the material (or "trash" as Milton calls it) used in the building process is quite obviously putrefaction of the worst sort (consider the meaning of "Abominations" alone). It is no coincidence, then, that Satan's "Palace," the type of all loathsomeness, is described as a "Mount / Rais'd on a Mount."

What is overtly stated in the prose is covertly suggested in the poetry: the accumulation of the material in order to rival the spiritual has its basis in perversion.[14] Satan attempts to imitate the sublime mountain of generation and creates instead an illusory and obscene mountain of degeneration. Indeed, his self-idolatry will find its analogue in history when Solomon "led by fraud" will "build / His Temple right

---

[12] Samuel Taylor Coleridge, "Milton" (1818), *Milton Criticism: Selections from Four Centuries*, ed. James Thorpe (New York, 1950), p. 95.

[13] Ibid.

[14] Cf. Brown, *Life Against Death*, pp. 254 and 302.

against the Temple of God / On that opprobrious Hill"
(I, 401–403). There Josiah will cause that "Hill of scandal"
(I, 416) to become defiled (2 Kg. 23:10–13) by "ordering
the former sites of the shrines to be used for the disposal of
refuse."[15] Milton leaves little doubt about his attitude concerning those who exalt themselves, as Satan does on his
"far-blazing" seat, through the vain illusion that they can
contend with God.

The unbearable irony of Satan's self-deception is that he is
never able to comprehend its absurdity. For even after he has
fallen, Satan exalts himself upon the identical "seat" of
selfhood.

> High on a Throne of Royal State, which far
> Outshon the wealth of *Ormus* and of *Ind*,
> Or where the gorgeous East with richest hand
> Showrs on her Kings *Barbaric* Pearl and Gold,
> Satan exalted sat.
>
> (II, 1–5)[16]

In Hell Satan re-enacts the physical attempt at omnipotence
in order to simulate the omnipotence of God. There is the
same avaricious predisposition to accumulate as much
wealth as possible in order to substantiate the illusory belief
in one's own grandeur. The barbarity of such wealth contrasts
sharply with the divinity of God's spiritual wealth. However,
the brilliance and luxuriance of the physical aspects merely
reinforce the sense of illusion.

The entire construct is illusory. Exaltation is the offspring of

[15] Prince, ed., *Paradise Lost: Books I and II*, p. 122n.

[16] In *The Dunciad*, interestingly enough, the Miltonic idea of "showering"
pearl and gold on Kings is "interpreted" by Pope as the showering of the
"fragrant Grains" of chamber pots—that is, excrement:

> High on a gorgeous seat, that far out-shone
> Henley's gilt tub, or Fleckno's Irish throne,
> Or that where on her Curls the Public pours,
> *All-bounteous, fragrant Grains* and Golden show'rs,
> Great Cibber sate.
>
> (II, 1–5; italics mine)

despair, and inspiration is the product of self-deception (II, 10). Despite the material wealth that surrounds him, however, Satan's fate is to remain "insatiate": his impulse is ever to destroy, to pursue "vain Warr" (II, 8–9). The Satanic consciousness can never be satisfied, regardless of the luxury of its illusions; the projection of the self into the illusion of its omnipotence causes the insatiable sense of unfulfillment.

The image of self-exaltation re-emerges when Satan returns to Hell in the tenth book and invisibly ascends "his high Throne," which is placed "in regal lustre" at the "upper end" of the "*Plutonian* Hall" (X, 444–446):

> Down a while
> He sate, and round about him saw unseen:
> At last as from a Cloud his fulgent head
> And shape Starr bright appeer'd, or brighter, clad
> With what permissive glory since his fall
> Was left him, or false glitter.
>
> (X, 447–452)

The pattern of making a sudden appearance from a state of invisibility re-echoes the motif of sight and lack of sight asserted in the fifth book. The unfallen angels are able to "behold" the Son, but when they fall, they are "cast out" from "blessed vision" and made to dwell in "utter darkness" (V, 611–615). Consequently, the "vision" of Satan in Hell becomes a mockery of the divine "vision." Satan's appearance from a cloud, moreover, parodies God's act of appearing in a cloud to show his power and great glory (Luke 21, 27, etc.), for man cannot look upon God's face unless he die.

Satan himself involves the illusion of sight: he becomes the deceptive, visionary wish fulfillment of the blinded fallen angels, who crave the ability to see:

> All amaz'd
> At that so sudden blaze the Stygian throng
> Bent thir aspect, and whom they wish'd beheld.
> (X, 452–454)[17]

---

[17] The "sudden blaze" in which Satan appears recalls "Lycidas":

Satan answers their wish by suddenly appearing to them, but that mode of sight is entirely illusory. It suggests the entire predicament of the fallen angels, who must create their own world of fantasy in order to be "productive." As Satan's "sea" was given a "shore" in Chaos, the blindness of the angels is given a supposed object of sight in Hell.

Satan's appearance is dream-like. The head and body emerging from a cloud involve the same distortion that characterizes fantasy. Like the Son upon his throne at the day of "begetting," Satan "begets" himself through his sudden transformation from invisibility to visibility. The act is that of a trickster who would fool his audience with a parody of parthenogenesis.[18] Within the context of generation, Satan's head becomes an object of derision: as the Son's "Head" implies creativity, Satan's head is "fulgent" because it gives forth light and radiates its "glory" to the astonished angels.

Milton immediately undercuts this image by relating it to the idea of "false glitter." The light emanating from Satan's head is both unreal and artificial; its insubstantiality merely indicates something that glitters. That notion returns us to the so-called "regal lustre" of Satan's throne and to the fabricated constructs of gems, diamonds, gold, and pearls

---

> But the fair guerdon when we hope to find
> And think to *burst out into sudden blaze*,
> Comes the blind Fury with th'abhorred shears
> And slits the thin-spun life.
> (ll. 73–76; italics mine)

There is a similar sense here of belief in an illusion which one creates himself. A sudden illusive flame of light is destroyed by a loss of vision reminiscent of the "*blind* Fury" (italics mine) destroying the illusion. True vision is that which concerns the reality and stability of Heaven.

[18] C. G. Jung, *The Archetypes and the Collective Unconscious*, trans. R. F. C. Hull (New York, 1959), pp. 255–256. The trickster is the archetypal "ape of God." He is a devil who has a "fondness for sly jokes" and "malicious pranks." He has the ability to change his shape, and he represents a parody of the figure of the savior. He changes himself often into the form of an animal (cf. Satan's bestial transformations), and as a devil he complains of being a "soul in hell." Finally, the trickster is always the butt of the joke (cf. Satan's forced transformation into a serpent in Book x).

that are the creations of pride both in Heaven and in Hell. All such luster is the result of that which is material, illusory, and ultimately debased. Such an idea contrasts sharply with the true glory of the faithful angels, who, as Abdiel says, are "more il*lustr*ious made" (italics mine) by their faith, for their brilliance and luster are spiritual rather than artificial.

Corresponding to Satan's visual deception through artifice, furthermore, is his gathering of the angels under him to his seat in the north, where he perpetrates a verbal deception. While the palace of diamond and gold simulates the grandeur of the holy mount, Satan's words simulate the veracity of the holy utterance. He calls "all his Train" to his palace, only "pretending" that he will "consult / About the great reception of thir King" (v, 768–769). The falsity of his intentions is reinforced by the pretentiousness of his palace. When they assemble, he "[holds] thir ears" with "calumnious Art / Of counterfeted truth" (v, 770–771). Through the artifice of verbal deception, which is as counterfeit as the illusion of Satan's own godhead, Satan's "calumniates," that is, slanders and causes to become depraved, that which is holy. Utterance for the Satanic consciousness is vilification. Satan's "Word" does not create: it debases. It causes a defamation and therefore an uncreation of what has been "begotten," that is, created and anointed.

Satan first addresses the angels by those titles which God ascribed to them in their glorification, and his very mode of address questions the true substance of such titles:

> Thrones, Dominations, Princedoms, Vertues, Powers,
> If these magnific Titles yet remain
> Not merely titular, since by Decree
> Another now hath to himself ingross't
> All Power, and us eclipst under the name
> Of King anointed.
>
> (v, 772–777)

Satan ascribes to God the very act of calumniation for which Satan himself is responsible. The Arch-Deceiver accuses God of depriving the angels of their "titular" power, but, of course, in deceiving the angels about the true meaning of the Son's glorification, Satan is himself causing those titles to become hollow, "merely titular." Moreover, by saying that God's "Decree" has allowed the Son to "ingross" all power, Satan not only causes God's act of glorification to become vilified, but he reveals precisely his own mode of vilification.

"Ingross't" here has at least two meanings, each of which reinforces the other. The word initially implies the idea of accumulating possession, indeed, of even taking over that which rightfully belongs to another. That is exactly what Satan is doing: he plans to possess, to take over God's rightful throne. In addition, the Satanic lust to possess connotes in its materiality the debasement associated with Satanic wealth. In line with such debasement, the word likewise implies the act of making gross or filthy, which is also what Satan is doing in his defamation of God. Finally, Satan's complaint that God's "Decree" has allowed the Son in his anointing as King to "eclipse" the angels reveals what Satan is himself doing to those under him. For Satan will cause the angels to become "eclipst," to be lost in a blackness devoid of the Son's divine light, to be cut off from "blessed vision."

The imagery of artificial creation is continued in Satan's assumption that the angels must "devise" honors to receive the Son. The "devising" of anything implies its artificiality, the counterfeit nature of its creation. The honors that the Son desires spring naturally and spontaneously from love. But in Satan's mercenary mode of thought, the Son is envisioned as one who demands the payment of a debt, as one who is coming to receive "Knee-tribute yet unpaid" (v, 781–782). Satan can think of glorification only in artificial, material terms, indicative of his own servile angels, who are required to bend the "supple knee" (v, 788). The "prostration vile" (v, 782) by which Satan characterizes their obligation to honor the Son as an image of God (v, 784) is most fittingly applied to Satan himself. For Satan pays such "prostration vile" to his own self-image: he "prostrates" himself to the "vileness" of his own personality. Moreover, he demands that such "prostration vile" be paid to him by his underlings. Finally, and most ironically, Satan will pay that "prostration vile" in his fall, when he is made to "prostrate" himself to the "vileness" of his calumniations against God.

In addition, when Satan refers to God and the Son in terms of duality, he confuses the creation of his own image, which he worships, with the creation of the Son. He says in reference to God that devotion is

> Too much to one, but double how endur'd,
> To one and to his image how proclaim'd?
>
> (v, 783–784)

Satan mistakenly concludes that, with the begetting of the Son, he will have to honor a double form of the godhead. He thereby separates the unity which the Father-Son relationship represents in the same way that he destroys the union of God and the angels under one individual soul. He does not realize that devotion to the Son is simultaneously devotion to the Father.

In his unwillingness to honor the Father, Satan would have the angels believe that they now must honor two rulers instead of one. He can conceive of creation only as a destruction of unity, a breaking of harmony as he himself has destroyed the harmony by creating and worshiping his own ego. Through his mode of creation God achieves unity, synthesis, harmony; through his mode of "creation" Satan causes disruption, division, a breaking away, discord.

Satan's false pleas for freedom and equality in his palace intimately concern his particular mode of "creative" dialectics. In reaction to his unwillingness to honor the Son, Satan would have the angels "erect" their minds as a means of casting off the supposed "Yoke" of God's jurisdiction (v, 785–786). "Erect" here implies a standing up in defiance as opposed to a bowing in submission. The angels will break out of their imprisonment by standing erect. But "erection" also has overtones of self-exaltation, of asserting the ego and then worshiping it as an icon; and exaltation is closely associated with generation as "self-begetting." Thus "erect" also means to build or fabricate. God says of Satan at one point:

> such a foe
> Is rising, who intends t'erect his Throne
> Equal to ours, throughout the spacious North.
> (V, 724–726)

The angels will beget themselves or individualize themselves in order to be free from obedience to God.

"Erect" has another meaning, however, that emerges when we consider that ordinarily the erection of a standard follows the act of territorial possession. In mythopoeic thought, these acts have definite creational relationships. According to Mircea Eliade, "when possession is taken of a territory . . . rites are performed that symbolically repeat the act of Creation; the uncultivated zone is first 'cosmocized,' then inhabited," and presumably one aspect of these rites is the erection of a standard.[19] The mythopoeic dimension certainly applies to Milton when we recall Satan's promise to Chaos and Night that he will "reduce / To her original darkness and [Chaos'] sway" the realm which the "Ethereal King / Possesses lately" and "once more / Erect the standard there of ancient *Night*" (II, 977–986). Implicit in Satan's statement is the idea that erection symbolizes not only the right of possession but the act of uncreation. Such a concept is tenable, of course, because "possess" is used as a synonym for "create." Ironically, Satan is at pains to reverse the very act of possession that erection celebrates: the "transformation of chaos into cosmos," to use Eliade's phrase.[20] Consequently, when the word "erect" or "possess" is applied to Satan, it has exactly the opposite meaning.

Within this creative framework, what are we to make of Satan's reference to God as a "usurper"? If to usurp is to

[19] *Cosmos and History*, pp. 9–11.
[20] Ibid., p. 10.

take over the possession of another, then Satan is merely
transferring his own uncreative policy of dispossession to
God. And yet Satan would have his cohorts believe that God
is the uncreative party. He says:

> ye know your selves
> Natives and Sons of Heav'n possest before
> By none.
>
> (v, 789–791)

"Possession" as it is used here intimately concerns the concept of nativity. Since no one, Satan argues, possessed
Heaven before these angels were created, it belongs by right
to Satan and his crew. Thus Satan implies that he is justified
in the assertion of his deity and equality "to win the Mount
of God" (VI, 88). The lust to possess becomes an integral
part of Satan's desire to accumulate wealth in defiance of
God. And that desire, as suggested, approximates the urge
to "create" in artifice what God has created in spiritual
glory. Consequently, "possession" is not only an uncreating
act for Satan but, in the exercise of its materiality, an act of
defilement. The need to "possess" and the need to "erect"
are aspects of the same compulsion to assert the ego and to
break away from God. In such a way Satan proclaims his
"freedom" and "equality."

Satan's references to freedom are deceptive and, in contrast to the freedom that results from obedience, contradictory. Desiring to maintain his own omnipotence and yet
at the same time to convince the angels to rebel against the
omnipotence of God, Satan must manipulate his terms so
that they will serve his own purpose. He says to the angels
that even if they are not "equal all," they are still "free,"

> Equally free; for Orders and Degrees
> Jarr not with liberty, but well consist.
>
> (v, 792–793)

Implying his own superiority over the angels, Satan tells
them that they are not all equal and yet states that they are

"equally free." Their "equality" ultimately resides in their own unswerving obedience to Satan, and their "freedom" involves the necessity to become servants of Satan's tyranny. Satan wishes to maintain the "Orders and Degrees" as aspects of servility to a master rather than as aspects of glorification. In reality, "Orders and Degrees" do not "jarr" with "liberty," but in reference to God Satan would have the angels believe so and thus cause them to rebel. Without applying equality and freedom as synonyms in the relations of the angels toward himself, Satan would have the angels apply those terms as points of rebellion against God's omnipotence. That is, Satan wishes the angels to rebel against what he considers God's presumptions of "Monarchie over such as live by right / His equals" (v, 794–796). In his rebellious attitude, Satan equates freedom and equality with reference to God in order to reveal the supposed injustice of God's dominion over the angels, but he does not in the least equate these terms with reference to his own assumed omnipotence. With respect to God, the angels are equal and free; with respect to Satan, the angels are free but not equal. Consequently, God has no right to "introduce / Law and Edict on [them]" who "Err not" and who therefore need no law (v, 797–799).

Abdiel alone first challenges Satan's statements concerning the consecration of the Son. To oppose Satan's rebelliousness, Abdiel argues, as I shall attempt to show, from a generative point of view:

> Shalt thou give Law to God, shalt thou dispute
> With him the points of libertie, who made
> Thee what thou art, and formd the pow'rs of Heav'n
> Such as he pleas'd, and circumscrib'd thir being?
> (v, 822–825)

The entire argument about equality and kingship resolves itself into a question of generation, for God's creative power, both in God's ability to create and in his ability to exalt, becomes the ultimate object of dispute. The implication of

God's having created the "Pow'rs of Heav'n" is that God has the right to expect obedience from his offspring. God not only created Satan and the angels, but he simultaneously glorified them. Coincident with the act of creation is the act of consecration. Abdiel says to Satan:

> the mighty Father *made*
> All things, ev'n thee, and all the Spirits of Heav'n
> By him created in thir bright degrees,
> *Crownd* them with Glory.
> (v, 836–839; italics mine)

Being crowned with glory follows naturally from being created: in both senses is one "begotten." The Son himself is paradoxically "begotten," that is, crowned and created, on the one hand, and made the agent of "begetting," that is, of glorifying and creating, on the other. Thus Abdiel develops the concept of the creative process still further when he says that God created Satan and "all things" through the agency of God's "begotten Son" as through God's creative "Word." Again there is an identification of "begetting" as consecration and "begetting" as generation.

As God pronounces his decrees verbally through the Word, the Son is both animated and becomes the means by which things are created. The Son as anointed and created offspring of the Father is thereby synonymous with the Word or utterance, God's verbal offspring. Deific utterance, then, is by its very nature creative: the Word itself is not only begotten, that is, consecrated and generated, but is the source of existence for others.[21] Thus the Word as it is uttered

---

[21] Jung (*Psychology of the Unconscious*, p. 177) aptly correlates the relationships between "mouth" and "word" as creative entities. Thus "mouth" is "invested with a procreating power" concerning the "sexual or creating libido." Jung quotes a passage from the *Aitareyopanishad* to reveal the mythical attitude of utterance from the mouth and its relation to birth: " 'Being brooded-o'er, his mouth hatched out, like as an egg; from his mouth (came) speech, from speech, the fire' " (p. 178). Moreover, according to Cassirer (*Language and Myth*, trans. Susanne K. Langer [New York, 1946], p. 45): "All verbal structures appear as *also* mythical entities, endowed with certain mythical powers, that the Word, in fact, becomes a sort of primary force in which all being and doing originate"

becomes "Omnific" (VII, 217), that is, all-creating, because it contains within its verbal structure all the possibilities of life. Finally, inherent in God's decrees is this "creativity," and to disobey them is to cut oneself off from the source of life. The Word as it is uttered involves a sense of obedience to a command.

The argument that Satan uses to counter Abdiel's statements may be characterized as "uncreative." Satan in his pride has the audacity to deny God's creative power and thereby God's right to expect obedience from his creatures. Satan's downfall, therefore, stems from his uncreative approach. He replies to Abdiel with a logic of absurdity:

> That we were formd then saist thou? and the work
> Of secondarie hands, by task transferd
> From Father to his Son? strange point and new!
> Doctrin which we would know whence learnt.
>
> (v, 853–856)

Immediately, Satan misinterprets the creative act as one which implies the transference of a task from one party to another rather than as one which implies the performance of that which is joyous through the operations of a creative agency. Satan's logic is depreciatory: it assumes that if there is any process of creation at all, it involves the menial labor of a subordinate who is required by his superior to do the work. Thus, not only does Satan confuse the idea of agency with the idea of transference, but he deprives the Creator both of his willingness to create and of his joy in creating.

In response to a doctrine so basic to the concept of godhead as that of the ability to create, moreover, Satan dares question "whence" this doctrine was "learnt." Milton would seem to imply that every creature knows instinctively that God is, by his very nature, a Creator. It is not a doctrine which has

---

(p. 45). Further, continues Cassirer, "in the creation accounts of almost all great cultural religions, the Word appears in league with the highest Lord of creation" (pp. 45–46).

to be learned at all but a fact that is instantaneously perceived by any creature born with a sense of intelligence. He who dares deny such a doctrine denies both his own existence and the existence of God: Satan does just that. He says:

>   who saw
> When this creation was? remembrest thou
> Thy making, while the Maker gave thee being?
> We know no time when we were not as now;
> Know none before us.
>
>   (v, 856–860)

Satan argues from the point of view of an atheist; by questioning God's creative power, Satan professes his disbelief in God. And, indeed, Satan and his cohorts are later referred to as the "Atheist crew" (vi, 370). Through a false logic which appeals in a quasi-empirical manner to sight and to memory, Satan in his pride "disproves" the existence of an exterior force responsible for his own making. He assumes absurdly that because the "time" of his creation is beyond the context of his own experience, there was never a time when he was not. Thus God had nothing to do with creating him.

The speciousness of his argument carries him to the final *reductio ad absurdum* of his uncreative train of thought. He transfers all power of creation and, therefore, all the Maker's right to expect obedience from God to himself. Indeed, Satan maintains with reference to himself and to the angels that they were

>   self-begot, self-rais'd
> By [their] own quick'ning power, when fatal course
> Had circl'd his full Orb, the birth mature
> Of this [their] native Heav'n, Ethereal Sons.
>
>   (v, 860–863)

The pride involved in Satan's assumption that he was "self-begot" and "self-rais'd" is the pride that causes his "selfunbegetting" and "self-descent." "Self-begot" refers here both to the idea that Satan was the cause of his own creation and to the idea that he was the cause of his own glorification. Moreover, "self-rais'd" is associated with the concept that Satan was responsible in his self-creation and glorification for the establishment of his own stature as an angel.

Satan maintains that it was his own animating power that caused him to exist and be glorified and not the creative power of God. He completely dissociates his creation as an event from the will of God. Indeed, he suggests that if he was created at all, he caused himself at that "fatal" hour to come full-blown into existence as a "birth-mature." His obligation as a "son" in that sense is one which concerns his owing his entire obedience to himself and to that which he conceives to be his place of nativity, that is, Heaven. Of course, the implications of "Heav'n" and "Ethereal" in this context are no longer associated with the divinity of God; these ascriptions have become desecrated in Satan's dissociations of them from the godhead. Heaven as a place of nativity loses its meaning and becomes associated with the absurd self-generation of demons.

In the assertion of his defiance, Satan "glorifies" himself by rebelling against God. His "self-begetting" causes him and his crew to declare their creative independence in order to prove that their "puissance is [their] own, [their] own right hand / Shall teach [them] highest deeds" (v, 864–865). What Satan deems his "own right hand" represents a parody of the power and creative energy of God. At a later point, when Satan confronts Abdiel again, Satan boasts that Abdiel has returned to receive "the first assay / Of this right hand provok't" (vi, 153–154). Satan is soon to learn, however, that the Son is "dextrous to subdue" the "Rebels" (v, 741–742), that the "dexterity" (right-handedness) of the Son as an agent of God may be used to destroy as well as to create. With "Victorie" sitting "Eagle-wing'd" at his "right hand" (vi, 762–763), the Son sets out to destroy the apostate angels:

> Full soon
> Among them he arriv'd; in his right hand
> Grasping ten thousand Thunders, which he sent
> Before him, such as in thir Souls infix'd
> Plagues.
>
> (VI, 834–838)

Thus the rebel angels become aware of the destructive power of God's "red right hand" (II, 174) and "red lightning" (I, 175) which are used to "plague" the angels.[22] Satan and his crew experience the process of uncreation enacted upon themselves, so that that process becomes for them a reality. They experience what it is to be destroyed by the same hand that would otherwise have sustained them in bliss.

As Abdiel warns:

> for soon expect to feel
> His Thunder on thy head, devouring fire.
> Then who created thee lamenting learn,
> Then who can *uncreate* thee thou shalt know.
>
> (V, 892–895; italics mine)

The dialectics of creation and uncreation are at the very heart of the conflict. Abdiel employs the "head" as a representation of a creative center to demonstrate the effects of uncreation.

---

[22] Biblical allusions to the "right hand" are plentiful. See Mk. 14:62: "and ye shall see the Son of man sitting on the right hand of power" and Mk. 16:19: "So then after the Lord had spoken unto them, he was received up into Heaven, and sat on the right hand of God." Cf. also Rev. 6:4. In *Paradise Lost* the left hand is associated with the underworld. For example, after Sin and Death have made their ascent out of Chaos, they see Hell appropriately "on the left hand" (X, 322). Moreover, if, as Harry F. Robins argues ("Satan's Journey: Direction in *Paradise Lost*," pp. 92–93), God faces east in a square Heaven, then Satan's palace in the north is located on the left side of Heaven. According to Robins, the "right stands for good and left for evil. Our word 'sinister' is, of course, Latin for 'left hand'" (p. 94). It is not surprising, consequently, that Sin and Eve are both born from the left side of their progenitors (II, 755–758; VIII, 465–467). Moreover, Jung, in his introduction to R. J. Zwi Werblowsky's *Lucifer and Prometheus* (London, 1952, p. x), notes the "conception of Christ as the right hand and the devil as the left hand of God." In another context Jung identifies the right hand with the conscious and the left with the unconscious processes (*Psychology and Alchemy*, p. 121).

Satan's head is no longer associated with any generative possibilities suggesting sublime creativity but is made to undergo God's "Thunder" and "devouring fire." The implications of "devour" here are of an explicitly uncreative nature: they imply the consuming properties of fire, which takes all into itself and returns nothing, and they imply the act of ravenous eating, which is an operation indicating something which preys upon something else in order to satisfy its own insatiable hunger. And, indeed, Satan and his crew are made to experience in Hell, the "huge convex of Fire, / Outrageous to devour" (II, 434–435). Satan, then, learns by force the lesson of creation, for by uncreating Satan, God ironically reveals to Satan who created him. Satan becomes aware of God's power to create through God's act of reversing that process.

Now that Satan's confrontation with Abdiel has ended, the War itself may commence. That is, the preliminary steps of verbal struggle may now be actualized in physical combat. Having been prepared through a prefatory movement from union to disunion, we may now witness the full effects of the process of uncreation. That experience, I believe, will serve to emphasize the importance of the battle to the central meaning of the poem. For here Milton will enact symbolically the poem's dialectical structure.

Chapter 4

The War in Heaven

REBELLION AND REUNION

T HE USUAL METHOD of describing warfare is to focus upon individual confrontations (soldier against soldier) or mass combats (army against army). Milton employs both methods. Like Homer in the *Iliad* and Vergil in the *Aeneid*, Milton concentrates upon large-scale figures, in addition to whole armies. His narrative runs the gamut of the experience of war. If, on the one hand, Satan and Abdiel (or, later Satan and Michael) meet face to face like Turnus and Aeneas, on the other hand, the entire force of the unfaithful angels meets its match in the force of the faithful angels. The narrative technique, however, is in no way arbitrary, but follows a definite and discernible pattern.

In general, Milton moves from a personal, close-up perspective to a more objective, distant perspective. The heroism of Abdiel and Michael's individual strokes against Satan finds its counterpart in the mass retaliation by Satan and his crew the following day. And the assault with cannons is met, in turn, with torn-up mountains. As Milton backs further and further away and as his perspective becomes more objective, the "heroic" qualities of the War seem to degenerate, to become a mockery of their own uselessness, a veritable Chaos controlled by Chance. At this point, Milton's focus has become so objective that the War is seen not from the limited eyes of the warring angels but from the eternal perspective of God on his holy Hill. Such is, briefly, the major pattern of the poem: a movement away from the immediate and toward the changeless. From that point of view, the Son as God's agent quells the battle and thereby, as I shall show, causes order to come out of disorder, creation out of Chaos, reunion out of rebellion.

The beginning of the War in Heaven is signaled in part by God's speech of praise to Abdiel. The Father exhorts the faithful angel: "the easier conquest now / Remains thee, aided by this host of friends, / Back on thy foes more glorious to return" (VI, 37–39). The original generative image of cyclical return and renewal within the womb-like state of bliss, in which everything received sustenance through the act of giving, now becomes an image which suggests the act of returning in order to destroy. The initial union of cyclical give-and-return is broken: "return" now signifies not sustenance within the "individual Soul" but an uncreating and rooting up of a foreign body that has disturbed the blissful equilibrium. The rebel angels must be driven out of the bliss of Heaven. The "wrauth" of God has been "awaken'd," and God returns in omnipotence through his faithful sons to reverse the process of creation.

At God's "command" "the Powers Militant, / That stood for Heav'n, in mighty Quadrate joyn'd / Of Union irresistible" (VI, 61–63). The union of birth becomes the union of destruction: the "Powers Militant" prepare to destroy by "joining" or "coupling" themselves within an "irresistible" union. Their army becomes a self-enclosed and self-sustained world, in which all the members depend upon other members for support. These "Saints" are "inviolable," that is, not subject to destruction, profanation, or corruption, and.they are "invulnerable" and "impenitrably arm'd" (VI, 398–400).

The ranks of the faithful angels "stood for Heav'n" not only by upholding Heaven but by symbolizing Heaven. Because the quadratic shape of their militant union is also the shape[1]

---

[1] Robins, "Satan's Journey: Direction in *Paradise Lost*," pp. 92–95. Milton emphasizes the three-dimensional quality of the angelic phalanx by calling it cubic (VI, 399), a most appropriate figure, since the angels move sublimely through the air (VI, 71–73), thus revealing all their sides. Both in movement and in shape, the angelic phalanx takes on important overtones. In its sublimity of movement (which, as I shall discuss, has specific creative connotations), it enacts symbolically the very spiritualizing that man might undergo if he remains

of Heaven, their "Cubic Phalanx" (VI, 399) represents Heaven's perfection (VI, 71).²

The entire movement of God's army has creative overtones. Inspired to glory by the wrath of God, they are upborne within the air (VI, 71–73), and their flight itself is seen creatively. Raphael develops the metaphor of flying by comparing the coming of the angels to the "Birds" who were "summond over Eden to receive / Thir names" from Adam (VI, 73–76). The implications of this analogy are not only those of "accommodation," which would allow Adam to experience the flight of the angels visually through a homely

---

² The idea is a pervasive one with Milton. Cf. *The Reason of Church-Government*, I, 789, in which Milton refers to "those smaller squares in battell [that] unite in one great cube, the main phalanx, an embleme of truth and stedfastness."

---

obedient (V, 469–484; VII, 156–161). The possibility of man's movement toward perfection (and, by extension, the futility of Satan's own attempts at aspiration) is figured here.

The overtones, however, extend still further into the realm of hieroglyph. Man's world is orbicular (cf. the Son's act of circumscribing the "O World" [VII, 231]), while God's is square. The spiritualizing movement to perfection represented in the flight of the faithful angels, then, finds its counterpart in the very shape of the angelic phalanx. If man's attempt to ascend to God involves becoming a part of God's holy union, then his ascent is symbolized by the squaring of the circle, a feat which is impossible without God's aid. (Cf. the "holy Mathematic" of Andrew Marvell's "Upon Appleton House," ll. 46–47, 52).

From the infernal point of view, on the other hand, we find a disuniting, a separation of square and circle as a means of frustrating God's plan. (Cf. Sin's statement in Book X concerning God's quadrature and what in man's fall becomes Satan's orbicular world [ll. 379–381].) Both in movement and in shape, then, the angelic phalanx comes to have complex associations; and, although we hardly need to go outside the epic for this information, Jung's observations are pertinent here. In his cultural studies, Jung (*Aion: Researches into the Phenomenology of the Self*, trans. R. F. C. Hull [New York, 1959], p. 264) finds that the quadrature of the circle is commonly related to the "four-cornered phalanx" and the "four-sided line of battle." (The specific alchemical overtones of the quadrature are discussed in the Appendix, n. 6.)

If we explore the shape of Heaven and the angelic union even further, we will see that the square (and, by extension, the circle) has definite mythological, religious, and psychological overtones. In his discussion of "mandala" (Sanskrit comparison. The summoning of the birds also has generative overtones. As the "total kind / Of Birds" (vi, 73–74) refers to their genus as creatures of the air, which genus Adam will make specific by naming the birds, the coming of the angels is also creative since they have been summoned by God to receive their names as God's glorious offspring. They will receive their names by performing meritorious acts in war. They will thus be "begotten" or glorified as a genus: their "kind" will be known as the faithful offspring of God.

In his account of the War to Adam, Raphael recognizes how the idea of union and unanimity has become inverted. He says to Adam:

> though strange to us it seemd
> At first, that Angel should with Angel warr,
> And in fierce hosting meet, who wont to meet
> So oft in Festivals of joy and love
> Unanimous, as sons of one great Sire
> Hymning th'Eternal Father.
>
> (vi, 91–96)

---

for "circle") and "temenos" (a taboo area), Jung (*The Archetypes and the Collective Unconscious*, p. 388) notes: "The 'squaring of the circle' is one of the many archetypal motifs which form the basic patterns of our dreams and fantasies. But it is distinguished by the fact that it is one of the most important of them from the functional point of view. Indeed, it could even be called the *archetype of wholeness*.

Because of this significance, the 'quaternity of the One' is the schema for all images of God, as depicted in the visions of Ezekiel, Daniel, and Enoch." In another context (*Psychology and Religion* [New Haven, 1938], p. 96), Jung suggests that squareness is a symbol both of God and the type of "union" that I have been discussing in this and the last chapter: within the interior of the quadrangle resides the "Holy of Holies with its magical agent, the cosmic source of energy" (Jung, *Psychology and Alchemy*, p. 124). The Eastern Heaven is a square, "and equally in the Western mandalas of medieval Christendom the deity is enthroned at the centre, often in the form of the triumphant Redeemer together with the four symbolical figures of the evangelists." Finally, the square is traditionally a generative symbol, since the quaternity contains within it the prime matter from which is created physically and psychologically the sense of form and personality. The square container represents the womb (Ibid., pp. 124, 137–142).

The pun on "unanimous" is certainly pointed: the previous "meeting" of the angels was in a state of "union." Their blissful intercourse in "Festivals of joy and love" had creational significance because the union was a festival in which the "sons of one great Sire" glorified the Father through hymns and in which the Father responded by returning that glory upon the sons. These festivals represented the all-sustaining and all-animating union itself. Thus the reciprocal action of such a cyclical event had to do with the very existence of the angels: mutual dependencies were sustained by one great source, which in turn was glorified by its offspring.

The inversion of that previous state of union to a state of destruction is what Raphael finds so strange. "Meeting" in "unanimity" has now become an uncreative act, for the "intercourse" is one of war. The angels "meet" in "fierce hosting" rather than in the interchange of "host" and "guest" on festive occasions. The effect of what was previously a creative union now becomes a "joining" whose purpose, that of uncreation, is, as Raphael says, "hideous" (VI, 107): the "Hosts" stand "Front to Front"

> in terrible array
> Of hideous length: before the cloudie Van,
> On the rough edge of battel ere it joyn'd.
> (VI, 106–108)

Union in war has become a mockery of the divine union. The joining is now uncreative, so that union in this inverted sense implies an unnatural coupling. Indeed, Abdiel himself characterizes the impending "union" or "antiunion" of "fierce hosting" as "brutish" and "foul" (VI, 124). And in the strokes of Abdiel and Michael, Satan will experience to his dismay the foulness of that coupling.

Appropriately, Abdiel is the first to execute God's fury on the "Head" of the enemy. By striking Satan (VI, 189–191), Abdiel obeys God's command to "return" back upon his foes. Satan had refused to bow to the "Scepter" because he had considered the act of "bending the knee" to the Son beneath his dignity. Now, however, he is made to undergo a parody of that very movement through the force of Abdiel's blow:

> ten paces huge
> He back recoild; the tenth on bended knee
> His massie Spear upstaid.
>
> (VI, 193–195)

He must pay "knee-tribute" now in humiliation rather than in glory. Abdiel's blow and Satan's reaction enact metaphorically the entire process of uncreation in the fall, for ultimately the Son is to return upon his foes, as I shall discuss, in order to bruise the serpent's head (XII, 150).

Michael's blow also has creative ramifications if we view his wounding of Satan within the context of some of the woundings that occur in the poem. Michael's sword "deep entring shar'd / All [of Satan's] right side" (VI, 326–327) with the result that

> The griding sword with discontinuous wound
> Pass'd through him, but th'Ethereal substance clos'd
> Not long divisible.
>
> (VI, 329–331)

I shall argue that the opening and closing of the wound and the substance that "issues" therefrom (VI, 332) repeat a similar movement that characterizes the poem's major generative pattern. We may begin in Heaven, where a "wound" originates with the forced opening of Heaven's side to let forth its "issue" followed by the consequent closing of the "breach." In Hell, as I shall discuss, Satan and his crew inflict a "wound" on the soil as a prelude to the creation of Pandaemonium (I, 689). The prime example, however, occurs on earth.

With the creation of Eve, the inflicting of a wound becomes a glorious act, and the blood streaming from the opening does not stain or pollute (as does the issuing of

Satan's humor [v, 331–334]) but aids in the creative act. The Maker, Adam relates,

>   stooping op'n'd my left side, and took
> From thence a Rib, with cordial spirits warm,
> And Life-blood streaming fresh; wide was the wound,
> But suddenly with flesh fill'd up and heal'd.
>
>   (VIII, 465–468)

Inherent in the description is the same pattern of an opening, the presence of blood, and the closing of the wound. That basic pattern, however, becomes the vehicle for antithetical meanings. In both cases an exterior force causes the wound, but whereas Michael wishes to destroy, God wishes to create. The idea of birth becomes the vehicle for both acts, one of uncreation and the other of creation. In both cases we find a closing of the wound, as of a closing of a womb after the birth process is completed.

Despite their similarities, however, the two processes differ markedly in one important respect: whereas the infliction of the wound upon Satan causes a great deal of pain, the infliction of the wound upon Adam is painless. The experience of pain is the result of the fallen condition. Pain, as Satan says at one point, "debases" and "enfeebles"; Adam is exempt from such "wounds" (IX, 486–488). When Adam and Eve do fall, however, the effect is that of a cosmological wounding: "Earth felt the wound, and Nature from her seat / Sighing through all her Works gave signs of woe, / That all was lost" (IX, 782–784). The wound which was previously a creative vehicle now assumes antithetical meanings. Adam and Eve experience the wounding of Satan.

Returning to the War in Heaven, then, we see that Milton causes apparently unrelated incidents to become parts of a larger pattern. He causes, as I also attempted to demonstrate, the same thing to happen to words. Indeed, if we view his language within this larger perspective, we can discern a great deal occurring in local instances that we might not otherwise have been able to see. To demonstrate my point, let me exercise my assumptions upon a passage that describes the retreat of Satan and his crew after the initial conflict has ended. In my analysis, I shall draw upon meanings presumably established earlier in the study. Having called his "Potentates to Councel," Satan "with his rebellious *disappeerd* / Far in the dark *dislodg'd*, and *void* of rest" (VI, 414–416; italics mine). A reading of the italicized words situates us semantically at various points in the epic. For example, "disappeerd" characterizes Satan's deceptiveness, his penchant for evasion and for causing that which appears perceptible and meaningful to lose its validity. The sleight-of-hand approach indicates his attitude toward the entire created world. Thus Satan in his "atheism" causes the validity of believing in the created godhead to lose its meaning, just as he causes the power of the created Word to disappear.[3]

"Dislodg'd" returns us to the creative and uncreative ideas of "possess" and "dispossess." The dislodging of something from its proper sphere is most characteristic of Satan's uncreative approach. As Satan and his crew are "dislodg'd" within the "dark" of the battlefield in Heaven, so they will be forcefully "dislodg'd" within the darkness of Hell. Furthermore, the movement within the confines of the dark in order to hold secret "Councel" suggests the movement within Pandaemonium. Such a movement suggests a return to a dark place in order to create something out of that darkness. The "dislodgment" of the angels is associated with their disappearance, for in their fall they will be made to "disappear" into Hell and thus be made inconsequential to the blissful state of Heaven, to the faithful angels, and to God in his holy rest.

The idea of holy rest is also associated with the third italicized word. "Void" characterizes the future experience of Chaos that the rebel angels will have to undergo in their fall. Their present deprivation of rest will manifest itself on a higher level when they encounter that uncreated world whose

[3] Satan's propensity for causing words to lose their meaning is discussed by Ferry, *Milton's Epic Voice*, pp. 117–121.

very nature is one of deprivation and confusion. Finally, that "void" is exactly what Satan and the rebel angels would cause in Heaven in their desire to destroy God's holy rest. Such is the richness of Milton's use of language, that his words contain within them reverberations of the entire generative pattern.

The personal conflict is completed; it remains for Satan to retaliate and for Milton to change his focus from primarily individual combats to mass warfare. The shift is made especially dramatic by the interlude in which Satan and his crew hold their meeting after the first day's battle. The preparations for retaliation have a direct bearing on the idea of creation in the poem.

In the "Councel" scene Nisroc longs for a "deliverer" to "invent" something that would "offend" the rebel angels' "yet unwounded Enemies" (VI, 464–466). "Invent" suggests the idea of mechanical creativity, the purpose of which here is to destroy. Satan, the prime "inventor" or fabricator, answers Nisroc's call for a "deliverer": "Not uninvented that, which thou aright / Beleivst so main to our success, I bring" (VI, 470–471).

Satan then assumes the role of a teacher who indoctrinates his pupils into the ways of creation. Because this War is based upon the very principles of creation, those who are fighting must understand those principles. Satan, therefore, explains to the rebel angels what he has discovered. Since part of Satan's fallen condition involves his violation of the secrets of generation, his disobedience of God has carried him beyond the "surfaces" of the created universe and has indoctrinated him into what lies beneath the surface. He imparts such forbidden knowledge to his followers as part of their own degradation:

Which of us who beholds the bright surface
Of this Ethereous mould whereon we stand,
This continent of spacious Heav'n, adornd
With Plant, Fruit, Flowr Ambrosial, Gemms and Gold,
Whose Eye so superficially surveys

These things, as not to mind from whence they grow
Deep under ground, materials dark and crude,
Of spiritous and fierie spume, till toucht
With Heav'ns ray, and temperd they shoot forth
So beauteous, op'ning to the ambient light.

(VI, 472–481)

Satan has described the entire process of creation; indeed, the passage, taken out of context, is almost a celebration. It reveals an essential aspect of the creative process associated with divinity. Heaven itself had to be created by an exterior force, and it was not created out of something that was as beautiful as the finished product. Rather, it was created out of that which is the antithesis of beauty, that which is "dark" and "crude" and "spiritous" and "fierie."

Beauty has its source in darkness, which represents the inability to behold beauty, and crudity, which represents the absence of healthful creativity. When these materials of origin come in contact with that which is creative, Heaven's "ambient light," they react to the ray by shooting forth into a state of beauty. They "open" in their receptiveness to the all-encompassing light: a union of creative interchange is therefore established between divinity and the thing created. Satan's attitude toward creation, however, is ultimately more concerned with that dark, crude, and fiery world beneath the surface than with that beautiful world above the surface. Satan has not been satisfied with Heaven's apparent bliss but has felt compelled in his discovery of the source of beauty to devote himself wholly to the negative properties of that source.

Such properties reveal themselves in Satan's very descriptions; that is, the language Satan uses to deal with origins of his creation is as perverse and crude as the origins themselves. His vocabulary has markedly sexual overtones that reflect Satan's depraved preoccupation with birth:

These in thir dark Nativitie the Deep
Shall yeild us, pregnant with infernal flame,

Which into hollow Engins long and round
Thick-rammd, at th'other bore with touch of fire
Dilated and infuriate shall send forth
From far with thundring noise among our foes
Such implements of mischief as shall dash
To pieces, and orewhelm whatever stands
Adverse.

(VI, 482–490)

Here we have even further indication that Satan's violation of the created universe extends to his penetrating its surface and tampering with that which should be left to God alone. By dissociating God from the creative act, Satan has taken upon himself the responsibility of the creator. His mode of "creativity," however, may be equated with defamation: he will violate the "pregnancy" of the "Deep," whose "yielding" is of a sexual nature. Satan will take the state of pregnancy and cause it to give birth not to beauty but to weapons opposed to beauty, weapons whose purpose is to return that which has been created beautiful to its previously uncreated state.

The marvelous engines of destruction which will effect the Satanic "return" emerge from Satan's world of defilement. The connotations of the language that describes these engines reveal that aspect of debasement. Thus the engines are "long," "round," "thick," and "dilated" or swollen instruments that "send forth" their contents furiously. The act of "sending forth" as an aspect of uncreativity offers fit contrast to the beauty that these same materials "shoot forth" when "temperd" with Heaven's light. The Satanic image concerns the perverted tampering of cosmic disorder as a means of effecting disorder; the deific image concerns the restraining of disorder as a means of effecting order. The conflict between the two acts finds expression through the same image of "shooting forth." Even under Heaven there lies the womb of destructive primeval elements that are continuously warring with one another, until God's creating light causes beauty to be born from Chaos.

In response to Satan's lecture on creation, the entire host of rebel angels "admire" their new "inventor" as they might admire God for his ability to create:

Th'invention all admir'd, and each, how hee
To be th'inventer miss'd, so easie it seemd
Once found, which yet unfound most would have
                                                                 thought
Impossible.

                                                        (VI, 498–501)

Such admiration has overtones of dramatic irony. In contrast to sublime and natural creativity stands artificial and ingenious invention. Indeed, "invention" becomes a term of disparagement when applied to Satan, whose ingenuity in finding something out (and therefore "inventing") opposes God's spontaneous creativity. Furthermore, the manner in which God's creatures "admire" their Creator's works is far different from the way in which Satan's followers "admire" their master's inventions. God's creatures celebrate God as a sublime Creator without reservation; however, Satan's followers admire Satan as an "inventer" with a touch of envy. They wish that they could have come up with such an invention before Satan had. Consequently, Satan's original envy of God's creations has been transferred to his own followers, who direct it toward their master.

After Satan completes his lecture, the rebel angels set about their new "creative" mission with renewed hope. Their creation of the instruments of destruction is an act that brings to mind a sexual violation and an assault. In the perverted attitude of an offender performing a gross operation, the rebel angels "turn" up "Wide the Celestial soil, and [see] beneath / Th'originals of Nature in thir crude / Conception" (VI, 509–512). The turning up of the "Celestial soil" reiterates the pattern of creating an opening as a prelude to the "creative" act. Their peering into the opening at the "originals of Nature" recalls Satan's perverted peering into the hole of Chaos as a violation of privacy. The term "originals," which are disturbed in their "crude conception," unmistakably refers to images concerning the reproductive organs. The "crudity" by which the "originals" are characterized reflects their generative state: they are not yet entirely created but merely "conceived," that is, present in their "substantial" form. Because in their perverted creativity the rebel angels are debasing the sublimity of God's creative act, the term "crude" might also apply morally to the actions of Satan's crew. By turning up the soil of Heaven, these angels confront the "Entrails" (VI, 517) of the "Deep" and create weapons out of the vitiated material. Their process of creation is metaphorically anal: they create engines of destruction out of putrefaction.

After the engines have been created, the troops of the faithful and the rebel angels face each other again. In striking contrast to the glorious military formation that God's army assumes is the simulated union of the rebel angels. They are described in the language of their own obscenity as a "Foe / Approaching *gross* and *huge*" (VI, 551–552; italics mine). The language is covertly sexual in its application to the distasteful figure the unfaithful angels make in their formation. The sense is that of a perverted exhibitionism: the grossness and hugeness of their own affront to God is compared to the "dilated" engines that they have created. The "Foe" approaches "in hollow Cube / Training his devilish Enginrie, impal'd / On every side with shaddowing Squadrons Deep / To hide the fraud" (VI, 551–555).

As the "Quadrate" that the faithful angels form "stands for" or symbolizes the perfection of Heaven, the "hollow Cube" that the rebel angels form represents the grossness of their perverted sexuality. The word "hollow" is applied both to the "Cube" or military formation of the fallen crew and to the machines they have invented, so that the hollowness of their devices is associated with the nonproductivity of Hell and Chaos, both of which are characterized as "hollow" (I, 314; II, 518). Nothing productive can issue out of the emptiness of any of these worlds: if anything does issue out, we recall, it is monstrous and perverted. Such monstrous perversion is exactly what the rebel angels are hiding in their formations: that instrument which has already been characterized in phallic terms as "hollow" and "swollen."

Within their formations, the fallen angels "train" or "aim" their "devilish Enginrie" at the faithful angels before they expose their "distasteful" creation. Immediately Satan gives the command: "Vanguard, to Right and Left the Front unfould; / That all may see" (VI, 558–559), and their "gross" creation is revealed as the "Front unfoulds" and exposes suddenly to the view what has been hidden all along. At the sight of so base an object prepared to vilify the purity of the faithful angels, the unfallen reaction of the faithful to something so "new and strange" (VI, 571) is that of bewilderment. They in "suspense, / Collected stood within [their] thoughts amus'd" (VI, 580–581).

That startling sight is followed by the igniting and firing of the weapons.

> Immediate in a flame,
> But soon obscur'd with smoak, all Heav'n appeerd,
> From those *deep-throated* Engins *belcht*, whose roar
> *Emboweld* with outrageous noise the Air,
> And all her *entrails* tore, *disgorging foul*
> Thir devilish *glut*.
>
> (VI, 584–589; italics mine)

Here we have the imagistic justification of God's statement that the Satanic world is one of "draff" or refuse and "filth" (X, 630). Such an attitude, as suggested, necessarily accords with Milton's polemical purpose in the epic. Logically, since Satan is the complete antithesis of God, his acts of defilement must be the absolute antithesis of God's acts of purity. Consequently, the engines' giving forth of fire that creates a "thundring noise" (VI, 487) when forced out of an opening is associated with perversion of the worst sort. The previous images of phallicism are fused here with those of anality to represent a debasement of God's creativity. The phallus, ordinarily a symbol of procreation, is here related to the anus as a symbol of the voiding of waste material. Satan's invention, then, partakes entirely of the obscene as opposed to the sublime. To complete the debased associations, anal and oral images (compare also the gaping "mouths" and "hideous orifices" of VI, 576–577) are combined to effect a most "outrageous" sense of Satanic evil.

As mouths, the "deep-throated Engins" not only belch out their inwards but vomit up the disgusting contents within them. "Disgorging" as the result of having been "gluttonous" relates the act of vomiting to that of "emboweling" and of causing "entrails" to be torn in the process. The consequences of the devilish devices are in keeping with their obscene implications, for their use results in "foul dissipation" and "indecent overthrow" (VI, 598–601).

In a reverse parody of the warring giants of the earth, the faithful angels defend themselves against the unexpected onslaught by tearing up the hills from their foundations and piling them upon the rebel angels' heads (VI, 639–655). The result is that "Hills amid the Air encountered Hills" until Heaven begins to undergo a transformation: it experiences, as suggested earlier, the process of uncreation, of return to its chaotic state. Indeed, Heaven is not only becoming Chaos but is taking on some of the "infernal" characteristics of Hell (VI, 666–667).

Here the "heroic" qualities of individual combat begin to degenerate. Milton no longer refers to the fighting of angel with angel. Rather, he describes objects encountering objects. The battle has become completely depersonalized, and seen objectively, it represents the warring of the elements.

If the tearing up of the hills suggests the reduction to Chaos, then the return of the hills to their proper places suggests the restoration, and, indeed, generation of order. It is important to recognize the symbolical overtones of these antithetical motions, for such a recognition allows us to see what God's uncreating of the angels through the agency of the Son really implies. Paradoxically, the Son's uncreating of Satan and his crew is not an uncreative act. Unlike Satan, who destroys for the sake of destroying, the Son destroys in order to create.

That generative fact is symbolized in the Son's returning of the hills to their proper places. As an aspect of his uncreating the rebel angels, the Son causes creation to evolve from the Chaos of war:

> At his command th'uprooted Hills retir'd
> Each to his place, they heard his voice and went
> Obsequious, Heav'n his wonted face renewd,
> And with fresh Flowrets Hill and Valley smil'd.
>   (VI, 781–784)

With the return of the uprooted hills to their proper places, a consequent sense of renewal and rebirth occurs. Such a word as "obsequious" recalls the original image of divine creativity: the holy Hill itself with its "obsequious" offspring light and dark (VI, 4–10). Chaos becomes creation through the all-creating voice of the Son.

The same creative act is described in God's generation of the earth, when, in reaction to God's voice "Immediately the Mountains huge appear / Emergent, and thir broad bare backs upheave / Into the Clouds, thir tops ascend the Skie" (VII, 285–287). The emerging of the hills in the creation of the earth is prefigured here by the hills' taking root again at God's Word. Both are creative acts: one indicating re-generation in Heaven, the other indicating generation in earth. The motion of the hills' taking root is a symbolical comment on God's ultimate purpose: even when he has come through the agency of his Son to uncreate (to "uproot" Satan), his intentions are creative. Such is the tenor of all God's actions: uncreation is merely an aspect of the creative or re-creative act.

With the coming of the Son on the third day, the perspective comes full circle in its return to the personal, except that now one against the many rather than individual warfare (soldier against soldier) is depicted. The final perspective for the Christian poet is the most glorious, for here is the grand example that all men must follow in order to be redeemed. Here is the trial of the "greater Man" confronting and over-coming the wicked multitudes.

The situation prefigured in Abdiel is now fulfilled sym-bolically in the Son. As I shall discuss, the pattern will continue throughout history in such figures as Enoch, Noah, Abraham, Moses, and David (Books XI and XII), and it will culminate in the Son as Messiah who will withstand all adversity and return again at the Apocalypse to defeat the forces of evil eternally. The present routing out of the angels foreshadows that final act, and the tone of the poem accor-dingly adapts itself at the conclusion of the sixth book to the sense of apocalyptic vision.

The Son arrives, as suggested, to uncreate (and thereby symbolically re-create) in the same Paternal Chariot that carries him on his creative mission into Chaos in Book VII. Milton's adaptation of Ezekiel's vision is particularly relevant to the creational imagery.[4] As a revelation of divine and living wrath, the Chariot's "multitude of eyes" (VI, 754–756, 845–847) deprive the rebel angels of their strength, "And of thir wonted vigour left them draind, / Exhausted, spiritless, afflicted, fall'n" (VI, 849–852).

The Spirit that imbues the vehicle of revelation is the same Spirit that gives life and strength to all created things, and in a reversal of that process can at will deprive all created things of their vital energy. Such a Spirit vivifies the Chariot and operates through the eyes. This is the "blessed vision" (V, 613) become an instrument of wrath: it is revealed to the sight of both the rebel and the faithful angels. Both sets of angels respond to the revelation in an antithetical manner, one set almost in a trance of disbelief and astonishment, the other set in a trance of enlightenment and respect. The rebel angels respond to the revelation with dread: their experience of revelation is, ironically, one of being "insensate" with "hope conceiving from despair" (VI, 787). The faithful angels

---

[4] Its alchemical significance is discussed in the Appendix, n. 6.

glory in the revelation and receive their strength from it: they stand as in a trance, "Eye witnesses of [God's] Almightie Acts" (VI, 882–883). Thus, the living vehicle of both God's wrath and creativity becomes the instrument of sight, of revelation that, with its multitude of eyes, causes trances in others. The vision results either in stupefaction and an ultimate deprivation of sight or in glory and respect and a celebration of the ability to see. Spiritually blinded and deprived of strength, the fallen angels may now experience the full repercussions of their rebellion. The consequences of the fall as they manifest themselves first in Hell and later on earth, consequently, will be of major concern in a discussion of uncreation.

Chapter 5

Satan's Fall & Its
Immediate Consequences

IN ORDER TO have some idea of how Satan and his crew react to their perdition, we must first view them in Hell's confines immediately after they have fallen. What they do (or are allowed to do) at that point will have repercussions throughout the poem. We must accordingly focus upon their plight with a knowledge of what that plight will lead to both immediately, as they are revived and then sit in council, and ultimately, as they corrupt man through Satan. The immediate consequences of their fall will, therefore, be our initial concern.

We see Satan and his cohorts in Book I lying "vanquisht, rowling in the fiery Gulf, / Confounded through immortal" (I, 52–53). Paradoxically, their immortality does not preserve them from destruction, for they are still "confounded." Indeed, even after they have "escaped" the "fiery Gulf," they still "feel by turns the bitter change / Of fierce extreams" (II, 598–599), in which they are rushed from fire to ice and then back to fire. Caught in a paralysis of unfillment, Satan and his crew act, as previously suggested, in the illusion that they yet have the power to act. But in making their actions contrary to God's, they are forever bound in a Hell of contraries, and if they act at all, their mobility is only temporary and is effected only through the will of God (I, 209–213).

Ironically, Satan never admits that what he feels to be the sense of renewal after the fall has any connection with divinity. Characteristically, he attributes his revivification to his own native powers: "for the mind and spirit," he supposes, "remains / Invincible, and vigour soon returns" (I, 139–140). Thus he has no conception of the extent to which he has been uncreated; and the only thing he has learned in his fall is that God is stronger than he. Satan is to discover, of course, that not only is he a subject to "torture without end," but he is a perpetual prey to a "fiery Deluge," whether external or internal, that is forever uncreating him, since it is "fed / With ever-burning Sulphur unconsum'd" (I, 68–69).

In addition, Satan mistakes the extent of God's strength, first by dissociating God's will from his own supposed revivification after the fall, and second by assuming that he will in his new freedom be able to pervert God's ultimate ends. Appropriately, Satan feels that the way to counter those ends is to thwart God as a Creator. That is, if God will create goodness out of evil now that Satan has fallen and evil exists (at least potentially), Satan will "pervert that end, / And out of good still . . . find means of evil" (I, 162–165). Finding means of evil implies two acts: as discussed, it implies the returning of creation to Chaos, but it also implies creating evil out of good. (Ultimately, of course, Satan's uncreative activities will serve "but to bring forth / Infinite goodness" [I, 217–218] and thus fulfill the *felix culpa*, a concept to be dealt with at greater length. My immediate point is that in concerning ourselves with the concept at all, we must simultaneously concern ourselves with birth in the epic.)

If the repercussions of creating evil out of good became evident in Satan's creation of cannons in the War in Heaven, the impulse to pervert and debase reveals itself most dramatically in Hell. Indeed, the nature of Hell reinforces the horror of Satan's negative approach, for Satan is made to inhabit

> A Universe of death, which God by curse
> Created evil, for evil only good,
> Where all life dies, death lives, and nature breeds,
> Perverse, all monstrous, all prodigious things,
> Abominable, inutterable, and worse

Then Fables yet have feign'd, or fear conceiv'd,
Gorgons and *Hydra's*, and *Chimera's* dire.
(II, 622–628)

A world characterized by its birth, Hell becomes the creation
of a curse and the procreator itself of cursed things. It
becomes, that is, a place where the concept of uncreation
manifests itself procreatively in a "perverse," "monstrous,"
"prodigious," "abominable," and "inutterable" brood. And
as the primal center of the absurdity and degeneration that
uncreation represents, Hell stands as the fit antithesis and
obscene parody of Heaven. In sum, we may expect to find
uncreation in *Paradise Lost* revealed through an imagery
of ugliness as opposed to beauty, of sickness as opposed to
health, of illusion and materiality as opposed to reality and
spirituality, of lust and unfillment as opposed to love and
fulfillment, and of guilt and disobedience as opposed to
innocence and submission.

From the point of view of uncreation, then, we will be
able to see how Satan and his activities ironically further
God's creative ends. With a knowledge that Milton invites
us to interpret Satan's posture, his gestures, indeed his very
physical presence within the context of birth, we may
return to the original image of Satan on the burning lake.

With Head up-lift above the waves, and Eyes
That sparkling blaz'd, his other parts besides
Prone on the Flood, extended long and large
Lay floating many a rood, in bulk as huge
As whom the Fables name of monstrous size.
(I, 193–197)

Although the image of Satan floating upon the waves is
covertly sexual, its phallicism[1] is strong enough to suggest
associations with the idea of uncreation. The "huge," indeed
"monstrous," figure "extended long and large" is prone
upon an element mythologically as well as imagistically

[1] See J. B. Broadbent, "Milton's Hell," *ELH*, XXI (1954), 175–176, for a discussion of phallic implications pertaining to Hell.

related to procreation. Mythologically, if the substance that has received Satan's body is the river Lethe ("th'oblivious Pool" [I, 266]), then it is traditionally the element from which souls drink before they are reincarnated.[2] Imagistically, Milton often causes water to become an element of birth, as we saw in his account of the earth's creation in the "Womb . . ./ Of Waters" that "Fermented the great Mother to conceave, / Satiate with genial moisture" (VII, 276–282). Because we are in the presence of an uncreated being, however, we are required to see water acting uncreatively. Unlike the "genial" or life-giving "moisture" that both sustains and allows the "great Mother" earth to "conceave" healthy offspring, the fiery deluge causes unfulfillment, the heat of lust,[3] and, through Satan, debased offspring. It is not enough, on the other hand, to see Satan as the progenitor of Sin and Death in *Paradise Lost*; prone on the flood and floating in his own "genial moisture," Satan suggests additional uncreative ideas.

The degradation and impotence of Satan's prostrate posture after his fall are repeated in the figure of fallen Adam:

> On the ground
> Outstretcht he lay, on the cold ground, and oft
> Curs'd his Creation.
>
> (X, 850–852)

In both figures we are presented with the uncreative mode of thought. There is a similar bodily extension in both, and whereas in Hell the element of Satan's unfulfillment is expressed in the heat of fire, in Eden the element of Adam's

[2] See, for example, the *Aeneid*, VI, 713–715. Appropriately, the fallen angels are not allowed to drink from Lethe (II, 604–614).

[3] The extremes of unfulfillment, lust, and frigidity are fused in the barrenness which is Hell. Thus the "parching Air / Burns frore, and cold performs th'effect of Fire" (II, 594–595). In this place, the elemental qualities of fire and water and ice combine in a language of oxymoron to reveal the incongruity and absurdity of the fallen state. The imagistic offspring themselves are of an impossible and contradictory nature: darkness becomes visible (I, 63), water burns with fire (I, 68), and frozen air causes parching and "burns" with cold (II, 595).

unfulfillment is expressed in the coldness of "damps and dreadful gloom" (x, 848). In both cases the atmosphere of the fall is one of extremes: there is no longer the unfallen climatic or psychologic temperance of "cool" and "mild" (x, 847). Creation as the product of such temperance is denied in both, and what we have, rather, is a cursing of creation (Hell, we recall, is created as the result of a curse [II, 622–623]). Impotency is the punishment of such an uncreative posture, so that with respect to both Satan and Adam, one cannot be productive within the fallen, uncreative condition.

Satan is, however, able to revive the "associates and copartners" who "lye thus astonisht on th'oblivious Pool" (I, 265–266). Indeed, in reviving them, Satan will, as I shall argue, assume the Mosaic function of a deliverer, and the imagery accompanying the delivery will recall, ironically, Satan's initial posture of defeat. That is, the phallicism of Satan floating in his "genial moisture" will become transformed into the image of Moses extending his "potent Rod" creatively "Over the Sea" (XII, 211–212). As a result, revivification and delivery will become fused in an image suggesting the ultimate destruction of evil. Before we discuss Satan's Mosaic role, let us discuss his revivifying one.

As Satan feels that he is responsible for his "own recover'd strength" and not dependent upon the "sufferance of supernal Power" (I, 240–241), so Beelzebub feels that his master will be able to re-create the fallen angels with the sound of his creating voice. Beelzebub says of the angels:

> If once they hear [Satan's] voyce,
>
> .   .   .   .
>
>   they will soon resume
> New courage and revive, though now they lye
> Groveling and prostrate on yon Lake of Fire.
>   (I, 274–280)

Beelzebub has transferred his allegiance from God as Creator to Satan as creator through his belief in the creative potentialities of Satan's voice. And Satan's act of revivifying the angels becomes a parody of God's bringing substance to life through the Word.[4] Thus Satan "call'd so loud, that the hollow Deep / Of Hell resounded" (I, 314–315). The tone of his creating voice is, ironically, one of contempt and disparagement toward the object which it is bringing to life, rather than one of glorification characterized by God's creating voice. Satan upbraids the "abject posture" (I, 322) of his fallen cohorts and warns them that they are in for a further defeat from Heaven's angels if they remain in that posture (I, 323–329). Like Adam, Satan "curses" his creation as a means of vivifying: "Awake, arise, or be for ever fall'n" (I, 330). The reaction of the fallen angels to the feeling of being re-created is not one of glory but of "dread" (I, 333). They are "abasht" (I, 331) or confounded in astonishment, and they awaken through Satan's supposed creativity not to a sense of celebration in a new life but to "fierce pains" (I, 336).

Now we are prepared to see the Mosaic aspect of Satan's revivifying activities. To appreciate Satan as a Moses figure, we must explore Milton's figurative language. In describing the prostrate angels before they are revived, Milton moves from a seasonal image to an historical one. He compares the angels first to "Autumnal Leaves" and "scattered sedge" and then, by implication, to the Egyptians defeated upon the Red Sea while the Hebrews look on from the shore in safety (I, 304–312). The first image implies natural loss and dispersion, the second a contrast between those evil forces that are destroyed and those good forces that are saved. (Among other things, the comparison suggests the idea of the faithful angels, safe within Heaven's bounds, viewing the overthrow of the rebel angels.) If we reconsider the action that follows and relate it to the simile, however, we may be surprised to find that the Egyptian forces do not remain long defeated. Reversing Moses' role as deliverer of

[4] The counterpart of Satan's Word, according to Northrop Frye, *The Return of Eden*, p. 19, is Death.

the Hebrews, Satan delivers his own host and thereby lets loose, at least potentially, the powers of destruction upon the world. Ignoring for the present man's role and responsibility in allowing evil to enter his life, we are made to respond by asking why evil should be allowed to reassert itself and what its presence signifies. Is this how Milton justifies God's ways to men?

The Mosaic context, however, is not yet complete, for the idea of Satan as Moses reappears shortly in another figure that becomes a counterpart of the first one. Whereas originally Satan's revivification of the angels is seen implicitly as the bringing back to life of the Egyptian host, the second simile causes revivification to mean something entirely different. Satan becomes Moses again, but this time Satan's act of delivery is self-defeating: in reviving his cohorts, he now calls up a "pitchy cloud / Of *Locusts*" with his "potent Rod" (I, 338–341). The purpose of the locusts, of course, is to destroy the Egyptians (I, 342),[5] with whom the rebel angels have just ironically been compared. Consequently, if Satan is able to deliver his rebel angels as Moses delivered the Hebrews, he must also destroy his cohorts in that very revivification. As I see it, the combination of the two figures implies what Milton is to make clear in the action of the poem: evil becomes self-defeating and thereby generates itself in order to destroy itself. Satan's enactment of birth is simultaneously his enactment of self-destruction; Satan fulfills God's divine plan by creating temporarily in order to destroy himself ultimately. With Moses and his "potent Rod," we return to Satan impotently prone upon the burning lake.

Before we may see that return ultimately effected, however, we must first discern the immediate repercussions of Satan's creativity. That is, if we view Satan's revivification of the angels dialectically, we must also recall that when Satan creates, he uncreates. Milton dramatizes this idea, I

[5] The locusts are the means of exodus, but they are also associated with Apollyon of Rev. 9.

think, as he further describes the way in which the angels are revived. Satan with his "uplifted Spear" like Moses with his "potent Rod" causes the birth of a "multitude, like which the populous North/Pour'd never from her frozen loyns" (I, 351–352). In Satan's uncreative world, the frigidity of "frozen loyns" produces offspring, and the nature of that offspring is monstrous, hideous, and "barbarous" (I, 353). We are reminded of the hideous births that characterize Hell. The purpose of the hideous creatures that Satan brings to life is, of course, to cause further corruption. As creatures of uncreation, they would uncreate others by causing those who obey them to "forsake / God thir Creator" (I, 368–369). And the result of forsaking one's Creator, as I shall discuss in much greater detail, is to "transform" oneself into the "Image of a Brute" (I, 370–371). What should concern us now is the idea that in considering any of the fallen angels individually, we are dealing with uncreated forms. Indeed, Milton emphasizes the creational dimension when he refers to the fallen angels through their future roles as deities in the world of man.

Appearing first in Milton's catalogue of the fallen angels, Moloch is described as the

> horrid King besmear'd with blood
> Of human sacrifice, and parent tears
> Though for the noyse of Drums and Timbrels loud
> Thir cries unheard, that past through fire
> To his grim Idol.
>
> (I, 392–396)

Moloch's characteristics accord precisely with the idea of uncreation that Satan and his crew represent. The furnace contained within Moloch's brass statue,[6] for example, suggests more than a place of horrible brutality. If we view the furnace mythopoetically as a "mother symbol, where [ironically] . . . children are produced,"[7] Moloch's furnace

---

[6] Tillyard, ed., *Paradise Lost: Books I and II*, p. 128n.
[7] Jung, *The Psychology of the Unconscious*, p. 184.

becomes a veritable place of uncreation, where children are consumed. Moloch, then, symbolizes in his sacrifices a perversion of the generative idea. Indeed, Milton underscores that pervision by directly associating Moloch with the fallen angel that follows. As the "obscene dread of *Moabs* Sons" (I, 406), Chemos or Peor "entic'd"

> *Israel* in *Sittim* on thir march from *Nile*
> To do him wanton rites, which cost them woe.
> Yet thence his lustful Orgies he enlarg'd
> Ev'n to that Hill of scandal, by the Grove
> Of *Moloch* homicide, lust hard by hate.
>   (I, 413–417)

According to Joseph Summers, the "juxtaposition of 'lust hard by hate' prevents our misunderstanding."[8] The homicidal destructiveness found in Moloch becomes a counterpart of the obscenity and lust found in Peor. In Milton's moral universe, "lust is particularly congruent with hatred."[9] Moloch and Peor reveal themselves, therefore, as variations of the same uncreative impulse in *Paradise Lost*.

Next follow Baalim and Ashtaroth, through whom the "Race of *Israel*" bowed "lowly down / To bestial Gods" (I, 434–435). Ashtaroth or Astarte demands the corruption of healthful love in having virgins pay "Vows and Songs" to her "bright Image nightly by the Moon" (I, 440–441). "Milton," according to Summers, "considered both the devotion to the 'image' and virginal vows as perversions of human love."[10] As the culmination of such perversion, Thammuz next appears:

> [His] annual wound in *Lebanon* allur'd
> The *Syrian* Damsels to lament his fate
> In amorous ditties all a Summers day,
> While smooth *Adonis* from his native Rock

---

[8] *The Muse's Method*, p. 90. My discussion of the pagan deities is heavily indebted to Summers.
[9] Ibid.
[10] Ibid.

> Ran purple to the Sea, suppos'd with blood
> Of *Thammuz* yearly wounded.
>
> (I, 447–452)

In the wounding of Thammuz we may find debased the pattern of death and regeneration that characterizes the Son's sacrificial wounding and consequent rebirth. As we discussed with the wounding of Satan in Heaven, the wound may degrade as well as glorify. Here its overtones are those of perverted sexuality as opposed to spiritual transcendence. Whereas the Son's sacrifice for humanity represents divine love, Thammuz's death epitomizes the idea of pagan carnality found in Milton's allusion to the Adonis legend. The damsels' amorous mourning for Thammuz indicates fallen love as *eros*, the so-called courtly passion that Milton spurns in his celebration of wedded love (IV, 750–770). *Eros*, of course, is opposed to unfallen love as *agape*, the "unlibidinous" love between Adam and Eve (V, 449) and the love of God in transcendent vision.[11] The love that Thammuz represents, then, is seductive: it causes "Damsels" to turn away from the adoration of God and to worship the selfishness of earthly love, which is transient rather than permanent. Such carnality is associated with death rather than with life, and it is conducive to the "heat" of "wanton passions" (I, 453–454), which are unhealthy and degenerate and which cause one to be consumed wholly with the self. And to be consumed wholly with one's ego, as I shall discuss, results in the "confusion of sexual desire with the desire for death."[12]

The "deities" that follow represent in their distorted shapes the extreme of sexual corruption. Thus Dagon's physical unnaturalness—"Sea Monster, upward Man / And downward Fish" (I, 462–463)—approximates his moral

[11] For a discussion of *eros* and *agape*, see M. C. D'Arcy, *The Mind and Heart of Love* (2nd. edn. rev; Cleveland, 1962), p. 63. Also Campbell, *The Hero with a Thousand Faces*, p. 6, distinguishes between death as *thanatos* or *destrudo* and love as *eros* or *libido*. See, however, Boyette, "Something More About the Erotic Motive in *Paradise Lost*."

[12] Summers, p. 91.

nature and foreshadows in his bipartite division the description of Sin. Dagon is one of the "monstrous . . . prodigious things" (II, 625) that Hell "breeds" as part of its creativity. Other such perversities are "*Osiris, Isis, Orus* and thir Train" (I, 478), whose physical proportions are "monstrous" and "brutish" (I, 478–481) and who cause similar monstrosities in men. Thus, states Summers, "from Thammuz the descent is clear: after those false gods who are part monster and part man are those who take 'brutish forms / Rather than human' (I, 481–482)."[13]

And the last and greatest of all representatives of sexual perversion is Belial himself,

> then whom a Spirit more lewd
> Fell not from Heaven, or more gross to love
> Vice for it self.
>
> (I, 490–492)

As Summers says,

> Belial is at the bottom of the infernal hierarchy. The 'grossness' of his combination of injury and outrage with insolence and wine finds its proper type in the impersonal rape of the matron by the group which wished to rape the supposedly masculine angel [I, 492–505].[14]

The remainder of the pagan deities are alluded to peripherally, yet generatively. For example, Milton mentions "*Titan* Heav'ns first born / With his enormous brood, and birthright seis'd / By younger *Saturn*" (I, 510–512), so that even with this brief allusion are sounded the primary uncreative motifs of monstrous offspring and the son's violation of the father's "birthright" from one generation to the next (I, 512–513).

As we can see by the examples cited, the immediate consequences of the fall upon the faithful angels have far-

---

[13] Ibid.
[14] Ibid., pp. 91–92.

reaching effects and contain many of the poem's major implications. Through Milton's description of the fallen angels both as they are revived in Hell and as they are characterized in the world of man, we are able to perceive the importance of corrupt and unhealthy creativity to the action of *Paradise Lost*. That perverted creativity lies at the heart of the unfaithful angels' existence, however, is nowhere more apparent than in Pandaemonium. There, the act of creating in a debased manner dictates the very verbal response of the angels to their fall.

Moloch's stern admonition of his fellow sufferers will offer a fit point of departure:

> them let those
> *Contrive* who need, or when they need, not now.
> For while they *sit contriving* . . . .
> (II, 52–54; italics mine)

What association the italicized words have with generation may not be immediately apparent. To point up the relationship, let me refer to a passage in which the association is apparent: the Spirit of God "Dove-like satst brooding on the vast Abyss / And mad'st it pregnant" (I, 21–22). (That image in turn recalls the "Birds of Calm" that "sit brooding on the charmed wave" [l. 6 in the "Nativity Ode"].) Here we have the essential combination of the physical and, by implication, mental postures that in *Paradise Lost* represent the sublime process of causing birth. Impregnation, at least imagistically, becomes the result of sitting, on the one hand, and brooding (both physically and mentally), on the other. We recall that the poet must also meditate or "brood" in order to give birth to his poem. Dialectically, the fallen angels re-enact the same pattern of sitting and brooding in order to effect their uncreative ends. When Moloch says "sit contriving," then, Milton is allowing him to draw upon the very images that describe the Spirit of God's "physical" and "mental" postures in the creative act.

Moloch's use of the word "contrive" is, of course, ironic:

it suggests the artificiality that characterizes debased creativity. (As suggested earlier, the cannons invented in Heaven
are artificially "contrived," as opposed to God's works,
which are naturally generated.) Indeed, the entire council
in Pandaemonium implies a debasement of sublime generation, for when the fallen angels attempt to "contrive"
through deception and fraud a means of overcoming God,
their solution is uncreative and results in their ultimate
defeat. Furthermore, as that which is "contrived," the
democratic atmosphere of debate in the council becomes a
façade that serves only to glorify Satan's predetermined
plans. Finally, the cognitive process associated with "contrive" results in the predicament of those fallen angels who
later

> sat on a Hill retir'd,
> In thoughts more elevate, and reason'd high
> Of Providence, Foreknowledge, Will and Fate,
> Fixt Fate, free will, foreknowledge absolute,
> And found no end, in wandring mazes lost.
>
> (II, 557–561)

Cognition here becomes a continuous internalizing of one's
dilemma, which results in being lost in labyrinthine mazes
that preclude productivity.[15] Ironically, as I shall discuss,
such labyrinthine internalizing finds expression in the figure
of Sin, who also characterizes herself as sitting "pensive"
before she gives birth to Death (II, 777–780).

If we trace the pattern of sitting and brooding even
further, we shall see how pervasive that pattern is in describing
the situation of the fallen angels in Pandaemonium. We
might, for example, consider Beelzebub, in whose "Front
engrav'n / *Deliberation sat*" (II, 302–303; italics mine). He
speaks in a language that draws upon (and debases) the
posture of sublime creativity when he says, "What *sit* we

---

[15] Adam, when he falls, finds himself in a similar cognitive—and, therefore,
creative—predicament. He is also in "wandring mazes lost" (IX, 1121–1131;
X, 715–862).

then *projecting* peace and Warr" (II, 329; italics mine),[16] and when he refers to the angels who "*sit* in darkness here / *Hatching* vain Empires" (II, 377–378; italics mine). In the second instance, the sublime image of the bird-like Spirit "brooding" over the darkness of the Abyss is parodied by the image of the angels "hatching" in the darkness offspring which are "vain." Such offspring exhibit in their vanity a sense of emptiness, uselessness, and pride. Once again, the process of cognition and physical birthgiving in the seated position refers to the same creative metaphor. Whereas God's "brooding" is fruitful—it brings forth a world "Answering his great Idea" (VII, 557)—the fallen angels' "contriving," "projecting," and "hatching" are the direct antitheses of God's creative act.

The original generative pattern of "brooding" upon Chaos as a bird in a sitting position is finally contrasted in the figure of Satan himself when he sits like a cormorant on the Tree of Life "devising Death / To them who liv'd" (IV, 194–198). The same metaphor of sublime generation acts in an antithetical manner. God's cognitive and physical act of "brooding" life becomes the diabolic act of "devising" or creating that which destroys life. And, ironically, Satan performs that uncreative act on the Tree of Life itself. As a further contrast to the original image, the dove-like quality of God is perverted in the cormorant-like quality of Satan. The protection provided by the dove is here debased in the analogy with the bird of prey. If the end of Satanic creativity is one of destroying, of returning life to its uncreated form, the figure of the cormorant is appropriate (compare Isa. 34:11), for the cormorant as a bird that devours is like Death, who is always ravenous to devour or prey upon life (II, 845–847). Appropriately enough, of course, Satan sits like a cormorant in the process of metaphorically giving birth to Death.

Returning to the council, let us explore Moloch's proposal

---

[16] With reference to its creative connotations, "projecting" is a psychological term referring to the creation of fantasies.

for revenge. His "sentence is for open Warr" (II, 51) and for "Turning [their] Tortures into horrid Arms / Against the Torturer" (II, 63–64). What this suggestion has to do with the idea of creativity will become clear if we recall the nature of the union in Heaven. As suggested, the basic idea relating to the union is that of reciprocity: the faithful angels return to God to celebrate him and to receive sustenance from him. Moloch's suggestion perverts the creative concept because it desires that the angels return to God to torture him. As I shall discuss in greater depth, such a perversion of creativity occurs allegorically in Hell with the hellhounds of Sin returning to her womb to torture her. The return to torture, then, becomes a debased counterpart of the return to glorify. Both acts are based antithetically upon the idea of creativity.

In opposition to Moloch, Belial counsels "ignoble ease, and peaceful sloath" (II, 227) and thereby counters the absurdity of a direct siege with the ignominy of total inaction. Therefore, Belial's approach is as uncreative in its inactivity as is Moloch's in its misdirected activity. Just as much as the other angels, Belial attempts to solve his dilemma by means of deception: he would have the fallen angels dupe God into thinking that God's enemies are no longer rebellious but docile. Indeed, Belial imagines God to be as slothful as he when he says that God will "not mind us not offending" (II, 212). The language here debases the entire situation: if we leave God alone, Belial implies, perhaps he'll leave us alone. The interchange is of an infantile nature, and such is exactly the way Belial in his own perverted infantilism conceives of God. That is, he opposes the lewdness and filth within his own mind to his version of a God that does not think dirty thoughts but is "pure," "incorruptible," "unpolluted," and "incapable of [the] stain" of Belial's "mischief" (II, 134–142). Such is the nature of Belial's perverted sexuality, which reduces the grand omnipotence and creativity of God to the lewdness of Belial's own infantilism.

The next to speak in the council is Mammon, whose approach is as uncreative as Moloch's and Belial's. Mammon

would have the angels "seek" their "own good" from themselves, so that their "greatness will appear / Then most
conspicuous" when they "can create" "great things of small /
Useful of hurtful, prosperous of adverse" (II, 251–260). Like
Satan, Mammon would have the angels glorify the self and
receive sustenance and strength wholly through self-
assertion. By these means the fallen angels would supposedly
assert their own greatness in defiance of God. Mammon's
world is totally one of delusive appearances based upon the
vain idea that that which looks impressive is so. (For example,
he would have the fallen angels "imitate" God's "Light"
[II, 269–270][17] and out of Hell's soil "raise / Magnificence;
and what can Heav'n shew more" [II, 271–273].) Thus the
angels would overcome their torments by creating that which
is beneficial to them out of those torments. As a means of
defying God, they would create in the illusion of their own
ability to create and thereby blind themselves to the reality
of their own impotence.

To summarize, then, we might say that in the council each
of the fallen angels characterizes God according to the
peculiarities of his own fallen nature. To Moloch, who
would cause so much torment in others through brutal
sacrifices, God is himself a "Torturer." To Belial, whose very
existence is based upon lewdness, God is no more than one
able to resist the infantile and perverted mischief of a Belial.
To Mammon, who derives his sustenance from the vanity of
appearances, God is none other than a creator of surfaces.
The impotence of all the fallen angels appears in the impotence
of these three angels as they attempt to "contrive" a fruitful
solution to their dilemma.[18] Since they cannot truly mitigate
the condition of their fall by "creative" means, however,
their only recourse is to try to frustrate God's creativity and

[17] Ironically, Mammon ascribes to God his own fallacious and imitative mode
of creativity, for just as Mammon suggests that the angels "imitate" God's
"Light," he also implies that God *imitates* the fallen angels' "darkness."

[18] Even Moloch, who blames the other angels for "contriving," would create
weapons out of his tortures.

goodness by causing God's most recent offspring to experience their creative deprivation.

As a culmination of the uncreative impulse, Beelzebub suggests that the fallen angels destroy the "new Race call'd *Man*" (II, 348) either by "wasting" or "possessing" God's entire "Creation." ("Waste" and "possess," we recall, are intimately associated with Milton's language of birth.) Beelzebub's suggestion is clearly a perversion of the generative idea: revenge becomes the impotent joy felt by the angels in hampering God as a Creator. Indeed, Beelzebub would have God's newly created race undergo the same process of uncreation that the angels themselves experienced. Such an act, Beelzebub thinks, would cause God to turn against his own works and "abolish" them (II, 364–370), thereby "justifying" the angels' fall and invalidating his own animating impulse. Appropriately, this "devilish Counsel" was "first devis'd" by Satan, the "Author of all ill," from whom was born "So deep a malice, to confound the race / Of mankind in one root" (II, 379–383). The "one root," of course, refers to Adam and Eve, who, Satan hopes, will pollute their own offspring as a result of their fall. In this way, Satan seeks impotently to revenge himself upon his Creator. Consequently, from our very first view of Satan prone on the burning waves to our view of him in Pandaemonium, we have seen that his impotence expresses itself as a corruption of creativity. As we shall continue to see, these immediate consequences of Satan's fall extend themselves even further in the course of his uncreative mission.

Chapter 6

Satan's Fall & Its
Extended Consequences

THE GENERATION OF SIN AND DEATH

IF THE IMMEDIATE consequences of Satan's fall are apparent in the scenes involving the burning lake and the council in Pandaemonium, the extended consequences are discernible in the figures of Sin and Death. Centered in them are the primary motifs through which the perverted form of the dialectics manifests itself.[1] Sin and Death become pivotal figures through whom all the varieties of sexual perversion, including incest and narcissism, find expression. Conception, pregnancy, birth and offspring in their most degenerate forms originate here.[2] To have any conception of what the absolute antithesis of sublime creativity suggests, to have any insight into the absolute horror of uncreation at its greatest extreme, is to understand the meaning of Sin and Death, and that implies an understanding of both the immediate and extended relationships to which these figures give rise. Therefore, in this and the next chapter, I shall explore the various motifs initiated in Sin and Death by tracing the implications of those motifs throughout the entire poem.

On his journey to seduce man after the council has concluded, Satan flies toward the gates of Hell, where he confronts what will be revealed to him as his dearly beloved

[1] I stress the importance of these figures so strongly because it seems incredible to me that Saurat, *Milton, Man and Thinker*, pp. 284–285, could have made the following statement: "The repulsive idea of incest seems quite gratuitous, a mere indulgence in the horrible on Milton's part."

[2] In the words of Joseph Summers, *The Muse's Method*, pp. 88–89, the "relation between Satan, Sin, and Death include narcissism, rape, sadism, and almost baffling complexities of incest."

offspring (II, 648–673). In a dramatic situation, Satan comes to terms with these figures concurrently with the reader. He is educated, along with the reader, in the atrocities of his uncreative acts. Satan has violated sublime creativity, and these are the offspring of his violations. The father-husband meets his daughter-wife and son-grandson. The Arch-Demon is compelled to learn of Sin "what thing [she is] thus double-form'd, and why / In this infernal Vale first met [she] call'st / [him] Father, and that Fantasm call'st [his] Son" (II, 741–743). With a sense of repugnance, Satan says to Sin: "I know thee not, nor ever saw till now / Sight more detestable then [Death] and thee" (II, 744–745). The situation is simultaneously comic, absurd, and horrible, for horror is, at its worst, laughable when viewed against the sublimity and stability of God's eternal world.

Each aspect of the description of the two figures has creational overtones. For example, Sin, when Satan sees her, is both beautiful and ugly: the appearance and reality of her situation confront him immediately. She is only apparently beautiful, and her beauty is seductive. In reality, she is monstrous and ugly, and her ugliness is repellent. She represents in her bipartite (and implicitly bisexual) figure the two aspects of the sinful experience: that aspect which seduces and tempts with appearances of beauty and pleasure before the sinful act has been committed, and that aspect which repels with the reality of its ugliness after the sinful act has been consummated.[3] And the nature of that sinful act is generative: for the ugliness we encounter in the description of Sin herself is centered in the area of reproduction, where the hellhounds bark about her "middle" and then "creep" into her "woomb." The serpentine aspect of her disfiguration

---

[3] Cf. Spenser's "Errour" in *The Faerie Queene* (references are to *The Poetical Works of Edmund Spenser*, ed. J. C. Smith and E. De Selincourt [London, 1912]), from which Milton's description of Sin is drawn:

> Halfe like a serpent horribly displaide,
> But th'other halfe did womans shape retaine,
> Most lothsom, filthie, foule, and full of vile disdaine.

has phallic connotations that suggest perversion: instead of the phallus impregnating, it destroys with its "mortal sting."[4]

Sin with her hellhounds is, finally, compared to two figures, whose imagistic situations have marked overtones of sexuality and birth. She is likened first to the bathing figure of Scylla "vex'd" by her own barking dogs (II, 660): the presence of water and its transforming powers (here in a hideous manner) returns us to the figure of Satan upon the flood. Secondly, she, with her dogs, is likened to the "Night-Hag" Hecate followed by her demons,

> when call'd
> In secret, riding through the Air she comes
> Lur'd with the smell of infant blood, to dance
> With *Lapland* Witches, while the labouring Moon
> Eclipses at thir charms.
>
> (II, 662–666)

The secrecy of the act, the situation of flying as the result of being "lur'd" by the diabolic, and the implications of magic and "charms" that one possesses when he participates in the act draw upon perverted sexuality. In her debased form, Hecate is a type of debased Diana, goddess of chastity, and

---

[4] See Jung's discussion of the phallic implications of the feminine *anima* with her poisonous power in *Aion: Researches into the Phenomenology of the Self*, pp. 15–16.

> And as she lay upon the durtie ground,
> Her huge long taile her den all overspred,
> Yet was in knots and many boughtes upwound,
> Pointed with mortall sting. Of her there bred
> A thousand yong ones, which she dayly fed,
> Sucking upon her poisonous dugs, eachone
> Of sundry shapes, yet all ill favored:
> Soone as that uncouth light upon them shone,
> Into her mouth they crept, and suddain all were gone.
>
> (I, i, 14–15)

One need look little further than such a passage to realize from what source Milton draws his own generative vocabulary. In one figure, we have the filth, the foulness, and the vileness of Satan's own world. There is little need to question here (as in Milton) the sexual implications of what is "horribly displaide" in serpentine form or what associations the image of "sucking" on "dugs" suggests.

the sexuality that her image evokes certainly concerns generation, for the "Night-Hag" responds to the "smell of infant blood," to the odor of that which has been newly born and then destroyed. And the eclipsing of the "labouring Moon" relates both to the magic involved and to the maternal idea of pregnancy and giving birth.

The description of Death also has creational overtones: the figure of Death is one which has not been fully generated. The "shape" does not partake fully of birth but remains in an area between reality and unreality, between substance and shadow. It is unformed and perpetually shifting between the created and the uncreated states. And yet the horror that it represents is real and is to be reckoned with. Like Sin, Death is "arm'd" with a "dreadful Dart," so that the phallicism of Sin's serpentine shape appears here in the weapon that Death wields.[5]

Those who are made to succumb to Death's destructiveness confess his kingship and confess that what seems to be his head is wearing what seems to be a crown. Here we have Milton's vision of what a creature who is, by his very nature, the absolute antithesis of creation might look like if he were born and did appear as a created entity. Death is not absolutely —that is, substantially—generated, because the mere nature of his presence denies the very fact of generation. He does, however, present a most terrible threat because he causes others to succumb to his uncreative powers. On the other hand, for those who will achieve immortality through God, Death becomes, as I shall more fully discuss, a means of birth to another life and is in his destructive powers unreal (XII, 571). To Satan Death is not only very real but is his "King

---

[5] "When *animus* [Death] and *anima* [Sin] meet, the *animus* draws his sword of power and the *anima* ejects her power of illusion and seduction" (ibid., p. 15; italics mine). Inherent in the description of Sin and Death is a parody of Cupid and his mother. Being wounded by Cupid's dart causes the type of erotic pining (cf. *eros*) associated with the earthly beauty of Venus, whose true carnality is made apparent in the ugliness of the "Night-Hag" Hecate and who offers an obvious contrast with the Heavenly Aphrodite implicitly celebrated in Milton's poems.

and Lord" (II, 699); and the two are about to destroy each other until Sin intervenes with her genealogical explanation.

Sin's relation of her genealogy and Death's begetting initiates the primary uncreative motifs that permeate the epic. Sin first reveals herself as Satan's original paramour and, ironically, his offspring. She relates her birth in the following terms:

> All on a sudden miserable pain
> Surpris'd thee, dim thine eyes, and dizzie swumm
> In darkness, while thy head flames thick and fast
> Threw forth, till on the left side op'ning wide,
> Likest to thee in shape and count'nance bright,
> Then shining heav'nly fair, a Goddess arm'd
> Out of thy head I sprung: amazement seis'd
> All th'Host of Heav'n; back they recoild affraid
> At first, and call'd me *Sin*, and for a Sign
> Portentous held me; but familiar grown,
> I pleas'd, and with attractive graces won
> The most averse, thee chiefly, who full oft
> Thy self in me thy perfect image viewing
> Becam'st enamour'd, and such joy thou took'st
> With me in secret, that my womb conceiv'd
> A growing burden.
>
> (II, 752–767)

To rebel against God is to give birth to Sin: the process is explicit. Satan's alienation from God causes him to generate another being—but a being unsanctioned by divine creativity (and therefore "essential" rather than "substantial"). The idea of uncreating oneself by splitting off from God is expressed in creational terms as a birth of that which is ultimately monstrous and involves the sexual perversions of narcissism, incest, and illicit love.

The act is one associated with death rather than with life. The generation of Sin alludes to Athena's birth out of the head of Jove, and the left or "sinister" side out of which Sin is born looks forward to Eve, who is born out of the left side of Adam (VIII, 465) and whom the fallen Adam in his anger calls his "part sinister" (x, 886). In Sin's birth, the head, as previously noted, becomes a creative center, a source of life, an idea which is reinforced by the metaphor of "brooding" or cognition. Consequently, Satan's ultimate punishment—the bruising of the serpent's head by the Son (x, 181)—is one of Satan's being deprived of his creative vitality, of his ability to create: Eve's offspring, whom Satan caused to be un-created, will, in turn, cause the final uncreation of Satan.[6]

The means by which Sin is born also has interesting ramifications. Satan's eyes become dim, and he experiences dizziness and pain. The mode of creation is unholy; it is completely deprived of the agency of God, so that contrary experiences, such as dimness, dizziness, and pain are present.[7] These unpleasant experiences are absent in the creation of Eve (VIII, 452–477). Satan's "trance" of birth is degenerate and parodies the situation of unfallen Adam's creative sleep. Satan is completely responsible for the conception and birth of Sin, who is brought forth not in glory but in pain and astonishment. (The "Host of Heav'n" react adversely to this being instinctively, and as if the name contained the essence of its meaning, they call her by that name which she represents.)

The recoil is followed by a return, and Sin seduces her creator, her father, into having incestuous relationships with her. For Satan views in Sin his "own perfect image," falls in love with his image, and copulates with it. Thus are the perversions of incest and narcissism combined as Satan in his revolt against God engenders his own self-image—his daughter Sin—and, like Narcissus consumed in his egocentric world, becomes "enamour'd" of himself and copulates

---

[6] Perhaps the remainder of the punishment—that the serpent will "bruise" the Son's "heel"—implies that Satan will harm temporarily only the least creative part—the "heel"—and that the Son will be reborn after death. (Cf. also the relationship between man's temporal frailty and Achilles' heel.)

[7] As part of the birth experience, it becomes reminiscent of the "labouring Moon," whose "eclipse" has overtones of fallen generation (II, 665–666). There is also implied a reversal of the eclipse of the sun at the crucifixion.

incestuously with the self. The <u>result</u> of such a perverted, internalized relationship is <u>the death of the individual.</u>

The narcissistic pattern is reiterated in the figure of Eve, who tells Adam about the day of her birth. She lays herself down "to look into the cleer/Smooth Lake" (IV, 458–459), and she continues:

> As I bent down to look, just opposite,
> A Shape within the watry gleam appeerd
> Bending to look on me, I started back,
> It started back, but pleas'd I soon returnd,
> Pleas'd it returnd as soon with answering looks
> Of sympathie and love; there I had fixt
> Mine eyes till now, and pin'd with vain desire,
> Had not a voice thus warnd me, What thou seest,
> What there thou seest fair Creature is thy self
> With thee it came and goes.
>
> (IV, 460–469)

The water that reflects Eve's image is both the holy water of birth and, because it is "Pure as th'expanse of Heav'n" (IV, 456), that substance which mirrors the world of Eve's spiritual origin. The water is also a vehicle of birth in the sense that it helps to generate a new awareness in Eve, an awareness that concerns true knowledge of the self. The shape within the water, the reflection of the self, is first dissociated from its owner because it is not known. Eve inhabits the world of the infant, who loves itself without being guilty of pride because it does not know that it is itself that it loves.

With Eve's becoming enamored of herself, we discover the natural disposition of every creature for self-love and therefore pride. Indeed, she would have "pin'd with vain desire" had she not been warned by the voice that the other image is herself. Now that she has been made aware of the nature of the other image, she is in the position of accepting the responsibility of being a human being with the power of choice. Thus pride results in the loving of the self with full recognition that it is self-love.[8] In that way, Satan has loved the self and copulated with his self-created image rather than having joined in union with his Creator's image in himself.

Unfallen Eve is to direct her love to God by uniting with Adam, through whom she was created and through whom she may unite with God. The voice says to Eve:

> but follow me,
> And I will bring thee where no shadow staies
> Thy coming, and thy soft imbraces, hee
> Whose image thou art, him thou shall enjoy
> Inseparablie thine, to him shalt bear
> Multitudes like thy self, and thence be call'd
> Mother of human Race.
>
> (IV, 469–475)

Eve's relation with Adam, whose image she is, will result in healthy and glorious offspring; on the other hand, Sin's relation with Satan, whose image she is, will result in monstrous offspring. The reason for this is that Adam's image in Eve is ultimately God's image, whereas Satan's image in Sin is nothing more than Satan himself. Sin's copulation with Satan is perverted sexuality, fusing narcissism and incest as counterparts of pride. Such copulation is of the lowest and most selfish kind, and it is a parody of Adam and Eve's copulation, which is neither narcissism nor incest because God is the Creator. Adam becomes the medium by which Eve is divinely created and through which Eve unites with God. Satan, on the other hand, has created his own partner, a projection of himself, and his love of

---

[8] According to Havelock Ellis (*Studies in the Psychology of Sex* [Philadelphia, 1928], VII, 348), the "figure of Narcissus was . . . clearly predestined to be the emblem of the absorbed self-love of youths and maidens who had not yet reached the stage of falling in love with another person of the opposite sex." Milton's Eve, like Narcissus who loved his reflection without knowing that it was himself, represents the "typical Narcissistic attitude of adolescence before she had met Adam" (pp. 348–349). Narcissism in the case of Satan, however, is a form of egoism: "Libido and ego-instincts dwell together still, unified and indistinguishable in the self-sufficient Self" (p. 359).

Sin's image in no way leads to God but leads inwardly and back again to the self.[9]

When Eve sees Adam for the first time and begins to flee him, Adam cries:

> Return fair *Eve,*
> Whom fli'st thou? whom thou fli'st, of him thou art,
> His flesh, his bone;
>
> .   .   .   .
>
> Part of my Soul I seek thee, and thee claim
> My other half.
>
> (IV, 481–488)

Adam as progenitor requires union with Eve in order to spread God's image through their offspring. Adam alone is incomplete: he needs to be completed generatively by Eve. Adam's seeking and claiming his other half is good and healthy because in the completion of his soul the fulfilled image of God is made manifest. Satan's seeking of Sin as a projection of himself is not good and is unhealthy, because that part of himself which he seeks was not made by God in order to spread God's image but was created by Satan in disobedience. Satan and Sin's offspring will not only be products of such disobedience, but, as the creations of self-love, will be unhealthy, deformed, and monstrous.

A further instance of the narcissistic pattern occurs when Adam willingly falls prey to Eve's charms and eats the fruit. He says:

> So forcible within my heart I feel
> The Bond of Nature draw me to my own,
> My own in thee, for what thou art is mine;
> Our state cannot be severd, we are one,
> One Flesh, to loose thee were to loose my self.
>
> (IX, 955–959)

[9] Whereas Satan's progeny (Sin and Death) are "essential" (and therefore "nonsubstantial") in their generation, God's progeny (e.g. Adam and Eve) are both "essential" and "substantial" (substance vitalized with spirit) in their generation.

Adam is drawn to himself; his only wish is to possess the self; his only fear is to lose the self. In submitting to Eve and in disobeying God, Adam is essentially committing the act of narcissism. He is loving his own image in Eve rather than God's image in himself. Eve becomes his mirror, his pool, and he yields to what the mirror reflects. Consequently, Adam's disobedience is not sacrificial but selfish. It is uncreative and egoistic and "effeminate." By disobeying his own Creator, he relinquishes his right as a creator over those below him.

If Satan's rebellion against God and his attempt to ascend to God's height involved the generation and narcissistic love of his own image in Sin, Adam's disobedience follows a similar pattern. It involves Adam's submission to his own image in Eve followed by his tasting of the Fruit as a means of ascending, "which cannot be / But to be Gods, or Angels Demi-gods" (IX, 936–937). And like Satan's self-generation of Sin, that ascent is described in the language of birth, for when Adam eats, "Earth trembl[es] from her entrails" as if in "pangs," and Nature "groan[s]" (IX, 1000–1001). The cosmos is undergoing a birth: it is Adam himself who, in one respect, is being born into the fallen world and who, in another, has just uncreated himself.

Adam, like Satan, becomes the creator of his own fallen image: with reference to Satan that image is Sin; with reference to Adam that image is Eve. The result of that creation is the experience of libidinous desires to copulate incestuously with one's offspring, one's self-created image:

> As with new Wine intoxicated both
> They swim in mirth, and fansie that they feel
> Divinitie within them breeding wings
> Wherewith to scorn the Earth: but that false Fruit
> Farr other operation first displaid,
> Carnal desire enflaming.
>
> (IX, 1008–1013)

On the occasion of this new birth, this new "breeding,"

they copulate in lust, the "Seal" of "thir mutual guilt" (IX, 1043), and the offspring of that copulation is death. And thus does Milton sing in the proem to Book I "Of Mans First Disobedience, and the Fruit / Of that Forbidden Tree, whose mortal tast / Brought Death into the World, and all our woe" (ll. 1–3).

Allegorically, it is Sin who first gives birth to Death. She continues to relate to Satan that after he had copulated with her and after they had fallen,

> Pensive here I sat
> Alone, but long I sat not, till my womb
> Pregnant by thee, and now excessive grown
> Prodigious motion felt and rueful throes.
> (II, 777–780)

The experience of birth in the fallen environment gives rise to horror rather than joy, to excess rather than temperance. The womb becomes a place of defilement and horror, and the language that describes the perverted process of birth takes into account the meaning of such defilement. If "excessive grown," for example, refers not only to the enormity of the womb but to the idea of "groaning" loudly, then the imagery is oral as well as procreative. Furthermore, "prodigious motion" suggests the excessiveness of the growth and of the life within, and it indicates the type of monstrosity that is to be born from the womb.

Additional debased connotations will assert themselves as Sin continues her narration:

> At last this odious offspring whom thou seest
> Thine own begotten, breaking violent way
> Tore through my entrails, that with fear and pain
> Distorted, all my nether shape thus grew
> Transform'd.
> (II, 781–785)

Ironically, the mother introduces the son to the father and explains the manner of birth. As the offspring is "odious" (that is, hateful and repugnant), deformed, unhealthy, the manner of birth is violent and horrible, and it causes a transformation in the birth giver that is also deformed and monstrous. The monstrosity of Sin is manifested in the monstrosity of the offspring. The area of conception, of pregnancy, and of birth becomes as deformed as the thing it gives birth to. As noted before, this is the center of the poem's uncreative dialectic, and it has repercussions throughout the poem.

For example, after Eve tempts Adam and they copulate with each other in "foul concupiscence" (IX, 1078), they realize what the shame of nakedness means. Adam says:

> But let us now, as in bad plight, devise
> What best may for the present serve to hide
> The Parts of each from other, that seem most
> To shame obnoxious, and unseemliest seen,
> Some Tree whose broad smooth Leaves together sowd,
> And girded on our loyns, may cover round
> Those middle parts, that this new commer, Shame,
> There sit not, and reproach us as unclean.
>
> (IX, 1091–1098)

In the transformation from the act of love to the act of lust, a metamorphosis has occurred metaphorically. The male and female reproductive organs suddenly take on the aspects of shame and even ugliness, and their "deformity" must be covered because they are "unseemly" and "obnoxious" (therefore, "deserving of censure"). In addition, the personification of Shame sitting about the "middle parts" and reproaching them as "unclean" relates to Death's reproaching Sin by sitting before her in "opposition" and setting the hellhounds on her (II, 803–804) as a means of torment. In that way, the reproductive organs of Adam and Eve are transformed as part of the fallen experience, and, indeed, in another context fallen Nature herself experiences Sin's generative metamorphosis, for, as Milton had recounted earlier in "On the Morning of Christ's Nativity,"

Nature tries to "hide her guilty Front with innocent snow," so that God will not see her "foul deformities" (ll. 39–44).

In the tradition of Nature's attempting to cover her deformities, Adam and Eve take refuge in the covering offered by that "Figtree," which produces "Daughters" from the mother's "Armes,"

> Braunching so broad and long, that in the ground
> The bended Twigs take root, and Daughters grow
> About the Mother Tree.
>
> (IX, 1104–1106)

The "Figtree" represents, according to Kester Svendsen, fallen fecundity "expressed as a cycle of human generation."[10] "The twigs," notes Svendsen, "still bound to their mother fall to earth, root themselves, and rise again as daughters, one more among a hundred images of rhythmic fall and rise, rise and fall."[11] As a creational image of reproduction after the fall, the branching arms from which offspring are produced and which offer shade and protection recall the Spirit of God who "broods" with outstretched wings. There is something of sadness and divinity in the "Figtree" image: although fallen reproduction suffers the sin of the parents, it also experiences both the rising pattern of rebirth and the protective pattern of divine creativity, in which a brooding, melancholy awareness of the fall is ever-present.

Continuing with Sin's serpentine transformation, we are presented first with the image of the serpent and its sexual overtones and then with the image of transformations associated with the serpent. The very aspect of the serpent, even in the unfallen world, is one of deceit and hypocrisy, of something hidden, and of something ingratiating. The "sly," "insinuating" serpent reveals its "fatal guile" but is "unheeded" (IV, 347–350). The serpent is later described as the "suttl'st Beast of all the field, / Of huge extent sometimes,

10 *Milton and Science*, pp. 135–136.
11 Ibid.

with brazen Eyes / And hairie Main terrific," although "not noxious" to the unfallen Adam, but "obedient" to his "call" (VII, 494–498). The sexual implications here are unmistakable. Fallen sexuality is played off against unfallen sexuality as Raphael refers to the serpent and its relation to Adam.

The subtlety of the serpent implies its secrecy, its penchant for that which is hidden from sight and revealed in a clandestine manner. Its ability to dilate, indeed, to grow "huge," coupled with its "brazenness" and "hairiness," tends to locate it in a sexual environment. "Brazen Eyes" suggests shamelessness and boldness and recalls Satan's perverted acts of spying secretly on that which is private and should not be disturbed. The idea of hairiness in its association with "Main" suggests not only power and virility but that which causes fright or terror, since it is "terrific," and hairiness itself as a sexual image calls up the wilderness with its "hairie sides" (IV, 135–136) outside Eden. This is the imagery of a fallen environment where desires are untempered and libidinous. Yet that environment is not "noxious" to the unfallen Adam, who should have no fear of such a serpent as Raphael describes corrupting or hurting him as long as he remains unfallen. Rather, the serpent should obey him because Adam has control in his unfallen state over ungovernable passions. Reason still reigns and can channel desire to fruitful ends as God is able to create healthy offspring out of a Chaos that is obedient to God's will.

As a counterpart of Sin's nether transformation, we are presented with Satan's willing imbruting of himself in serpentine form. Satan's act becomes a parody of Christ's *kenosis* or emptying himself of his godhead in order to regenerate man.[12] Satan, on the other hand, assumes the serpent's form in order to uncreate man. His entering of the serpent

---

[12] Shawcross, "The Balanced Structure of *Paradise Lost*," pp. 698–699. In *The Psychology of the Unconscious* (pp. 415–417), Jung interprets the entering of the serpent as a meditative introverting or going down into oneself. The serpent represents the "introverting libido. Through introversion, one is fertilized, inspired, regenerated, and reborn from the God." The entering of the serpent

furtively has overtones of seduction and forbidden coition (IX, 88–91). And the "dark suggestions" which he "hides" in the serpent are "insinuations" that cause further thoughts to materialize. Satan impregnates the serpent with his "dark suggestions" as God uses the "dark materials" of Chaos to create more worlds (II, 916), but the effect is one of uncreation in the case of Satan rather than generation.

Before undergoing his parody of the *kenosis,* Satan laments:

> O foul descent! that I who erst contended
> With Gods to sit the highest, am now constraind
> Into a Beast, and mixt with bestial slime,
> This essence to incarnate and imbrute,
> That to the hight of Deitie aspir'd;
> But what will not Ambition and Revenge
> Descend to? who aspires must down as low
> As high he soard, obnoxious first or last
> To basest things.
>
> (IX, 163–171)

Satan himself seems aware in his soliloquy of the paradoxical implications of his *kenosis.* He complains of his "foul de-

---

as an archetypal situation approximates the creeping into oneself and becoming one's uterus, becoming pregnant with oneself in order to give birth. (Cf. the discussion of the poet's process of creation. The poet also fertilizes himself by entering his own womb through brooding or meditation.) The hero, who is to overcome death, broods upon himself in introversion, "coiling as a snake around its own egg," conquers himself and gives birth to himself again. Satan, of course, represents a parody of this entire situation. With respect to the coiling of the serpent around its own creative center, we are presented with the following image: Satan finds the serpent sleeping

> In Labyrinth of many a round self-rowl'd,
> His head the midst, well stor'd with suttle wiles.
> (IX, 183–184)

The "Labyrinth" re-enacts the circular process of return to the source indicative of the hellhounds' returning to devour the mother's womb. The movement is introverted or internalized. The serpent's head as the creative source is in the center, to which the labyrinthine coils lead. The image suggests Sin's generative organs which have become labyrinthine and to which the hellhounds periodically return.

scent," for his pride is immediately repelled by the idea that he who aspired to be God must now debase himself with "bestial slime."[13] The mere act of aspiring to be on God's level, however, involves a simultaneous debasement of the aspirer. Thus, as Satan himself recognizes: he "who aspires must down as low / As high he soar'd." Eve descended to lust with Adam as a consequence of their intoxicating feelings of aspiration in the fall. Likewise, the result of Satan's aspiring in Heaven is Sin's disfigurement in Hell. Consequently, Satan's lament is a waste of breath, for aspiration, by its very nature, is debasement, and "foul descent" is merely another term for Satanic aspiration.

The perversion of Satan's *kenosis* manifests itself in a seduction: impregnation results from Satan's entering the beast. Satan approaches the serpent, which was

> Not yet in horrid Shade or dismal Den,
> Nor nocent yet, but on the grassie Herb
> Fearless unfeard he slept: in at his Mouth
> The Devil enterd, and his brutal sense,
> In heart or head, possessing soon inspir'd
> With act intelligential.
>
> (IX, 185–190)

The image fuses the idea of masculinity with the serpent as that which impregnates and the idea of femininity with the serpent as that which is impregnated. Such a fusion is not unusual, since the image of Sin's serpentine nether parts combines both sets of associations, masculine and feminine. The same is true of Death with his mouth as feminine symbol and with his dart (compare Sin's "mortal sting") as masculine symbol. As masculine symbol, the serpent is not yet fallen: there is as yet no need for concealment (as Adam and Eve must conceal their reproductive organs when they fall), and there is no need to associate it yet with that which is "horrid" or that which is "dismal." As feminine symbol, the serpent

---

[13] Cf. Mother Mary Christopher Pecheux, " 'O Foul Descent!': Satan and the Serpent Form," *SP*, LXII (1965), 188–196.

is seduced or "enterd" at the "Mouth." Within, the birth process is enacted, for the "brutal sense" is "inspir'd." That is, life is breathed into it, and the tenor of its new life is to express itself "with act intelligential."

We have been dealing up to this point with the concept of transformation as it relates to the original image of Sin's giving birth to Death. In the description of that birth, however, we find a further aspect. Death is not easily born: indeed, he tears through Sin's "entrails," thereby causing his mother infinite pain. That aspect is reflected in God's curse on fallen Adam and Eve, who must suffer as progenitors. The "Oracle" proclaims the sentence on Eve first:

> Thy sorrow I will greatly multiplie
> By thy Conception; Children thou shalt bring
> In sorrow forth.
>
> (x, 193–195)

The sentence is generative: Eve as the progenitor of the race of man will give birth in torment and pain. Creation in the fallen world will have an aspect of sorrow about it. And the procreative judgment applies also to Adam, to whom the "Oracle" says:

> Curs'd is the ground for thy sake, thou in sorrow
> Shalt eat thereof all the days of thy Life;
> Thorns also and Thistles it shall bring thee forth
> Unbid, and thou shalt eat th'Herb of the Field,
> In the sweat of thy Face shalt thou eat Bread,
> Till thou return unto the ground.
>
> (x, 201–206)

Adam as a progenitor must suffer pangs and torments with respect to the land. These pangs and torments, it is made clear, are the masculine counterparts of a wife's labor pains. As Eve's womb is cursed in her fall, so is the ground for Adam's sake. The agricultural means by which Adam causes birth will bring forth unhealthy offspring, "Thorns" and "Thistles." Healthy birth, herbs and bread, will be the result of great "labor pains" causing sweat. And at the end of the tormenting process of creation, the progenitors of the land will return to that womb which gave them birth.

However, because man is capable of regeneration, whereas Satan is eternally damned, Adam and Eve will find recompense in their fall because of God's grace (x, 1050–1056). Adam and Eve are not wholly lost; even the generative curse pronounced upon them has positive ramifications. The "fruit" of Eve's womb, although painful in the bringing forth, is not necessarily a curse but may be joyous. Likewise, Adam as a progenitor will be able to provide sustenance through his labor.

Only when there is a joining with evil in the fallen world are the offspring monstrous. Such is the case with the sons of Seth, who joined with the evil daughters of Cain and begot giants (xi, 556–627). Michael says of the giants, who "multiply/Ten thousandfould the sin of him who slew/His Brother" (xi, 677–679):

> These are the product
> Of those ill-mated Marriages [Adam] saw'st:
> Where good with bad were matcht, who of themselves
> Abhor to joyn; and by imprudence mixt,
> Produce prodigious Births of bodie or mind.
> (xi, 683–687)

Here again is another variation of the central incest pattern, but now it is the evil joining of good (the sons of Seth) and bad (the daughters of Cain) that produces monstrosities. The joining of antithetical qualities in the fallen world produces "prodigious Births." Consequently, the third aspect, that concerned with the birth of Death as an offspring that is physically deformed, has repercussions in the world of man.

To trace the implications of Sin and Death's description and genealogy—Sin's illicit birth from Satan, her incestuous copulation with her father, her debased pregnancy, her giving birth to Death, and her resulting transformation—is to open innumerable avenues into the poem, and to follow those avenues is suddenly to see how rich and complex the design of the poem becomes. We are let into its internal world, its world beneath the surface and made aware of how vital its texture is, how the words, the images, the patterns, give life to each other and, like God's union of interdependencies, cannot function without each other. Such an interpretive approach, I think, shows that *Paradise Lost* is not one-dimensional, that the subtleties of its rhetoric repay close and careful scrutiny.

Chapter 7

Satan's Fall & Its Extended Consequences

THE INTERRELATIONSHIPS OF

SIN AND DEATH

S IN HAS EXPLAINED only a portion of her genealogy: she must still relate her rape by Death and the births that proceed therefrom. In that remaining description, a major portion of the poem is contained. As in the last chapter, I shall attempt to get at that portion through the basic ideas and patterns revealed in Sin's description. Her statements lead to such occurrences as Satan's soliloquy (Book IV), Adam's soliloquy (Book X), Eve's tasting of the Fruit (Book IX), Adam's witnessing of history (Book XI), Sin and Death's building of the bridge (Book X), and Satan's return to Hell (Book X). What these occurrences have in common is the way in which they are articulated: each becomes a variation of an essential unifying concept. And that concept finds expression in the complex image of birth initiated in Satan, Sin, and Death's perverted relationships.

As the dialectics of creation imply the obedience of the created to the creator, so the dialectics of uncreation imply the disobedience of the created to the creator. Both Sin and Death are the products of disobedience, and in the birth of Death from Sin, the son immediately becomes the mother's "inbred enemie" (II, 785). "Inbred" not only carries the sense of innate, as Death is by his very nature the enemy of her who created him, but reinforces the idea of incest that informs the entire Satan-Sin-Death association. With the stress upon inbreeding and offspring among the three diabolic figures, we are presented with the primitive idea that inbreeding is related to deformed, unhealthy, indeed, monstrous offspring.[1]

In that sense, Satan makes a point of alluding to Death's "miscreated Front" (II, 683), and Sin recounts the "inbred" disobedience of her offspring in the following manner:

> I fled, but he pursu'd (though more, it seems,
> Inflam'd with lust then rage) and swifter far,
> Mee overtook his mother all dismaid,
> And in embraces forcible and foul
> Ingendring with me, of that rape begot
> These yelling Monsters that with ceaseless cry
> Surround me, as thou sawst, hourly conceiv'd
> And hourly born, with sorrow infinite
> To me, for when they list into the womb
> That bred them they return, and howl and gnaw
> My Bowels, thir repast; then bursting forth
> Afresh with conscious terrours vex me round,
> That rest or intermission none I find.
>
> (II, 790–802)

The pattern of incest and its culmination in monstrosities continues right down to the relationship between Sin and Death and their offspring. The cycle begins with Satan the father copulating with his self-image in Sin the daughter, is

[1] See Edward Westermarck, *The Future of Marriage in Western Civilization* (New York, 1936), p. 258. The belief that the incestuous brood will be monstrous is common. See also Westermarck, *The Origin and Development of the Moral Ideas* (London, 1908), II, 375. "The belief in the supernatural, especially, has played a very important part in the ideas referring to incest, as in other points of sexual morality, owing to the mystery which surrounds everything connected with the function of reproduction." Ancient thought ascribed to the belief that incest "was always followed by the birth of monsters with . . . disfigurations."
Milton's belief that mixed procreation will produce monsters was made evident in the discussion concerning the sons of Seth and the daughters of Cain. But also consider Milton's statement in *Animadversions* (I, 720): "which poore and low pitch't desires, if they doe but mixe with those other heavenly intentions that draw a man to this study, it is justly suspected that they should bring forth a baseborn issue of Divinity like that of those imperfect, and putrid creatures that receive a crawling life from two most unlike procreants the Sun, and mudde." Relationships concerning the mixture of good and evil, as well as those concerning incest, result in deformed offspring.

followed by Death the son raping Sin the mother, and is completed in the monstrous hellhounds being perpetually born and perpetually ravishing the womb of their origin.[2] Not only are the monsters of incest "hourly conceiv'd / And hourly born," but they continuously rape the very source of their birth. The first incestuous rape begets a perpetuity of rapes. Finally, the whole incest pattern beginning with Satan and Sin represents a continuous return to the womb, in which the mother is forever made to have relations with her offspring.

Again, the circumstances are, at their most horrible, humorous, and Milton deepens the humor of the circumstances through a playful use of language. For example, when Sin recounts her rape by saying that Death "overtook" her, his own mother, "all dismaid," we can see how Milton causes his evil characters to make fun of themselves unintentionally. If in one respect Sin laments her experience of "dismay," in another she unknowingly laments her loss of maidenhead. The hint of maidenhead, with its connotations of purity and innocence as ascriptions of Sin, reinforces the absurdity of the horror. Through language, as well as through event, Milton thus invites us to laugh at what his evil characters view with utmost seriousness. But the idea of incest culminating in the return to the womb has even more extensive implications.

As noted in the discussion concerning the War in Heaven, the perpetual return to the mother as a means of monstrous

---

[2] The mythological and psychological importance of the incest pattern is discernible in Jung's description of a "syzygy" composed of a male (*animus*) and female (*anima*) figure. Associated with the personifying habits of the unconscious, the *anima*, the all-embracing, all-enveloping Mother, and the *animus*, the Son (and Father), engage in incest (*The Archetypes and the Collective Unconscious*, p. 284; *Aion*, pp. 10–12). Furthermore, the *anima* represents the illusory, self-devouring world of the unconscious. "Together [the *animus* and *anima*] . . . form a divine pair, one of whom [the *animus*], in accordance with his Logos nature . . . [is] ever-shifting [cf. the insubstantiability of Death], . . . while the other, in accordance with her Eros nature wears the features of Aphrodite, Helen, . . . Persephone, and Hecate [cf. the eros nature of Sin and Book II, 662]" (*Aion*, p. 21).

birth begotten of incestuous rape parodies the sublime and glorious return to God by the faithful as a means of renewal and sustenance. The pattern of continuous internalization suggested by Satan, Death, and the hellhounds' resorting to Sin as a vehicle of propagation is contrasted by God as a creative entity who is in himself "perfet" and in whom no "deficience" is found (VIII, 415–416). In addition, we have seen how Satan's desire to imitate God's state of perfect and absolute union with the self causes his downfall and his creation of the self imaged in the absurd propagations associated with Sin. Sin, as Satan's self continuously propagating, continuously being raped, and continuously being resorted to as the source of sustenance for its own creations, is the degenerate form of the sublime deific image. That pattern manifests itself in the torment of both Satan and Adam. Indeed, the idea of return actually becomes part of their vocabulary.

Satan in his uncreated state reveals his torment through a sense of destructive return. His own uncreated thoughts are forever recoiling back upon themselves (IV, 15–18 and IX, 171–172). Ironically, Satan even recalls his previous relationship with God according to the idea of return: "[God] deserv'd no such return / From me" (IV, 42–43):

> What could be less then to afford him praise,
> The easiest *recompence*, and pay him thanks,
> How due!
>
> (IV, 46–48; italics mine)

Satan himself is aware of the type of "return" on "recompence" God expected: the expression of gratitude that an offspring owes to his Creator. Of such a return Satan was entirely incapable. Now in his uncreated state, he feels the pangs of unfulfillment caused by the destructive, self-devouring awareness of return. He beholds the fulfilled union of Adam and Eve "Imparadis't in one another's arms" (IV, 506) and laments his having to experience the unfulfillment of Hell, that environment of extremes "where neither joy nor love, but fierce desire, /. . . Still unfulfill'd with pain of longing pines" (IV, 509–511). As a result, Satan directs his entire store of destructive energies toward returning the unfallen Adam and Eve to the uncreative state of "contraries" (IX, 122).

Ironically, Satan does not presume to lighten his own burden by returning others to his chaotic state but merely wishes to make others the same as he is in order to frustrate God's creative ends, "though," as he says, aware that his destructiveness will return only upon himself, "thereby worse to me redound" (IX, 126–128). Consequently, Satan experiences the full implications of the idea of return, both as that idea is related gloriously to God and as that idea is related ignominiously to Sin. In the first case, Satan realizes how incapable he is to effect such a return; in the second case, he manifests Sin's dilemma by being psychologically devoured through a return to Chaos. As an aspect of his own unfulfillment, he would effect the second sense of return on others.

Such an awareness of return is exactly what Satan does effect in Adam and Eve. The motif of the hellhounds, perpetually born and perpetually returning to devour the source of their birth, is repeated in the fallen Adam, who curses his procreative function. What had previously been a blessing to Adam now becomes a curse. In his language of complaint, the acts of reproduction and of eating are imagistically fused: "All that I eat or drink, or shall beget," laments Adam, "Is propagated curse" (X, 728–729). Eating and drinking become synonymous with begetting, and all these acts produce a blasphemous offspring. Adam therefore laments:

> O voice once heard
> Delightfully, *Encrease and multiply*
> Now death to hear!
> (X, 729–731)

Adam's role as begetter becomes distasteful to him; that

which was to be his glory as a progenitor now becomes his torment and punishment. Creativity, he feels, is turned against him as a means of hurting him. He will "encrease and multiply" nothing but curses that will return upon him from future ages (x, 731–737).

Adam as procreator now assumes the role of Sin, whose womb becomes the center of execration. He laments:

> so besides
> Mine own that bide upon me, all from mee
> Shall with a fierce reflux on mee redound,
> On mee as on thir natural center light
> Heavie, though in thir place.
>
> (x, 737–741)

The language itself re-enacts the sense of return to the origin of which Adam is so terrified. The word "mee" is repeated four times within three lines, and the repetition of the personal pronoun reinforces the idea of internalization and of return to the center. The curses of the previous lines here become offspring that in the future flow to their source. There is a giving forth, as the hellhounds are born and issue out of the womb, and a "fierce reflux," as the hellhounds rush back to the womb and devour it.

Psychologically, the continuous, unhealthy turning inward that Sin with her hellhounds represents is associated with the effects of perverted sexuality. F. T. Prince states the situation clearly:

> Sensuality, or lust, the pursuit of animal satisfaction, is intimately related to the fear of death, or the sense of mortality. In its turn sensuality leads to disgust, or disappointment, and a sense of guilt or fear; but guilt or fear brings back the need to escape by way of repeated sensuality.[3]

Therefore, lust implies the act of ultimate egotism, a copulating with the self, and that act is concurrent with the death

[3] F. T. Prince, ed., *Paradise Lost: Books I and II*, p. 165n.

wish, the destruction of the self. Finally, the offspring of such self-copulation are monstrosities.

The diabolic return to the womb that parodies the return enacted by God's faithful offspring, however, has still further implications. I refer to what in Milton becomes a fusion of two acts: sexual assault and diabolic eating. A debasement of the renewal and sustenance that the faithful angels experience in their return to God, these two acts, we recall, are portrayed by the hellhounds, who renew and sustain themselves by simultaneously raping and devouring the womb of Sin. That is, they "gnaw" Sin's "Bowels" as their means of sustenance. The motif of eating as it relates to the sexual act is not an unusual concept with Milton, for we find it expressed quite succinctly in the following line from "On Time": "And glut thy self with what thy womb devours" (l. 4). Such a fusion of oral-sexual imagery, then, finds expression early in Milton's poetry and culminates in the debased figures of *Paradise Lost*.

As a reinforcement of that basic idea, Death is simultaneously an object of lust and the very embodiment of a ravenous hunger that can never be satiated. Thus Death, we recall, sits in opposition to his mother in order to set the hellhounds on her and watches while they rape and devour her (II, 803–806). This act provides a kind of grotesque substitute-gratification for him, for he would devour her himself "but that he knows / His end with [hers is] involv'd" (II, 806–807). Nevertheless, we can see that in both figures sexual and oral aggression become different facets of the same idea. The act of devouring finds its counterpart in debased sexuality, neither of which can be fulfilled. We may recall from earlier discussions that the womb in the Satanic world implies its negation: a hole into which one enters to suffer unfulfillment and annihilation. Such, of course, is precisely in accord with the plight of Death, whose attempts to glut his ravenous maw are futile. Like the womb that devours, Death's maw takes life into itself and destroys it. In this respect Death becomes the type of the dilemma of the fallen condition, which, as I shall further discuss, is one of perpetual impotence in spite of lust and perpetual unfulfillment in spite of the gluttonous attempts to satiate. We should further remember, however, that unfulfillment may likewise express itself through un-creation, and here is where the dialectical framework of Milton's epic becomes so important. A summary statement is in order before we proceed further.

The dialectic which involves the fusing of sexuality with eating expresses itself in the following manner: gluttony is associated with lust and with the narcissism of self-copulation, the offspring of which are physically and morally deformed.[4] The gluttonous aspect of the narcissistic relationship begun by Satan and perpetuated incestuously in Sin, Death, and the ravenous hellhounds is manifested in the temptation and fall of Eve. Eve's gluttonous eating of the forbidden Fruit sym-bolically re-enacts the lust of Satan's original narcissism. After Eve has "pluck'd" the Fruit, she,

> Intent now wholly on her taste, naught else
> Regarded, such delight till then, as seemd,
> In Fruit she never tasted, whether true
> Or fansied so, through expectation high
> Of knowledge, nor was God-head from her thought.
> Greedily she ingorg'd without restraint,
> And knew not eating Death.
>
> (IX, 786–792)

As Adam comments, Eve has been "deflowrd" (IX, 901): like Sin, except in the true sense of the word, she has been "dis-maid" (II, 792). As in his narcissistic lust for his self-created image, Satan sinfully copulates with the self and begets Death, Eve, intoxicated with the presence of her newly found egotism, devours the Forbidden Fruit.[5]

---

[4] The hellhounds, we may remember, bark "with wide *Cerberean* mouths" (II. 655). "Cerberus, the three-headed dog who guards the threshold of Hades, is placed by Dante in the third circle (*Inferno*, VI) to punish those whose sin is gluttony" (B. Rajan, ed., *Paradise Lost: Books I and II*, p. 90n.).

[5] According to Jung (*Psychology of the Unconscious*, pp. 189–190), the forbidden act of plucking the apple from the Tree indicates masturbation, in which lust

Her eating is an act of lust, first because she is wholly consumed with the self to the exclusion of all else (she is not even aware that her seducer slinks stealthily away [IX, 784–788]), and second because the manner of her eating is gluttonous. Like Death, who in his lust rapes and devours, Eve "ingorg'd without restraint." There is the same sense of turning inward, of the hellhounds rushing into the womb and devouring and ravishing, in Eve's intemperate and unhealthy ingorging of the food. And whereas the love act is one of due regard for one's partner, Eve's entire lustful regard is for herself. Finally, as Death himself is the incestuous product of lust that would devour, Eve in her eating of the Fruit "eats" Death: she has been seduced into becoming a devotee of the gluttony and carnality that Death represents. She is "to Death devote" (IX, 901), for she is doomed.

That instance in which eating and uncreation reveal themselves most appropriately is the "Lazar-house." Adam beholds his fallen offspring, who have corrupted themselves with "Intemperance . . . / In meats and Drinks, which on Earth shall bring / Diseases dire" causing physical monstrosities (XI, 472–474):

> Immediately a place
> Before [Adam's] eyes appeard, sad, noysom, dark,
> A Lazar-house it seemd, wherein were laid
> Numbers of all diseas'd.
>
> (XI, 477–480)

The original act of gluttony found in the image of Death and the hellhounds, and the relationship of gluttony to lustful sexuality and the begetting of monstrous offspring are reiterated here in the fallen environment. Through gluttony man begets monstrosities in himself.[6] He becomes a deformed sight (XI, 494) as the result of intemperance.

---

and régard for none other but the self play dominant roles. The forbidden act is also related to incest, for copulation with one's own image is both onanistic and incestuous.

[6] See John M. Patrick, *Milton's Conception of Sin as Developed in Paradise Lost* (Logan, Utah, 1960), p. 48.

After being exposed to such a place, Adam laments:

> Can thus
> Th'Image of God in man created once
> So goodly and erect, though faultie since,
> To such unsightly sufferings be debas't[?]
> (XI, 507–510)

Adam does not understand how the beautiful and erect, therefore, generative, image of God created in man could have been transformed into so debased a monstrosity. To Adam's question why man should not be free from such deformities, Michael answers:

> Thir Makers Image . . . then
> Forsook them, when themselves they villifi'd
> To serve ungovern'd appetite, and took
> His Image whom they serv'd, a brutish vice,
> Inductive mainly to the sin of *Eve*.
> (XI, 515–519)

Like Satan, who lusted after his own image in Sin rather than obeying God's image in himself and thereby begot a race of monsters, these fallen offspring took the image of appetite for their god, so that God's image "forsook them" and thereby begot monstrosities in themselves. As Sin is a projection of Satan's own egotism, the image of appetite is likewise a projection of man's own selfishness, his need to take all into himself. He repeats Eve's act of "ingorging" and becomes monstrous and "defac't" (XI, 522) like Eve, who is at once "Defac't, deflowrd, and . . . to Death devote" (IX, 901). Consequently, Eve's original intemperance is consummated generatively in man.

Paradoxically, through gluttony God achieves creative ends. Referring to Sin and Death in language that fuses sexuality and gluttony, God says that he "drew" Sin and Death out of Hell to be his

> Hell-hounds, to lick up the draff and filth
> Which mans polluting Sin with taint hath shed
> On what was pure, till cramm'd and gorg'd, nigh burst
> With suckt and glutted offal, at one sling
> Of thy victorious Arm, well-pleasing Son,
> Both *Sin*, and *Death*, and yawning *Grave* at last
> Through *Chaos* hurld, obstruct the mouth of Hell
> For ever, and seal up his ravenous Jaws.
>
> (x, 630–637)

God will effect rebirth and redemption through a reversal of the very process by which Sin and Death hope to effect uncreation. As Sin's hellhounds devour her womb, which, because of its degenerate offspring, is associated with depravity, so God will make Sin and Death his hellhounds to devour the filth that they would create on earth. Sin and Death will "lick up" the draff that they cause man to "shed" as a result of his own sinning. Their devouring of others will result in their own destruction, their own experience of being devoured. Like hellhounds, they will devour man's "polluting Sin" until they are so "cramm'd and gorg'd" that they will nearly "burst" with their own contamination, their "suckt and glutted offal."

Both language and imagery reverberate with the offensive connotations of the gluttonous act. "Suckt" and "glutted," for example, are harsh and gutteral sounding. Imagistically, after Sin and Death are "cramm'd and gorg'd," the Son will destroy them by performing another act of cramming and gorging: he will hurl them, along with the open-mouthed "Grave," through Chaos and permanently "obstruct the mouth of Hell." Hell's ravenous hunger will then be sated. Gluttonous eating will then destroy itself and be destroyed, for God will use the filth of intemperance to obliterate intemperance. Nothing will issue out of Hell's opening then: the mouth will be closed, and all monstrous birth will be destroyed. But before that apocalyptic time, Sin and Death will issue out of Hell as a result of man's transgression, and the dramatization of that issuance is an integral part of the creational idea.

Adam and Eve's having fallen and having given birth to sin and death within themselves allows the allegorical figures of Sin and Death to be born into world of man. The mother and her incestuous son, who were "there in power before, / Once actual, now [arrive] in body, and [come] to dwell/ Habitual habitant[s]" (x, 586–588). Thus Milton establishes the psychological correlation between man and his psyche and the external universe and its cosmic realms. Adam and Eve's fall and Satan's success give Sin and Death immediate knowledge of their freedom. Sin says:

> O Son, why sit we here each other viewing
> Idlely, while Satan our great Author thrives
> In other Worlds, and happier Seat provides
> For us his ofspring dear?
>
> (x, 235–238)

The language is inherently generative: the mother talks to the son about their mutual father as God's offspring might talk about their provident "Author." In the case of Sin and Death, of course, the language merely serves to point up the absurdity of the whole incestuous relationship.

Aware of these circumstances, Sin continues to speak of their situation in the language of birth:

> Methinks I feel new strength within me rise,
> Wings growing, and Dominion giv'n me large
> Beyond this Deep.
>
> (x, 243–245)

Sin, ironically, experiences a sense of rebirth comparable to Adam and Eve's feeling of "breeding" wings when they eat the Fruit (IX, 1010). The connection thereby becomes a psychological one between Sin and Adam and Eve, as well as a cosmic one between Sin and Satan. Sin responds to the drawing power of both the psychological and the cosmic:

> whatever draws me on,
> Or sympathie, or som connatural force
> Powerful at greatest distance to unite
> With secret amity things of like kind
> By secret conveyance.
>
> (X, 245–249)

Like Adam, who, before he commits the transgression, feels the "Bond of Nature draw [him] to [his] own" (IX, 956), Sin speaks in the language of God's holy union of birth and sustenance when she refers to the mysterious "force" that secretly unites "things of like kind." Her language is a debasement of God's creative language, her situation a debasement of God's holy union. Sin, as well as Death, will be born from the deep of Hell to the upper world, as man's subconscious drives usurp his rational processes, over which Sin has new dominion.

In order to re-establish the demonic union, Sin and Death will, as "The Argument" of Book X states, "pave a broad Highway or Bridge over *Chaos*, according to the Track that *Satan* first made." The mode of creation involved in the building of Sin and Death's bridge is the direct antithesis of divine creativity. Once again, uncreativity or the return to Chaos appears in a metaphor of debased generation. Thus Sin and Death are described as "Hovering upon the Waters" (X, 285) of Chaos as God in the process of creation "moved upon the face of the waters" (Gen. 1:2). God's holy act here takes on a degenerate form: impregnation diabolically becomes a prelude to destruction.

Sin and Death first "drove" "what they met / Solid or slimie" to the "mouth of Hell" (X, 285–288): the process is one of the ingorging again of an opening, this time Hell's mouth. Then

> The aggregated Soyl
> Death with his Mace petrific, cold and dry,
> As with a Trident smote, and fixt as firm
> As *Delos* floating once; the rest his look

> Bound with *Gorgonian* rigor not to move,
> And with *Asphaltic* slime.
>
> (x, 293–298)

The description combines all the motifs which are the exact opposite of true creativity. Death's process of creation is described in destructive terms. For example, Death with his mace does not cause matter to come to life as did Moses when he caused the sea to part by stretching his "potent Rod" across it (XII, 211). Rather, Death causes matter to become petrified, to partake of a state that is drained of life, that has connotations of fear and the inability to act. Creation for Death is accompanied not by fluidity and warmth, which impregnate with a sense of security in and love toward the creator, but by coldness and dryness, which are "adverse to life." In contrast, when the Spirit of God creates, he infuses "vital vertue" and "vital warmth" and purges "downward" the "black tartareous cold infernal dregs" (VII, 235–238). If God's mode of creativity is vivifying, Death's is petrifying: the one causes life; the other negates it.

Whereas God in the likeness of a Dove spreads out his wings in creation as a symbol of protection from harm, Death destroys simultaneously as he creates, for he "smites" what is before him. As God's creatures receive life and the ability to move through God's "blessed vision," Death's creations are "bound" immovably through Death's petrifying "look," which, like the Gorgon, transforms life into stone. Finally, Death's creativeness suggests Satan's inventiveness, his mechanical ingenuity that allowed him to produce weapons in Heaven. Again, unnatural creativity is contrasted with God's natural and spontaneous creativity. The result of Death's creation, like all diabolic offspring, is monstrous: the "Bridge" is of a "length prodigious" (x, 302).

Satan's meeting with Sin and Death on the crossroads is expressed as a parody of the creative idea. Debased progenitor converses with degenerate progeny as God the Father would converse with his offspring. Satan's "Children dear" immediately recognize "thir Parent," even though he is disguised "in likeness of an Angel bright" (x, 326–331). When Satan meets his "Ofspring dear" (x, 349), his "fair / Inchanting Daughter" (x, 352–353) addresses him as "Parent," and Satan responds in like manner by addressing his offspring as "Fair Daughter, and thou Son and Grandchild both" (x, 384).

Because Satan is ultimately responsible for the Bridge, Sin addresses him as a creator:

> O Parent, these are thy magnific deeds,
> Thy Trophies, which thou view'st as not thine own,
> Thou art thir Author and prime Architect:
>
> . . . .
>
> Thou hast atchiev'd our libertie, confin'd
> Within Hell Gates till now, thou us impow'rd
> To fortifie thus farr, and overlay
> With this portentous Bridge the dark Abyss.
> Thine now is all this World, thy vertue hath won
> What thy hands builded not.
>
> (x, 354–373)

Although Satan's "hands" did not build this Bridge, he is still the creator or "Author and prime Architect."[7] For the Bridge is the result of Satan's deeds, and Sin and Death are the agents

---

[7] Although we cannot examine every word in the epic, Milton's language is so rich and so deceptive in the extent of its complexity that a dialectical examination of two words ("hands" and "won") might prove interesting. These two words are initially put into a creative context when Sin says that although Satan's "hands" did not build the Bridge, his actions have allowed the creation to occur. Furthermore, with its specific implications of power and creative potency, "vertue" (cf. God's infusing of "vital vertue" into substance to make it live [vII, 236]) reinforces this immediate creative framework, as well as points up the irony of Satan's "virtuous" actions. But a true understanding of what "hands" and "won" come to mean in a larger perspective involves a knowledge of Milton's dialectical strategies. Mario A. DiCesare ("Advent'rous Song: The Texture of Milton's Epic," *Language and Style in Milton*, p. 21) states that the "hand as creative instrument belongs mainly to God," whose "creating hand / Nothing imperfet or deficient left" (IX, 344–345; see also IV, 364–365; VII, 224; VII, 500) and "under [whose] forming hands a Creature grew" (VIII, 470). Dialectically, then, Satan's "hands" serve exactly the opposite purpose: to uncreate. And that is the way we must view their function, even when they are performing

of Satanic creativity. If it had not been for Satan, the Bridge could never have been built. Indeed, only through the union of Satan with his offspring Sin and Death was the Bridge built at all. Satan has achieved his offsprings' "libertie" and made it possible for Sin and Death to build. Through his deeds, Satan has "impow'rd" his offspring, given them "creative" power within the "fatal consequence" that unites them (x, 364). Such empowering of the offspring as agents of one's creativity becomes a parody of God's empowering the Son as an agent to create as a result of the animating interchange within the holy union. Sin and Death, as generative agents of Satan, counter the Son as the generative agent of God. If divine creativity ensues because of God, perverse creativity ensues because of Satan.

Enhancing the role of Sin and Death as agents of Satanic creativity, Satan's address to his offspring parodies God's address to the newly created Adam and Eve. Satan tells Sin and Death to "descend" "right down to Paradise":

> There to dwell and Reign in bliss, thence on the Earth
> Dominion exercise and in the Air,
> Chiefly on Man, sole Lord of all declar'd,
> Him first make sure your thrall, and lastly kill.
>
> (x, 399–402)

---

an ostensibly creative act. "Won" also becomes meaningful outside its immediate context.

Aside from the idea of "winning" something as in combat, "won" also implies generating birth out of Chaos, as when light is "won from the void and formless infinite" (iii, 12). What then can we say of God's having "won" the War in Heaven? Because of its essential associations with an underlying dialectical idea, that triumph necessarily becomes part of a pattern having to do with creation. Whenever the word "won" is applied "creatively" to Satan, however, its meaning is negated in its very statement, since Satan's having "lost" the War in Heaven becomes part of a dialectical pattern having to do with uncreation. (In the same way, as I have shown, the word "womb" is negated semantically as soon as it is applied to Satan.) Yet "won" (as well as "womb" and innumerable other words of the same type) is applied "creatively" to Satan because that is the way Milton dialectically reveals the polarities of good and evil—by expressing them paradoxically in the same terms. Our business in reading Paradise Lost is to learn the meanings of the terms before we can begin to know the meaning of the poem.

Sin and Death become the new Adam and Eve, the new pos-
sessors of paradise, where, like their once unfallen prototypes,
they will live and rule in bliss. And as man was once ruler of
those below him, Sin and Death will have dominion over
man, be able to enslave him and then destroy him. As Adam
and Eve's dominion was originally creative, helping things to
grow, Sin and Death's dominion will be uncreative, causing
things to die.

Satan's language parodies God's language of creation
originally heard by the unfallen Adam and Eve, to whom
God said:

> Not onely these fair bounds, but all the Earth
> To thee and to thy Race I give; as Lords
> Possess it, and all things that therein live,
> Or live in Sea, or Air, Beast, Fish, and Fowl.
>
> (VIII, 338–341)

God gave Adam and Eve, as well as their offspring, paradise
and "all the Earth" to "possess," that is, "create." The land,
the sea, and the air were given to them as creators. That
central pattern is exactly inverted when Satan makes his
children the rulers:

> My Substitutes I send ye, and Create
> Plenipotent on Earth, of matchless might
> Issuing from mee; on your joynt vigor now
> My hold of this new Kingdom all depends,
> Through Sin to Death expos'd by my exploit.
> If your joynt power prevail, th'affaires of Hell
> No detriment need fear, goe and be strong.
>
> (X, 403–409)

As Adam and Eve's great purpose was to increase and multiply, Sin and Death's purpose is a parody of that procreative
end. By destroying all life on earth, Sin and Death will be
"creative": they will perpetuate their all-powerful and fully
potent species on earth. As God is to create offspring through
man, Satan will create his offspring through Sin and Death,

whose race will be Satan's issue. By means of that race, Satan will be able to control earth. And as Adam and Eve were to copulate in order to perpetuate God's offspring in man, Death and Sin are instructed by their father to copulate with their "joynt vigor" to beget Satan's offspring in man. In that way, Hell will remain in power, and the Kingdom of God will die out. Satan approaches the destruction of man in the same language that God approaches the creation of man. Creation and uncreation, the birth of the uncreated out of Chaos and the return of the created to Chaos, are expressed ironically in a similar language of generation.

Following their father's directions, Sin and Death arrive in paradise, where Death will presumably be able to glut himself. Yet even with the prospect of all the food that is to come, Death remains unhappy, for he knows that he must always remain ravenous. Attempting to placate her son, Sin suggests how he might go about his meal.

> Thou therefore on these Herbs, and Fruits, and Flowrs
> Feed first, on each Beast next, and Fish, and Foul,
> No homely morsels, and whatever things
> The sithe of Time mows down, devour unspar'd.
>
> (x, 603–606)

There must be order and propriety in everything, even in the process of destroying order; consequently, Sin tells Death to start devouring the lowest things first, the plants, and then work up to such tasty morsels as animals, fish, and birds. But of course such is precisely the hierarchical pattern that God followed in his creations from plant, to beast, and to man. And of the last and greatest morsel, Sin implies that Death should wait until she "in Man residing through the Race, / His thoughts, his looks, words, actions, all infect, / And season him [Death's] last and sweetest prey" (x, 607–609). The process of creation will be reversed even to the point of following exactly the hierarchy established by the creative pattern. Sin will "infect" the race of man like a disease spreading throughout all his actions as preparatory to Death's devouring of the "last and sweetest prey." Man will be honored in his fallen condition, for he is at the top of the hierarchy in the process of uncreation.

After meeting with his children and returning to Hell to announce his victory over man, Satan, with his cohorts, experiences a metamorphosis that combines the motifs of being transformed and of having to devour, both of which are found in the metamorphosis of Sin and in the ravenous plight of Death. Having announced his success in the upper world regarding the perversion of man, the Arch-Demon expects loud acclaim, "universal shout and high applause / To fill his ear" (x, 505–506), but he hears instead "from innumerable tongues / A dismal universal hiss" (x, 507–508). Since the mouth in *Paradise Lost* is associated with the womb and that which issues from the mouth may be characterized as the verbal offspring, then the "hiss" here becomes the Satanic "Word" incarnate. The "Word" that debases appears full-blown in its true form. And concurrent with the verbal metamorphosis is the physical "rebirth" in the diabolic context:

> His visage drawn [Satan] felt to sharp and spare,
> His Armes clung to his Ribs, his Leggs entwining
> Each other, till supplanted down he fell
> A monstrous Serpent on his Belly prone.
>
> (x, 511–514)

Satan again physically manifests the filth and obscenity of the world he has created both for himself and for others. He becomes the degraded monstrosity of perverted sexuality in his transformation. His plight recalls his debasement after the fall when he lay prone on the flood, stretched out long and huge. The association with Sin's own serpentine transformation in the area of her reproductive organs need hardly be stressed. In any case, Satan's transformation has implicitly generative overtones.

Satan has fathered Death in Sin, and he has fathered death in Eve. The degraded transformation of the first reverberates through the second backwards upon the father, for in Eve

Satan has seduced not the offspring of his own imagination but the offspring of God. As a result, Satan is "supplanted," that is, "uprooted" as well as "tripped up"; he is again symbolically deprived of the root or source of life as he was in his fall from Heaven. His transformation re-enacts the fall. The foreshadowing of Satan's final degradation is represented in the metamorphosis. Satan, along with his cohorts, is "punisht in the shape he sin'd, / According to his doom" (x, 516–517).

To reinforce the idea that the metamorphosis is envisioned as an aspect of the birth metaphor, Milton allusively compares Satan's transformation to the Sun's having "Ingenderd in the *Pythian* Vale on slime, / Huge *Python*" (x, 530–531). The birth indicates the lowest, most degenerate of births, that referred to as spontaneous generation from slime, from filthy secretions and excremental waste products. Such organisms arising from putrid organic substances are the offspring we are to associate with this metamorphosis. Within a similar context, these "complicated monsters" (x, 523) are then allusively compared to those monsters that "swarm'd once the Soil / Bedropt with blood of *Gorgon*" (x, 526–527). That soil is, of course, "Libya, upon which blood dropt from the Gorgon Medusa's head when Perseus . . . was carrying it through the air"; the drops of blood then engendered the "serpents with which Libya swarms."[8] Thus in relation to the metamorphosis in Book x, we have the comparison of serpents springing from blood, which substance becomes the means of engendering monsters.[9] The figure also recalls the idea of the

[8] David Masson, ed., *Milton's Poetical Works* (London, 1874), III, 246n.

[9] Blood as a generative substance has both negative and positive connotations. On the one hand, it is related to "*Moloch*, horrid King besmear'd with blood / Of human sacrifice" (I, 392–393), to Thammuz, whose annual wounding becomes a mockery of the rebirth process (I, 451–452), to the death of Abel, who "Groand out his Soul with gushing blood effus'd" (XI, 447), and to Hecate's riding through the air "Lur'd with the smell of infant blood" (II, 664). On the other hand, it recalls Adam's lifeblood from which Eve is born (VIII, 465–468) and the rebirth associated with Christ's "more precious" blood (XII, 293). Cf. also blood as a medium of birth in "Sonnet 18": "Their martyr'd blood and ashes sow / O're all th'*Italian* fields . . . that from these may grow / A hundred-fold," and the association of blood and the purification from childbirth in "Sonnet 23."

head as a place of birth, and since the head here belongs to the
slaughtered Medusa, we are returned to the image of Sin
springing from Satan's head and made to look forward to the
bruising of the serpent's head as a part of God's curse on Satan.

Outside the hall, the transformed serpents are confronted
with a "Grove" which has "sprung up" to "aggravate / Thir
pennance" (x, 549–550). Like the hellhounds which devour,
like Death whose maw is never satisfied, like Eve who eats in
gluttony, these serpents are made to undergo the impotence
of unsatisfied hunger. In their state of unfulfillment, they are
tempted by a mockery of fulfillment, for the "Grove" is
nothing but the projection of their desires, the projection of
pride and selfhood. Fixing their eyes "on that prospect
strange," projecting or "imagining / For one forbidden Tree
a multitude / Now ris'n" (x, 553–555), they become Narcissus pining for his reflection and finding it nothing:

> Yet parcht with scalding thurst and hunger fierce,
> Though to delude them sent, could not abstain,
> But on they rould in heaps, and up the Trees
> Climbing,
>
> .   .   .   .
>
>   greedily they pluck'd
> The fruitage fair to sight, like that which grew
> Neer that bituminous Lake where *Sodom* flam'd.
>   (x, 556–562)

They unwillingly enact Eve's transgression, which they
themselves have caused. Their inability to abstain iterates the
idea of intemperance, which, as in the case of those in the
"Lazar-house," turns one into a monster. Furthermore,
intemperance is not only the counterpart of lust and perverted sexuality, but characterizes the idea of uncreation, which
is opposed to the tempering of elements in the process of
creation.

The reference to Sodom fuses a number of associations
that have a bearing upon creativity. First, the "bituminous
Lake" prefigures the perverted creativity of Nimrod and the

building of Babel, the city and tower of which are partially constructed out of the "black bituminous gurge" (XII, 41–44). Second, the "flaming" of Sodom connotes both its fiery destruction and those lustful perversions that caused its destruction. Third, the fair apples of Sodom have the semblance of that false beauty which entices but which is in reality bitter after the tasting.[10] Such is the experience of sin itself, which is attractive to the sight but repellant after the experience, fair above and monstrous below.

As the fruit or offspring of Sodom, these are the apples of deception, which the fallen angels have perpetrated on others and are now forced to experience themselves:

> they fondly thinking to allay
> Thir appetite with gust, instead of Fruit
> Chewd bitter Ashes.
>
> (X, 564–566)

The "bitter Ashes" and "soot and cinders" (X, 570) refer to the state of death, in which the living body resolves itself into ashes and dust. Unregenerative substances, the cinders and ashes are the remains of consuming fire, associated with the burning of Sodom and the self-consuming passions of lust. Finally, the eating of the ashes recalls God's curse upon the serpent that it shall "grovel" upon its "Belly" and shall eat "dust" (and, therefore, man who is dust) "all the days of [its] Life" (X, 177–178).

With Satan's return to Hell and consequent transformation, the extended effects of Satan's fall are clearly discernible, for such will ultimately be the fate of evil when it is eternally degraded, eternally humiliated, and no longer of any threat to God's creatures. In Sin's transformation, that degradation, that humiliation is prefigured. Even Sin and Death, ironically, have a premonition of their own end (II, 806–809). For us to have that same premonition, we must constantly be aware that *Paradise Lost* is, at each instance, revealing what the future will be. The extended consequences of Satan's fall are

[10] Merritt Y. Hughes, ed., *Paradise Lost*, p. 250n.

contained, indeed, defined by, the immediate consequences. When Satan greets Sin and Death, he greets his past, present, and future. To God they are all one, all instantaneous. To the poet writing a poem in time, they are made one by the essential dialectical technique that unifies *Paradise Lost*.

Chapter 8

The Temptation &
Fall of Man

THE ENTIRE STORE of motifs implicit in the relationships of Satan, Sin, and Death culminates in the fall of man. A full understanding of how those motifs operate throughout the poem involves a discussion of Satan's temptation of Eve, both when she is asleep and when she is awake. By concerning myself with the creational aspects of these temptations, I shall attempt to demonstrate how Milton causes the seduction of man to find a common dialectical referent in such ideas as pregnancy and birth. For like every other aspect of the poem, the temptation and fall are based upon the concept of generation.

In the dream temptation, the mouth again assumes its creative function as a fructifier. Thus Satan attempts to seduce Eve in Book IV, in which Ithuriel and Zephon find the Arch-Demon

> Squat like a Toad, close at the ear of *Eve*;
> Assaying by his Devilish art to reach
> The Organs of her Fancie, and with them forge
> Illusions as he list, Phantasms and Dreams.
>
> (IV, 800–803)

Responding to this image, Kester Svendsen notes the remarkable correspondence "between Satan's corruption of Eve through her ear . . . and the medieval notion that Mary was impregnated by the Holy Ghost through her ear."[1] Whether the correspondence is conscious on Milton's part or whether it is merely coincidental, the situation of Satan's assaulting the sleeping Eve is clearly sexual in its implications. Milton causes the situation to become sexual first by providing

[1] *Milton and Science*, p. 265n.

us with parallel instances and second by developing the image even further.

In order to know what temptation means in *Paradise Lost*, we need only examine the overtones of Satan's posture. For example, Satan's squatting position causes him immediately to be contrasted with the Spirit of God who "Dove-like satst brooding" (I, 21) or with Beelzebub who questions why the fallen angels sit hatching "vain Empires" (II, 378). We have already seen that the sitting position may be associated with the idea of birth when the connotations of such a posture accord with similar situations elsewhere in the poem. The same approach may be applied certainly to the act of whispering into an ear. The parallel situation is found in the implicitly sexual relationship, as John T. Shawcross has seen it,[2] between Milton and his Muse, who inspires or gives life to the poet nightly through his ear (IX, 47). Indeed, we may recall that preceding the War in Heaven Satan tempted his own cohorts by infusing bad influence into them (V, 694). That same idea of infusing or pouring into is iterated here and will be reiterated in the actual temptation scene in Book IX. And the meaning of infusing can be found in the central pattern—God's infusing of "vital vertue" and "vital warmth/ Throughout the fluid Mass" (VII, 236–237) in order to create the universe. All these creative parallels and more are present in the one image of Satan's squatting at Eve's ear. They all argue that a full awareness of an isolated incident involves an understanding of the complex variations that that incident may undergo throughout the poem.

Since Milton is creating an incident that contains sexual connotations, we may expect to find additional evidence of sexuality in the remaining description. Indeed, as Milton uses them, the "Organs of the Fancie" combine both psychological and creational overtones. Once these particular "Organs" are activated, for example, the potentially chaotic emotions, previously tempered by the rational faculties, gain sway. The

---

[2] "The Metaphor of Inspiration in *Paradise Lost*," pp. 75–76. See also Chapter 1 above.

impregnated "Organs" then give birth to "Illusions,"
"Phantasms and Dreams," in which world the fallen Satan
is himself forever confined. The description of the assault
continues:

> Or if, inspiring venom, he might taint
> Th'animal Spirits that from pure blood arise
> Like gentle breaths from Rivers pure, thence raise
> At least distemperd, discontented thoughts,
> Vain hopes, vain aimes, inordinate desires
> Blown up with high conceits ingendring pride.
>
> (IV, 804–809)

Satan wishes to initiate the process of impregnation and
consequent birth. The presence of such words as "inspiring,"
"animal" (from *anima* or spirit), "Spirits," "breaths," "raise,"
"blown up," and "ingendring" merely serves to reinforce
the idea previously mentioned. Underlying the imagery is
the concept of giving life through the breath as a breathing
into or inspiring. Ironically, Satan gives life in order to cause
death.

In the chain reaction of pregnancy and birth, the inspiring
of venom will corrupt those life-giving spirits that arise or
are themselves given life from the blood. These exhalations
or "gentle breaths" now become corrupt will in turn "raise"
or cause to be born the "distemperd, discontented thoughts"
and "vain" (therefore empty or devoid of life) hopes, aims,
and "inordinate desires." Further, such ascriptions as "distemperd" and "inordinate" are implicitly uncreative, for
healthful generation implies a tempering and ordering of
that which is chaotic and disordered. These births, however,
proceed from corruption and are the offspring of Chaos.
Other ascriptions such as "vain" imply not only a void or
lack of life, but as products of vanity they imply that which
is without direction, that which is purposeless and without
healthful fruition (compare the fallen angels "in wandring
mazes lost" [II, 561]), and that which is illusory and insubstantial. Finally, these monstrous offspring, these thoughts,

hopes, and desires, cause a further impregnation and birth. Because they are "blown up," and therefore full of wind (compare the Paradise of Fools in Book III), they engender "pride," which is itself hollow and characterized by the illusory nothingness of the Abyss.

To complete the generative cycle, Satan's being discovered itself results in a kind of mock birth. The idea of being fraudulently "blown up with high conceits" is transferred to a more spectacular "blow up." Ithuriel's touching Satan lightly with his spear causes Satan to reveal himself explosively. The act recalls the igniting of the cannon fuses in the War in Heaven when the cannons exploded their load of wasteful products upon the unsuspecting angels. Here, on the other hand, "truth" explodes "falsehood" with its store of debased associations, and the "Smuttie grain . . . inflames the Air" (IV, 810–818). The offspring of this explosive birth, Satan in his true shape, "resembl'st now /[His] sin and place of doom obscure and foul" (IV, 839–840).

Eve's relating of her dream in Book V foreshadows the libidinous sexuality made so apparent in the actual fall. As Eve describes it, the seduction begins when a voice calls her forth to admire the beauties of the night and, in doing so, flatters her in the following manner:

> now reignes
> Full Orb'd the Moon, and with more pleasing light
> Shadowie sets off the face of things; in vain,
> If none regard; Heav'n wakes with all his eyes,
> Whom to behold but thee, Natures desire,
> In whose sight all things joy, with ravishment
> Attracted by thy beauty still to gaze.
>
> (V, 41–47)

The mode of flattery here is extremely deceitful, because it shifts evasively from praise of the external world to direct, personal praise. In both cases, of course, Eve is the real object of flattery. The first instance works by indirection, for it assumes that it is useless for the night to be so beautiful, unless someone, namely, Eve admires it. That is, the beauty of the external world depends for its existence upon the admiration of man. Such a thought is not foreign to Eve, who had previously voiced the same idea to Adam before they had retired for the night. With reference to the stars, Eve had asked, "But wherefore all night long shine these, for whom / This glorious sight, when sleep hath shut all eyes?" (IV, 657–658). Adam had answered that the world can go on perfectly well without man to admire it. These stars, he had said, which keep Chaos and Night from regaining their former possession, "though unbeheld in deep of night, / Shine not in vain, nor think, though men were none, / That heav'n would want spectators, God want praise" (IV, 674–676). There are millions of other creatures who are God's offspring that praise God's creativity by night and by day (IV, 676–688). Thus Eve's question, though innocent at the time, had begun to take on a tincture of questioning God's creative purpose.

Satan makes full use of Eve's questioning when he tempts her through the dream. First, he makes Eve the end of all creativity by saying that the universe was created for her admiration and that without her presence God's creations would be useless. Then, Satan goes even further by suggesting that the universe receives its recompense by admiring Eve like a doting lover. Admiration has been reversed: not only was the universe created to be admired by Eve, but Eve was created to be admired by the universe. By making Eve the crown of all creation, Satan sets her up for the oncoming seduction.

When the voice that Eve believes to be Adam's leads her to the "Tree / Of interdicted Knowledge" (V, 51–52), the pattern of doting initiated with respect to Eve is now directed toward the tree. As Nature in the guise of a love-starved paramour would "gaze" on Eve's "beauty" with "ravishment," so the heavenly figure that Eve sees next to the tree also "gazes" or dotes upon it and addresses it as one would address a mistress:

> O fair Plant . . . with fruit surcharg'd,
> Deigns none to ease thy load and taste thy sweet,
> Nor God, nor Man [?]
>
> (v, 58–60)

The tree becomes an object of libidinous temptation, and its fruits or forbidden offerings excite the appetite. Within the creative context, the "fruit surcharg'd" has connotations of birth: the tree becomes pregnant with its burden or "load," and the easing of the load becomes synonymous with the completing of the birth process. With "ventrous Arm," then, the figure plucks and tastes, and Eve's instinctive reaction is one of repugnance at so bold an act (v, 65–66).

Such an act and its consequences, however, set a pattern before Eve's eyes and dupe her innocence. For when the heavenly figure praises the fruit for its godlike power and then offers it to Eve (v, 77–78), the seduction is successful. As Eve explains: "he drew nigh, and to me held,/Evn to my mouth of that same fruit" (v, 82–83). The fruit is brought right up to the mouth with the consequent entering of the opening as part of the birth pattern. And the result of the tasting is a type of sexual climax and postclimactic experience:

> Forthwith up to the Clouds
> With him I flew, and underneath beheld
> The Earth outstretcht immense, a prospect wide
> And various: wondring at my flight and change
> To this high exaltation; suddenly
> My Guide was gon, and I, me thought, sunk down,
> And fell asleep.
>
> (v, 86–92)

Eve's exaltation after tasting the fruit is expressed in terms of flying: with her seducer she flies up to the clouds as a representation of sexual excitement. Spirituality becomes debased in its equation with a sexual metaphor. Fulfillment is followed by the postclimactic experience of a sudden, unexpected drop and the disappearance of the seducer. Eve experiences a sinking feeling and a return to sleep.

Adam's interpretation of the dream has a direct bearing upon the creational idea, because it differentiates two modes of generation: the rational and the fanciful. After expressing his dissatisfaction with the dream, which he fears is "of evil sprung" (v, 98), Adam analyzes it by positing the idea of a hierarchy from Reason down to "Fansie." Both faculties are creators in their own way. Reason is the "chief" faculty, and "Fansie next / Her office holds" (v, 102–103). Through Fancy's forming of "Imaginations" and "Aerie shapes" by means of the senses, Reason joins what it considers appropriate and disjoins what it considers inappropriate (v, 103–108). Right Reason is the true creator, and when Reason retires, Fancy takes over the creative function by trying to "imitate" Reason's creativity. The effects of Fancy's performing Reason's office, however, become absurd:

> but misjoyning shapes,
> Wild work produces oft, and most in dreams,
> Ill matching words and deeds long past or late.
>
> (v, 111–113)

The misjoining of shapes is like the work of Chaos, which unites qualities haphazardly and creates "wild work." Such creativity in a demonic light characterizes the prodigious productions of Hell and in a satirical light the abortive creations of the Paradise of Fools. This is the realm of Fancy without the tempering power of Right Reason. In the dream world, according to Adam, the same "ill matching" occurs regarding words and deeds that we have experienced in waking life.

Despite his astute interpretation, however, Adam fails to realize what Eve's actions prefigure. For Adam actually takes hope from Eve's abhorrence of the dream:

> Which gives me hope
> That what in sleep thou didst abhorr to dream,
> Waking thou never wilt consent to do.
>
> (v, 119–121)

He should rather have taken heed from the dream itself: Eve has the propensity to disobey when tempted and, prefiguratively, will disobey if tempted.

The dream typology[3] of Books IV and V becomes a reality in Book IX. Eve's inclination to "divide [their] labours" (IX, 214) is the first mistake in a chain of mistakes that activate the process by which the fall may be effected. The bond or union of birth through which each partner completes the other cannot be severed if that union is to remain inviolate. Since Adam is not God, his labors must be united with those of Eve in mutual dependency. Neither Adam nor Eve is self-sustaining; like the angels, they depend upon each other, and finally upon their Creator for sustenance. Thus Adam calls his partner "sole *Eve*, Associate sole" (IX, 227): Eve becomes an entity only as she is associated with Adam. She is not only Adam's only associate, but she is his associate "soul," and the two halves complement each other in one whole union.

Adam attempts to preserve the union by assuring Eve that "These paths and Bowers doubt not but our joynt hands / Will keep from Wilderness with ease" (IX, 244–245). The joining of the hands becomes a symbol of the union, and the separating of the hands (IX, 385–386) becomes a breaking of the union. When they separate, Adam and Eve are incomplete; as long as they are together, however, they are able to work in unison. Moreover, Adam is afraid "least harm / Befall [Eve] sever'd from [him]" (IX, 251–252). The severing of the birth union is what disturbs the male counterpart; he fears that alone the female counterpart will be subject to a seduction, an "assault" (IX, 256). Adam, therefore, pleads in a language conscious of its generative implications: "leave not the faithful side / That gave thee being" (IX, 265–266).

[3] For further discussions of dreams and their importance, see Manfred Weidhorn, "Dreams and Guilt," *HTR*, LVIII (1965), 69–90; and William B. Hunter's two studies, "Eve's Demonic Dream," *ELH*, XIII (1946), 255–265, and "Prophetic Dreams and Visions in *Paradise Lost*," *MLQ*, IX (1948), 277–285.

Eve counters Adam's plea with what sounds suspiciously like an uncreative assertion regarding the Creator:

> Let us not then suspect our happie State
> Left so imperfet by the Maker wise,
> As not secure to single or combin'd.
> Frail is our happiness, if this be so,
> And *Eden* were no *Eden* thus expos'd.
>
> (IX, 337–341)

The apparent refusal on Eve's part to "suspect" that the Maker could have created anything "imperfet" is immediately undercut by the assumption that this might possibly "be so" and that Eden might possibly be "expos'd" as manifesting such imperfection. The assumption, even if negatively stated, at least hints at the possibility of Eve's doubting God's creative ability. Such a stance smacks of Satan's arguments against God's creativity in Heaven.

Adam, like Abdiel, with whom Satan argued, replies "fervently":

> O Woman, best are all things as the will
> Of God ordain'd them, his creating hand
> Nothing imperfet or deficient left
> Of all that he Created, much less Man.
>
> (IX, 343–346)

Adam is quick to recognize the possible hint of doubt in God's creative ability and is quick to defend God as a Creator. God, maintains Adam, creates everything in perfection. We are the ones who corrupt perfection and cause creation to become vilified (IX, 348–349). Man must be responsible for his own uncreation. Yet Eve persists and invites temptation, while Adam in the same vein warns her to perform her part as a created individual endowed with a sense of responsibility (IX, 375).

After Eve has parted from Adam's side, thereby symbolically severing the union of birth, Satan as an "Inmate bad" within the serpent (IX, 495) prepares to tempt Eve. The attitude toward the serpent at this point is ambivalent: although the serpent is corrupted because of Satan's presence, it is still unfallen. "Inmate" suggests not only a sexual joining but a perversion of sexuality, an incestuous inbreeding similar to the hellhounds' relationship to Sin. Since the serpent is not yet fallen, however, it is not yet

> Prone on the ground, as since, but on his rear,
> Circular base of rising foulds, that tour'd
> Fould above fould a surging Maze, his Head
> Crested aloft, and Carbuncle his Eyes;
> With burnished Neck of verdant Gold, erect
> Amidst his circling Spires, that on the grass
> Floted redundant.
>
> (IX, 497–503)

The serpent is still in the "erect" or generative position and not "prone" as Satan was "prone on the Flood." The serpentine convolutions move upward from a "circular base" to a crowned "Head." In that posture the serpent presents an imposing image. On the other hand, there are even here some characteristics that will take on negative connotations after the fall. For example, the serpentine folds within the context of fallen sexuality and Sin's nether transformation become associated with the labyrinthine aimlessness of those who are lost and alienated from God. Because the serpent uses its beauty for evil ends, it becomes with its "burnished Neck" and "Carbuncle" eyes an object of pride that attempts to appear greater through ostentation. Further, the ascription "redundant" involves the idea of that which "redounds" or surges back. Sin in her nether transformation experiences such a "redounding" with the "return" of the hellhounds to devour her womb. Finally, this particular serpent is immediately associated with the idea of transformations or metamorphoses like the one that Sin has undergone. Thus the loveliness of the serpent's shape is compared to such metamorphosed serpents as *"Hermione* and *Cadmus"* and those other serpentine metamorphoses reminiscent of the *"Amnon-*

ian Jove" and Roman Jove (IX, 503–510). With reference to the last two names, there are also seductions and begettings which prefigure the seduction of Eve that is about to ensue.

In such an aspect, then, Satan as the serpent "curld many a wanton wreath in sight of *Eve*, / To lure her Eye" (IX, 517–518). Here we have the fawning of the courtly lover upon his mistress, the subtle and devious advance, the appeal to pride through flattery and mock humility that have all the earmarks of seduction. The temptation is as "fraudulent" (IX, 531) as the beauty of the serpent becomes.

Satan's immediate appeal is one of flattery, of placing Eve at the center of the universe and of making her the object of all admiration. As an "insatiate" (IX, 536) lover, the Arch-Demon violates the created hierarchy: he places Eve above Adam by calling her the "Fairest resemblance of [her] Maker fair" (IX, 538). The technique of seducing Eve in her dream is repeated here: the universe becomes her pining lover that "gazes" on her and "adores" her "Celestial Beautie" with "ravishment" (IX, 539–541). Through flattery, then, the serpent fulfills those previous thoughts and desires bred of Fancy in Eve. That is, it is obedient to what Eve has already wished. And as the newly born Eve looked into the water and fell in love with the shape she did not know was herself, the serpent re-creates that self, that image of wish fulfillment, in the Fruit, so that Eve will pine again. Further, as Eve then did not know the reflection was herself yet loved it, she does not know that the Fruit is the Forbidden Fruit yet desires it. The voice of God told her then the meaning of the image and led her away from it; the voice of Satan now deceives her further about the meaning of the image and leads her to it. "Lead then, said *Eve*" (IX, 631), and the serpent obeys. It leads the credulous Eve to "Boggs and Mires," where she will be "swallow'd up and lost" (IX, 641–642) in the filth and waste of the fallen condition. The tragedy is a generative one: the Mother of man is led into the "fraud" represented by the "Tree of prohibition," which becomes the source or "root of all our woe" (IX, 643–645).

Eve's immediate reaction upon seeing the Fruit is that of disappointment: such Fruit is "fruitless" to her (IX, 648), for God has defined the Fruit as he had defined Eve's image in the water. This reflection of the self is forbidden, and to succumb to the self in defiance of God will result in death. Satan, then, must undermine that decree and seduce Eve into succumbing to this projection of the self in the same way that Satan had succumbed to the projection of his ego in Sin. Thus the serpent proceeds to tempt Eve into yielding to her own image as an icon that is higher than all else. It offers itself as an example of one who has tasted and not died, in order to deprive God's decree of its meaning.

Satan, therefore, repeats in Eve the very pattern, the very motivation of his own fall: a rebellion of the created against the Creator. God's decree, maintains the serpent, was made to keep his creatures subservient, to "awe" his creatures and keep them "low and ignorant / His worshippers" (IX, 704–705). And as Satan and his crew were cut off from "blessed vision," so Satan would have Adam and Eve deprived of that life-giving experience by promising Eve that if she eats, her "Eyes" shall then be "op'nd and cleerd," and Adam and Eve "shall be as Gods" (IX, 705–708). Further, Satan perverts the meaning of death, "whatever thing Death be" (IX, 695), into a type of fraudulent rebirth, for he promises:

So ye shall die perhaps, by putting off
Human, to put on Gods, death to be wisht,
Though threat'n'd, which no worse then this can bring.
(IX, 713–715)

The eating of the Fruit will cause them to die into a new life, to be reborn as Gods after putting off their lives as humans. Such is the meaning that Satan gives to death and the means of attaining such death by exhalting the self as it is projected in the Fruit. "And what are Gods that Man may not become / As they, participating God-like food?" (IX, 716–717).

As a final inducement, Satan employs the same mode of persuasion that characterized his argument with Abdiel in

Heaven. He presumes to deprive God of the power of his creativity by refusing to acknowledge God as his Creator:

> The Gods are first, and that advantage use
> On our belief, that all from them proceeds;
> I question it, for this fair Earth I see,
> Warm'd by the Sun, producing every kind,
> Them nothing.
>
> (IX, 718–722)

Satan again disputes divine creativity: he maintains that because man was created after the Gods, man is being duped into believing that all creation proceeds from the Gods. In accordance with his usual uncreative approach, Satan would dissociate creation from the Creator and would ascribe, rather, the engendering power of "this fair Earth" to the influence of the sun. The earth itself, rather than a divine power, becomes the cause of creation. Adam and Eve, then, are the offspring of the earth as Satan and his crew had been the sons of Heaven's soil. In this way Eve is released from her obligation to obey her Creator, who would, through envy, keep her ignorant and thereby subservient.

Eve has been given the provocation that she desires to disobey. As Satan had previously seduced Eve through the ear and impregnated her Fancy with his words, likewise now "his words replete with guile / Into her heart too easie entrance won" (IX, 733–734). She gazes as a pining lover upon the projection of herself, the interdicted Fruit, "and in her ears the sound / Yet rung of his perswasive words, *impregn'd* / With Reason, to her seeming, and with Truth" (IX, 736–738; italics mine). Already hungry because of the noon hour, she rationalizes the validity of disobedience; she disobeys; and after she has eaten, she talks like another person entirely.

The figure at the water's edge has been seduced into copulating with its reflection.[4] Eve has embraced the insubstan-

---

[4] After Eve has eaten of the Fruit, her "real value [becomes] self, and the Tree becomes a convenient external correlative of self" (Arnold Stein, *Answerable Style*, p. 95). The eating of the Fruit, then, represents a "return to the mirror-state" (ibid.).

doubt God's creative purpose. By questioning whether God as a Creator would truly destroy his creations if they disobeyed, Adam disputes the meaning of God's Justice as a counterpart of God's creativity. Adam says:

> Nor can I think that God, Creator wise,
> Though threatning, will in earnest so destroy
> Us his prime Creatures, dignifi'd so high,
> Set over all his Works, which in our Fall,
> For us created, needs with us must fail,
> Dependent made.

(IX, 938–943)

> do not charge most innocent nature,
> As if she would her children should be riotous
> With her abundance; she good cateress,
> Means her provision only to the good
> That live according to her sober laws
> And holy dictate of spare temperance.

(ll. 762–767)

Nature provides for those who know how to control their appetites and temper their desires according to that creative pattern by which God tempered the elements of Chaos in order to create the world. Comus, like Satan, would, through intemperance and gluttony, return created (and therefore "tempered") order back to uncreative Chaos. But, like Satan, Comus employs a dialectic of creativity concerned with Nature's overabundance in order to voice his destructive views. It is because man was gluttonous in his fall that he would have starved later had it not been for God's willingness to "provide" for man, "restore" man with Nature's offspring as food.

In her description of gluttony, furthermore, the Lady provides us with an image that prefigures Eve's own act of gluttony in her eating of the Fruit:

> for swinish gluttony
> Ne're looks to Heav'n amidst his gorgeous feast,
> But with besotted base ingratitude
> Cramms, and blasphemes his feeder.

(ll. 776–779)

Here we have Eve herself in her gluttonous act of "ingorging" the Fruit "greedily," intent wholly upon herself, never looking toward Heaven, regarding "naught else," but, like Death, cramming her maw in ingratitude to her Maker. The whole pattern of generation, then, has been foreshadowed in the earlier poetry. The dialectic becomes a means of speaking figuratively as a poet, and it is a mode of speaking that had occupied the poet early in his career.

Such a rationalization for disobeying God is important because it reveals how closely the idea of creation is associated with the idea of obedience in the poem. There is somehow a disbelief on Adam's part that his mere disobedience of a covenant could have cosmic consequences to the created order. God as Creator, Adam maintains, cannot be serious in his threats to destroy what he has created because of one transgression. The implication is that God's carrying through with such a threat would show folly. God would then be a faulty Creator who did not know what he was about when he generated his "prime Creatures" and dignified them over "all his Works." Through such rationalization, Adam, like Satan and Eve, not only questions God as a Creator, but relieves himself of the responsibility of maintaining his obedience. He does not believe that God shall "uncreate" and thereby frustrate his creativity (IX, 943–944); Adam does not realize, however, that he in his transgression will be uncreating himself, since divine Justice must be fulfilled if free will is to have any meaning. He is blind to the fact that God's decrees are not arbitrary but purposeful and that one must bear the responsibility for his own transgressions.

Adam's succumbing willingly and knowledgeably to Eve's temptation "concludes," on the human level at least, the antithetical process of the poem. Uncreation is fulfilled both in Heaven (Satan's fall) and on earth (man's fall). The second fall mirrors the first and yet differs radically from the first in that Satan's fall (from God's point of view and therefore absolutely) precludes reascent, while man's fall (because of God's grace) allows for restoration. The first fall is closed, complete, categorical, as it were; the second, although from man's point of view complete (because man alone is powerless to make it otherwise), is from God's point of view open (because God will provide a way to make it otherwise). The poem, as John T. Shawcross has shown, cannot be viewed solely from the perspective of Book IX ("Satan's climax"),[6]

---

[6]"The Son in His Ascendance: A Reading of *Paradise Lost*," 388–401.

for Satan's fall and his successful temptation of man are merely a means to God's end. Satan's importance as a figure diminishes after Book x, and the poem focuses upon the new creation effected by God through man. The argument of the poem is fulfilled, then, only when we see the full process: creation—uncreation—re-creation.

The Process of Re-creation

Chapter 9

Redemption

To discuss the idea of redemption in *Paradise Lost* is to
return to the central image of God's creating out of
Chaos.[1] Although the image is basically the same, the
circumstances of creativity are somewhat different: not so
much the original cosmic substratum (although that too) as
the human substratum (man taking on the characteristics of
Chaos) is the "matter" out of which God creates. That is, a
reorientation of the primal image occurs with fallen man as
the Chaos through which God achieves glory. God's glory,
as shall be shown, is even greater in the second case than in the
first. Because Milton is a Christian poet, he conducts his
"Argument" so that despite the nature of the situation
(whether creative, destructive, or re-creative), God is inevitably glorious. That we may better know what redemption
means in *Paradise Lost,* let us first explore the type of Chaos
out of which the new creation will emerge.

The fall of man results in a cosmic and psychological return
to disorder. Satan, at least temporarily, has accomplished his
uncreative ends of causing creation to be uncreated and partake of Chaos, Satan's own natural environment. Cosmically,
the process of uncreation manifests itself in various ways. The
sun moves in such a manner as to "affect the Earth with cold
and heat / Scarce tolerable," thereby creating winter and
summer (x, 651–656). The moon and other planets form a
type of uncreative union, a "joyning" in "Synod unbenigne"
(x, 656–661). In the fallen cosmos union is no longer a benev-

---

[1] According to Barbara Kiefer Lewalski ("Structure and the Symbolism of
Vision in Michael's Prophecy, *Paradise Lost*, Books XI–XII," *PQ*, XLII [1963], 28),
Milton's handling of redemption through Michael's prophecy "owes something
to the widespread tradition" that divides history into six ages of restoration
in order to balance the six days of creation. Such a tradition, notes Professor
Lewalski, "enables Milton to use the historical prophecy as a counterpart to
his earlier creation sequence."

olent source of birth. The universe becomes rather a veritable
Chaos of blustering winds that "confound" the sea, the air,
and the shore; and the thunder is taught "when to rowl /
With terror through the dark Aereal Hall" (x, 664–667).

Within the confines of the earth a return to Chaos likewise
ensues:

> Beast now with Beast gan war, and Fowl with Fowl,
> And Fish with Fish; to graze the Herb all leaving,
> Devourd each other; nor stood much in awe
> Of Man, but fled him, or with count'nance grim
> Glar'd on him passing.
>
> $\qquad\qquad\qquad\qquad\qquad$ (x, 710–714)

Disorder possesses the minds of beast, bird, and fish, whose
actions reflect the War in Heaven and Chaos itself. And since
a return to Chaos inevitably involves the act of devouring,
these animals devour each other or uncreate each other in a
process of self-destruction. Further, since the return to Chaos
is the result of man's disobedience to his Creator, fallen man
loses his creative power over those under him, so that those
animals which obeyed unfallen man before now either flee or
threaten him. The hierarchy of created cosmic order is over-
turned, and the world exists in an upside-down state.

As Sin felt the "growing burden" of Death within her,
Adam sees these "growing miseries" without and feels them
in an even more extreme degree within:

> And in a troubl'd Sea of passion tost,
> Thus to disburd'n sought with sad complaint.
>
> $\qquad\qquad\qquad\qquad$ (x, 718–719)

Psychologically, Adam suffers the consequences of being initiated as fallen man into the Chaos that composes his
subconscious mind. He attempts, like the fallen angels lost in
labyrinthine thought, to "disburd'n" himself of his troubles
through "sad complaint." Such an attempt at disburdening
or productive release, however, proves ultimately fruitless,
for complaining about one's situation does not improve it.

The person merely remains psychologically trapped in his chaotic condition. Adam, like Satan, is plunged into an "Abyss of fears / And horrors" out of which he finds no egress "from deep to deeper plung'd!" (x, 842–844).

The tenor of Adam's "Abyss" is one of generative horror: he proceeds through a chain of thoughts concerned with the idea of creation in all its forms to no positive resolution. As an offspring who questions his Maker's creative purposes he complains: "Did I request thee, Maker, from my Clay / To mould me Man [?]" (x, 743–744). Since he did not ask to be created, then, he feels, he is naturally absolved from responsibility and should be returned or reduced to the "dust" out of which he came (x, 746–752). In that way, his sin will not be passed on to his offspring. Then, from the point of view of the begotten, he assumes the viewpoint of the begetter and sees that his arguments are vain: "what if thy Son / Prove disobedient, and reprov'd, retort, / Wherefore didst thou beget me? I sought it not" (x, 760–762). And again Adam desires to be returned to the dust of his "Mothers lap" (x, 778). He is caught in the conflict of desiring immediate death without knowing what the experience of death will be.

Adam's final complaint concerns Eve and a questioning of God's purpose in creating woman. At this low ebb in his fallen condition, Adam feels that woman has no function, that she is nothing but the serpent herself, "false" and "hateful" and made to ensnare man (x, 867–873). Adam then proceeds to question the validity not only of creating woman at all but of the original creative union itself (x, 894–895). Such complaining, however, merely reveals Adam's own weakness, his own subservience to irrational and selfish impulses in himself. Blinded by his complaining, he cannot see how he failed in fulfilling his function in the union of male and female, how he inverted the created order by following Eve. (God must re-establish that order in his punishment of the couple; therefore, part of God's sentence is that the husband will rule over the wife as a means of maintaining the proper sense of the created hierarchy [x, 195–196].) As purposeless as it is, Adam's complaining reveals one important aspect of the poem's meaning. Whether in the form of Satan, Eve, or Adam, when a creature rebels against God, the essential mode of argumentation he employs in his rebellious stance is that concerned with creation. The rebel eventually winds up questioning God's creativity in some way, and ultimately, the means of his rebellion have undeniable creational consequences.

From a positive viewpoint, however, Eve's desire to re-establish the union of love likewise has creational repercussions. Unlike the fallen angels who selfishly exclude others by complaining about their own torments, Eve selflessly offers to undergo punishment for Adam as well as herself (x, 924–936). Her offer suggests a most important aspect of the union: a relinquishing of the self for the benefit of others. Indeed, her attempt to re-establish the union despite her fallen state is the essential preliminary step in the regaining of that holy union which existed before the fall. Eve's sacrificial offer recalls the spirit of the Son's offer to let divine Justice light on him. In her own way, Eve takes on the character of a deliverer, and her offer disarms the complaining Adam to such an extent that he assumes the same attitude and would be willing to accept the blame if it could alter divine Justice (x, 952–957). He knows, however, that Decree must stand and yet welcomes Eve's overture and tells her how to "rise" as a symbol of potential rejuvenation (x, 958). Finally, Adam responds in a positive manner to Eve when he suggests that they "no more contend" but "strive / In offices of Love, how [they] may light'n / Each others burden in [their] share of woe" (x, 958–961). Adam's gesture too is one of re-establishing a union in which each is dependent upon the other and shares with the other rather than regarding the self.

The re-establishment of the union, however, becomes liable to one setback that ultimately tests Adam's ability to resist temptation a second time and accept the procreative responsibility of God's judgment upon him. Eve suggests two ways of mitigating that judgment which so closely con-

cerns their roles as parents: barrenness or death. Although
Eve feels a sense of rebirth in being "restor'd" by Adam and
although she is "hopeful to regain" his "Love," she would
plunge them both back into the Abyss through her attempts
to provide "som relief of [their] extremes" (IX, 971–976). Her
torments are those of a future mother worried about her
inevitable offspring. She complains that the "care" of their
"descent" is what most perplexes them, for their offspring
must undergo unavoidable "woe" as victims who will be
"devoured / By Death" (x, 979–981). Her torment is, therefore, overwhelmingly procreative:

> miserable it is
> To be to others cause of misery,
> Our own begotten, and of our Loins to bring
> Into this cursed World a woful Race,
> That after wretched Life must be at last
> Food for so foul a Monster.
>
> (x, 981–986)

The entire creational idea is centered in such a statement:
the concept of birth is juxtaposed against antibirth or uncreation; for dying is synonymous with being devoured, and
the act of devouring in *Paradise Lost* becomes a metaphor for
returning that which has been created to that which is
uncreated.

Eve's solution to such a plight is "Conception to prevent"
(IX, 987), an act which implies violating that most holy of
acts that consummate the union of love. The suggestion is
blatantly adverse to their roles as procreators, and Eve
realizes it. She knows that the mere presence of male and
female in love necessitates intercourse and that abstinence
goes against nature (x, 992–998). Her alternative, then, is to
"seek Death, or he not found, supply / With our own hands
his Office on our selves" (x, 1001–1002). Eve places so little
value on life and the glorious act of God's having created life
that she would be willing to end it herself. Consequently, in
her attempts to find a means of frustrating God's essential

creativity, Eve resorts to the idea of uncreation. What Eve proposes is a denial of the very reason why she and Adam were created, a denial of God's entire creative existence. Eve suggests not only their own suicide but the suicide of the entire race of man before man has even had a chance to live. Like Satan, she would return creation to Chaos, and, as Adam fortunately realizes, she would prevent the ultimate triumph of good over evil through the birth of Christ and the ultimate regeneration of man in the afterworld of bliss.

Adam immediately perceives that Eve's suggestions, although apparently sacrificial in their concern for others, are actually selfish and spring from an overlove of pleasure. "Self-destruction" implies not Eve's contempt for this life "but anguish and regret / For loss of life and pleasure over-lov'd" (x, 1013–1019). Rather than submitting to these temptations suggested by Eve, Adam as the head suggests their accepting the holy responsibility of being prime progenitors and their remembering "with heed/Part of [their] Sentence, that," as Adam says, "thy Seed shall bruise/The Serpents head" (x, 1030–1032). Adam, to counter Eve's uncreative suggestions, begins to think in terms of regeneration, for the bruising of the serpent's head, as Adam interprets it, represents the crushing of Satan:

> to crush his head
> Would be revenge indeed; which will be lost
> By death brought on our selves, or childless days
> Resolv'd, as [Eve] proposest; so our Foe
> Shall scape his punishment ordain'd, and wee
> Instead shall double ours upon our heads.
> (x, 1035–1040)

Adam begins to recognize even now their ultimately regenerative purpose: to give birth to an offspring who will cause the destruction of that force which caused Adam and Eve to fall and allowed evil to enter the world. Yet they must propagate in order for that divine event to occur. To abstain from propagation or to seek death would be to frustrate their own regeneration and, like Sin with her hellhounds, double their destruction upon themselves. Consequently, Adam begins to adopt a renewed and healthful attitude toward their punishment; he begins to come to terms with their fate, to view the positive side of it. Even in their fallen state, Adam and Eve have the potentiality for regeneration. They are able to fall "prostrate" of their own free will before their God, confess their faults, and beg for forgiveness (x, 1087–1092). Such genuine humiliation and unwilling prostration the fallen angels could never be capable of and thus could never be restored, as man can be, to bliss.

The idea of regeneration as revealed in the fate of man finds expression in the last two books. Adam and Eve's willing submission to God is an aspect of the regenerative process within themselves, and the language which characterizes that process is markedly one of birth. As a result of their contrition, Adam experiences a new sense of return: not one of remorse but one of "peace," which, as Adam says, "returnd / Home to my brest" (xi, 153–154). Their repentance, then, is characterized in generative terms, for the grace of God "descending had remov'd / The stonie from their hearts, and made new flesh / Regenerat grow instead" (xi, 1–5). Through God's influence upon their submissive act, a process of regeneration occurs in which there is a growing of new flesh and the healing of a wound. Further, their prayer is compared to the petition of Deucalion and Pyrrha, who "before the Shrine/Of *Themis*," prayed for the restoration of "Mankind drownd" (xi, 10–14) and whose petition resulted in the springing up of a new race. That allusion also glances forward to Noah as the survivor of the Flood and the progenitor of the continuing race. The fall as destruction is associated with the Flood, from which there is a new birth, and Themis as the goddess of justice is associated with God's Justice, which paradoxically allows for new births through the mercy of the Son.

It is the Son who presents the prayers to the Father through a language of generation:

See Father, what first fruits on Earth are sprung
From thy implanted Grace in Man, these Sighs
And Prayers, which in this Golden Censer, mixt
With Incense, I thy Priest before thee bring,
Fruits of more pleasing savour from thy seed
Sow'n with contrition in his heart, then those
Which his own hand manuring all the Trees
Of Paradise could have produc't, ere fall'n
From innocence.

(XI, 22–30)

In a passage that ostensibly concerns such religious matters as
grace and prayers proceeding from contrition, Milton has the
Son talk about fertilizing, sowing, and reaping and, by extension, impregnation and reproduction, for as we have seen
earlier the two acts characterize the same metaphor. For
example, the Son reveals to the Father the "first fruits" or
first offspring created as a result of God's having impregnated
man with divine grace. Prayers thus become the offspring of
penitence, and the "savour" of these prayers is associated
with life. Furthermore, discernible here is a contrast between
creation in the states of innocence and contrition. Much more
pleasing to God than the smell and taste of unfallen fruits
are the smell and taste of those fruits that spring from repentance, because the latter offspring rely directly upon God's
grace for their birth, rather than upon man's own cultivating
practices. Consequently, in response to the Son's approaching
the Father, first as an interpreter of man's prayers and then
as a professed object of sacrifice for man's misdeeds, the
Father reiterates his acceptance of the Son as the means by
which man will be reborn.

Man, however, must first be ejected out of paradise,
which he will corrupt if he remains. Paradise will purge man
off "as a distemper, gross to air as gross," since man has been
"distemperd" by Sin, who has made all things corrupt (XI,
50–57). Here again we are given a direct relationship in
Milton's vocabulary between the ideas of distempering

(returning order into Chaos as opposed to tempering or causing order to come out of Chaos) and corrupting. The association is clear enough: Chaos (the result of distempering) is corruption, and corruption is, very simply, gross, vile, the antithesis of purity.

As Heaven ejected Satan and his crew before they could cause the purity of Heaven to become gross, Eden must eject Adam and Eve, who, in their fall, have become an "unharmoneous mixture foul" (xi, 51). The foulness and grossness attributed to them clearly have overtones of the vitiated qualities associated with Satan, and the "inharmoniousness" of the mixture applies to the "inharmoniousness" of Chaos, whose mixture of elements is opposed to the harmony of the created order.

With the regenerative potentialities that man now possesses, on the other hand, his corruption is not eternal, for God has "provided Death," which suddenly takes on positive qualities in its association with the idea of regeneration. Paradoxically, rather than negation, Death becomes man's "final remedie," a means of new birth:

> and after Life
> Tri'd in sharp tribulation, and refin'd
> By faith and faithful works, to second Life,
> Wak't in the renovation of the just,
> [Death] resignes him up with Heav'n and Earth renewd.
> (xi, 62–66)

The passage involves major aspects of the rebirth dialectic. Corruption or distemper must undergo a purgation through "sharp tribulation" and a process of refinement. That which is gross, inharmonious, and chaotic must undergo the trial of purification during this life as a way of restoring through the Savior what was previously harmonious and generative. After such tribulation and the pangs of death have been endured, man will ultimately awaken from a temporary sleep. He will re-enact permanently that initial sleeping and waking process that Adam first experienced when Eve was created. That Milton is careful to cast this process within a creative framework becomes evident from the following description.

In compliance with God's order that Adam and Eve be banished from Eden, Michael descends to indoctrinate the fallen couple into their future roles by allowing them as parents to witness the fate of their offspring. The indoctrination is expressed, appropriately, through a language of generation. While Adam ascends the Hill in order to awaken to foresight, Eve sleeps below. Milton deliberately describes the sleeping and waking here to Adam's once having slept while Eve "to life was formd" (XI, 366–369). Instead of Adam sleeping and Eve being created, Eve sleeps and Adam is "created," that is, awakened to foreknowledge and humanized by experiencing the torments of the future world.

If we wish to pursue the creational overtones even further, we might consider the name given to the Hill Michael and Adam ascend. Because Milton calls it the "top / Of Speculation," we may relate the name of the Hill to the process of meditation, which, as we have seen, refers to the idea of "brooding." On the "top" of "Speculation" Adam, like the Son in the act of creation, "broods" on the Abyss of human history which is revealed beneath him, and he is able to create out of that Abyss a sense of regenerative life within himself, a "Paradise within" (XII, 587). As fallen man, he confronts his own Abyss and gives it shape, and through the grace of God, he will be "much more cheer'd / With *meditation* on the happie end" (XII, 604–605; italics mine). By means of the education that Michael as an agent of God provides, Adam will be humanized through suffering as a parent the consequences of his fallen state.

One of the most important aspects of the humanization Adam undergoes is his experience of the "greater" men as types of the "one greater Man" (I, 4) or Messiah. Such men are those who, in their role as "deliverer," have a great deal to do with the concept of generation in the poem. This type of individual, for example, is Noah, who stands at the juncture "betwixt the world destroy'd and the world restor'd" (XII, 3), between Chaos and re-creation. And through that one righteous man, who alone has confronted an alien world, "Man as from a second stock" will "proceed" (XII, 7). Noah, then, becomes the type of Christ, from whom man receives renewed life as through a second root.

Another such "greater" man who continues the idea of generation is Abraham, from whom a "Nation" will "spring" (XII, 113). Like Noah, righteous Abraham turns away from an alien world and leaves his "Fathers house" (XII, 121) to travel into a land where God "from him will raise / A mightie Nation," and "in his Seed / All Nations shall be blest" (XII, 122–126). Through obedience to God, Abraham delivers the future race from the Abyss of iniquity; furthermore, Abraham is the progenitor in whose "Seed," Christ the "deliverer," "all Nations of the Earth" shall be "blessed" (XII, 147–149). Continuing the cycle of pregnancy and birth, through the grandchild Jacob the twelve tribes of Israel will be born.

The next great Messianic figure is Moses, who causes his people to be delivered from the confinement of Egypt. Like the Son in the act of creation when he confronts the Abyss and like Noah when he confronts the sea of destruction, Moses confronts the Red Sea, tames it, and delivers his people from its portending destruction (XII, 170–214). (The antithesis of all these deliverers is, of course, Satan, who confronts Chaos in order to deliver his crew from the bondage of Hell and whose "delivery" or metaphoric birth is, finally, illusory.)

After the account of Joshua and David as the types of Jesus, we are finally presented with a vision of the Messiah, who effects the ultimate regeneration; for by quelling the "adversarie Serpent," Christ shall "bring back / Through the worlds wilderness long wanderd man / Safe to eternal Paradise of rest" (XII, 311–314). As the apotheosis of the rebirth pattern, the Messiah causes the final return to the womb. He becomes the deliverer who causes birth to issue out of Chaos or wandering man to be born out of the wilderness of this world and to return to the paradise of the eternal realm of birth. His opposing type will then be defeated. Thus, as part of the vision, the Messiah's birth is celebrated (XII, 360–371), and Adam as prime progenitor is overjoyed at hearing the prophecy.

"Surcharg'd" (XII, 373), quickened by such inspiration, Adam "hails" the "Virgin Mother" and the fact that Mary as a progenitor of divinity must "proceed" from his "Loyns"; in that way God will "unite" with man (XII, 379–382). This ultimate and mysterious birth by which a physical, as well as a spiritual, union will occur between God and man becomes the triumphant object of celebration, for that is the birth of all births and the means by which man will finally be reborn in spiritual and apocalyptic union with God.

To Adam has been revealed the fortunate outcome of his fall, and he replies with a full awareness of how the Fortunate Fall relates to the ideas of creation and re-creation:

> O goodness infinite, goodness immense!
> That all this good of evil shall produce,
> And evil turn to good; more wonderful
> Then that which by creation first brought forth
> Light out of darkness!
>
> (XII, 469–473)

Adam rejoices at the generative paradox whereby evil shall, because of God, produce an "immense" good as opposed to the original evil which, without God's influence, produced only further evils. Indeed, such a paradoxical act of transformation in which evil turns to good is even a greater act of generation than that which characterized the first creative act of bringing light out of darkness. Regeneration is more wonderful than generation. Furthermore, the opposite of uncreation (Satan's copulation with Sin, Sin's transformation, and the consequent birth of Death and the hellhounds) is regeneration. That involves God's redemption of man through the Savior followed by the divine transformation of Satanic evil to deific good. The divine paradox informs the entire texture of the poem : as glorious as creation is, re-creation is that much more glorious because it triumphs over those forces that would have returned creation to its chaotic state.

In his joy Adam is "full of doubt" whether he should repent the sin of his fall "or rejoyce"

> Much more, that much more good thereof shall spring,
> To God more glory, more good will to Men
> From God, and over wrauth grace shall abound.
>
> (XII, 476–478)

Adam stands between the sin of his fall and the knowledge that because of his fall God's glory will be that much greater and man's happiness that much more abundant. God will re-create out of the uncreative nature of man's lapse a world far more glorious than the one he first created. Such ecstatic knowledge gives Adam hope in his fallen state: he now understands the divine paradox whereby "to the faithful Death [becomes] the Gate of Life" (XII, 571). Thus through the example of Christ the Regenerator, Adam has been taught the meaning of rebirth (XII, 572–573).

With his new knowledge, Adam has "attaind the sum / Of wisdom" (XII, 575–576): he has been humanized through vision. Eden loses the magnitude of its importance as it gives way to the Fortunate Fall with the promise of rebirth and the "Paradise within." Because Eden becomes just a place, Michael can say to Adam:

> then wilt thou not be loath
> To leave this Paradise, but shalt possess
> A Paradise within thee, happier farr.
>
> (XII, 585–587)

Satan has been dispossessed of paradise, and Adam and Eve, of the earthly paradise, but whereas Hell possesses Satan psychologically (as well as cosmically), Adam and Eve will now possess a psychological paradise. Since within the generative context, the idea of possession is coincident with the idea of creation, Adam and Eve will be able to create an internal paradise in the knowledge of man's future redemption. As a result of the vision of regeneration inherent in the last two books, paradise has been internalized, and its meaning has changed. It is no longer associated with an external environment generated cosmically but with an internal environment regenerated psychologically.

The entire cosmogony of the first ten books is viewed from a new perspective. That perspective embraces not only man's individual re-created psyche but a future cosmos in which "time stand[s] fixt" (XII, 555) in the apocalyptic "All in All." Until that event, when internalized paradise and externalized paradise are fused in an ultimate union, Adam and Eve must become part of the "Race of time" in "this transient World" "measur'd" by Michael in the vision (XII, 554). That is, they must become progenitors of that "Race" as well as undergo time's flight, but within themselves, they will be sustained by a timeless re-created realm. Although they are to be expelled into the fallen world after the loss of an insulated paradisiacal consciousness, their expulsion involves the redemption of man, that is, the creation of good out of evil, an event more wonderful than the original creation of "Light out of Darkness." Both Adam and Eve, then, find consolation in the promise that their offspring will fulfill. Humanized in the creation of a new consciousness, they are prepared to confront the world below.

The manner in which they are driven hence contains essential dialectical overtones. For example, the environment of their expulsion is associated with "Ev'ning Mist" that glides "o're the marish" and gathers quickly about the "Labourers heel / Homeward returning" (XII, 627–632). Foreboding and menacing in its associations, the mist returns us to Satan himself when he is in the act of leading Eve to her destruction.[2] He is described as a "wandring Fire / Compact

---

[2] Cf. also Book IX, 158–162, in which Satan is "wrapt in mist / Of midnight

of unctuous vapor" that "misleads" the "Nightwanderer" into "Boggs and Mires" (IX, 634–641). The contrast between the two occurrences is important. Now the wanderers are not deluded into being swallowed up in the marsh as they had been when they fell. Rather the image of banishment indicates that they will be able to avoid the dangers of the "Mist" by exiting out of Eden. Because their "guide" catches them by their hands "and to th'Eastern Gate / [Leads] them direct" (XII, 638–639), they are shown the way rather than being misled. Their escape from destruction is analogous to the escape of Lot and his wife, when the angels "laid hold upon [their hands] . . . and . . . brought [them] forth, and set [them] without the [doomed] city."[3] With Adam and Eve's delivery from the marsh into which they had been led by Satan, the final image of the foreboding "Mist" paradoxically reverses the Satanic process. The destructivity of the "Mist" and its relation to the "Labourer" glances ahead at the prophecy that the serpent will bruise the Victor's "heel" and cause temporal death, because the "Mist" is only allowed to reach the "Labourers heel" before he is shown the way "home." "Homeward returning," finally, allows us to see the banishment as a return to one's place of origin. The poem ends with the creative sense of return as opposed to the destructive return imaged in the hellhounds. Those figures capable of redemption enact the creative return, and indeed the Redeemer himself in *Paradise Regain'd* will enact that same pattern when he returns "home to his Mothers house" after his trial in the wilderness (IV, 639). Both *Paradise Lost* and *Paradise Regain'd*, then, culminate creatively in a movement towards the home.

vapor" in order to "glide obscure" on his destructive mission of finding the "Serpent sleeping." The mists and vapors have their counterpart in the "Exhalation," of which they are forms and which (as I shall discuss in the Appendix) is associated with the paradoxical idea of both death and creation. Furthermore, these destructive vapors should be compared with the "temperat vapors" "bred" from "pure digestion" attributed to the unfallen Adam (V, 3–5). Opposed to these "temperat vapors" are the "exhilerating vapour[s]" caused by the Forbidden Fruit (IX, 1046–1048).

[3] Masson (ed., *Milton's Poetical Works*, III, 271n.) citing Gen. 19:16.

The nature of Adam and Eve's expulsion, furthermore, offers an interesting parallel to Satan's. For instance, the "Chariot of Paternal Deitie" is present in both cases (VI, 750 and XI, 126–133). As with Satan, we find the element of destruction: the "torrid heat" of God's "brandished Sword" begins to "parch that temperate Clime" (XII, 633–636). That which was previously temperate, as opposed to the excesses of intemperate Chaos, begins to undergo a return to disorder. In addition, because Adam and Eve, like Satan, issue from the opening of a world that had previously sustained them in bliss, indeed, a world that we had previously associated imagistically with a womb, their expulsion draws upon the same pattern of birth found in the expulsion of Satan. Like Satan, they are figuratively born from the womb and become suffering inhabitants of the nether world that awaits them. Here is where the similarity ends, however.

That Adam and Eve are expelled from the "Eastern Gate" (XII, 638–639) by Michael, rather than from a forced opening in the side, implies that their birth is natural, not abortive like Satan's. It also implies that their birth is auspicious because the "Eastern" location of the exit suggests the promised regeneration. Furthermore, the fact that Michael leads the fallen pair to the "Gate" contrasts markedly with Satan's forced and violent expulsion. Because they are "led," indeed, shown the "way" out of the destruction into which they had been misled, Adam and Eve escape the permanent destruction experienced by Satan. Essentially, in having Adam and Eve banished from Eden, God provides the means for their re-creation. It is up to them to make proper use of God's Providence. The power to choose is theirs; their salvation or damnation is in their own hands. Although they are born united into the fallen world (since they walk "hand in hand"), their "way" is "solitarie" because they now become authors of their own fate (XII, 646–649).

With the banishment of Adam and Eve from Eden, the process of re-creation is, in one way, effected and, in another way, waiting to be effected. It is effected insofar as we have been taught along with Adam and Eve the meaning of re-creation; it is waiting to be effected insofar as history must commence before it can be realized. The poem's ending is our beginning: its sense of grand and quiet finality is made paradoxical by the feeling that things have just begun. As the poem closes narratively, it seems to open up, and we behold with our first parents our own world, which we view somehow for the first time, although we have viewed it already with them in vision. Only with the completion of our own lives (the working out of that part of the poem experienced in vision and therefore the working out and final obliteration of history itself) can the poem, or the dialectical process expressed by the poem, be fulfilled.

Conclusion

I N HIS DISCUSSION of the last two books of *Paradise Lost*, F. T. Prince generalizes about some critical approaches to Milton's epic. He says that

> modern methods of criticism are liable to fail us, based as they are on minute verbal analysis and on the search for implied ironies and ambiguities, for subtle correspondences between images and "themes." . . . The fact that Milton's poetry does not respond to this kind of analysis and appreciation, and that his work has therefore always been ranked low by the founders and followers of this school, suggests that we must find other methods of analysing the total effect of such a poem as *Paradise Lost*.[1]

These assumptions, I think, are dangerous not only for *Paradise Lost* but for poetry itself. They imply that texture is of little importance in determining the worth of at least certain types of poetry, that the concrete verbal details of which a poem like *Paradise Lost* consists are subservient to larger elements or "total effect[s]." It seems almost a truism, however, to say that those larger elements depend for their very existence upon the words that describe them, as Prince himself has demonstrated in *The Italian Element in Milton's Verse*.[2] And yet the above passage, which suggests an unwillingness to examine the interrelationships between terms, the connections between local poetic moments, is a (misdirected) reaction against what Prince implies is a definite mode of criticism that has presumed to look closely at Milton's poetic practices, only to find them inadequate.

The classic statement of disapproval was made by T. S.

---

[1] "On the Last Two Books of Paradise Lost," *Essays and Studies*, XI (1958), 47.
[2] (Oxford, 1954).

Eliot, who allowed Milton to be a "great" poet while not allowing him to be a "good" one.[3] The distinction is spurious; yet Prince inadvertently sanctions it when he says that Milton should be examined for his "total effect[s]" (similar in meaning to Eliot's "great") rather than for his verbal subtleties (similar in meaning to Eliot's "good"). Implicit here is the attitude that Milton's greatness must be viewed at a distance in order to be appreciated.

William Empson in at least one instance finds Milton strangely deficient when viewed closely.[4] For Empson, Milton's use of "all" in *Paradise Lost* reveals a poet who is an "absolutist, an all-or-none man," a rigid and "self-centered" man who lacks interest in the "variety of the world." Approach too closely, and we find inflexibility, single-mindedness ("all-or-none"), insensitivity, and perhaps dullness. Empson implies that Milton as a writer did not know what he was about:

> that [Milton's] feelings were crying out against his appalling theology in favour of freedom, happiness and the pursuit of truth was . . . not obvious to him, and it is this part of the dramatic complex which is thrust upon us by the repeated *all*.[5]

[3] "A Note on the Verse of John Milton" (1936), reprinted in *Milton: A Collection of Critical Essays*, ed. Louis L. Martz (Englewood Cliffs, New Jersey, 1966), p. 13. Eliot's 1947 recantation, one must admit, does little to modify this basic stance.

[4] *The Structure of Complex Words* (Norfolk, Conn., n.d.), pp. 101–104. See, however, Christopher Ricks' statement (in *Milton's Grand Style* [Oxford, 1963], pp. 8–9) about Empson's view of Milton as a "sensitive and subtle" poet who "*does* make use of expressive closeness to the senses when the occasion demands." Ricks is referring primarily, I think, to Empson's treatment of Milton in *Some Versions of Pastoral* (London, 1935).

[5] *The Structure of Complex Words*, p. 104. The importance of "all" that Empson seems to overlook concerns the poem's tone of affirmation. *Paradise Lost* is very much a celebration of the Deity's power to create and to redeem. The absolute presence (omnipresence), the absolute power (omnipotence), the absolute wisdom (omniscience) of God in the face of the negation which is Satan are suggested in Milton's repeated use of "all." The "All in All" (III, 341 and VI, 732) as a reference to the apocalyptic purification is drawn from Cor. 15:28.

Catchwords ("freedom," "happiness," "pursuit of truth") aside, such a statement can give a very distorted view of *Paradise Lost* and its poet.

A rebuttal of this point of view, however, should not assume that "modern methods of criticism are liable to fail us" and then go to the other extreme of avoiding contact with the verbal elements presumably because they do not "respond" to close analysis and appreciation. The point is that Milton's poetry does respond to this kind of analysis and that Milton as a poet was aware of what he wrote. Coming to terms with *Paradise Lost* must take account of its poetry, that is, its subtleties and complexities of meaning, its variety and flexibility of execution. A genuine assessment of *Paradise Lost*, I think, will reveal a very different performance from the insubstantial "greatness" that Eliot attributes to Milton's epic and the rigid, single-minded egotism that Empson attributes to it.

In my study, I have attempted to reconcile this disparity in critical attitudes by discovering a further means of understanding the expressive elements of *Paradise Lost*. To accomplish this, I have attempted to show how the poem manifests itself both in isolated instances and in large scale patterns according to the idea of creation. Such an approach, I think, has revealed one of Milton's basic techniques as a poet: the central method by which he conducts a poem of epic length is dialectical at its core. He employs the idea of creation—uncreation—re-creation as a way of dramatizing his argument. As I have suggested, the poem's various aspects (the temptation, the fall, the War in Heaven, the struggle of good and evil, redemption, and the vision of human history, among others) find their referent in the concept of birth. The consequences of my approach are apparent, for example, in the interpretation of Satan. With a knowledge of what creation means in the poem, the reader will better understand Satan's function. He will not think that Satan is a hero who gets out of hand in the beginning and whom Milton must degrade as the epic progresses. He will know that as Satan is in the very act of making his "heroic" speeches or performing his "heroic" deeds, he is degrading himself with a language that is given new meaning within the total context of the work.

Understanding the dialectical design of Milton's epic, the reader will be able to view *Paradise Lost* with a renewed sense of its complexity, to see the poem not as a one-dimensional performance but as a performance that is not even begun until it is completed. If the reader is not always able to appreciate how language operates within its total environment, he will at least avoid the mistake of thinking that the texture of *Paradise Lost* is immediately or locally ascertainable. He will not, for instance, presume to know the meaning of "possess" in the poem merely from his own experience but will realize that Milton veritably defines "possess" (or "erect" or "return" or "sit" or "disburden") according to a unifying dialectical concept.

If the idea of birth is not the only way of approaching Milton's poetry, or at least of approaching *Paradise Lost*, it is, I think, an important way. When applied to *Paradise Lost*, it reveals the poem's unity, organicity, and immense variety. It also provides a method of understanding Milton's epic without necessarily avoiding the language, as Prince suggests, because that language is unsatisfactory, as Eliot suggests, or inflexible, as Empson suggests. Rather, it views the language as vital, as constantly defining and redefining itself within the poetic framework, in which the interrelationships of words form an essential part of the poem's existence. As obvious as that idea sounds, we can see from the critical attitudes briefly examined above that it cannot be overemphasized in a consideration of *Paradise Lost*.

Appendix

the *lapis* or Philosopher's Stone here is even associated with Urim and Thummim, the mysterious stones in *"Aarons Brestplate"* (III, 598). Within the earth the sun's radiant light acts simultaneously as an impregnating and transmutational force. Through its alchemical powers, which "Philosophers in vain so long have sought" (III, 601), it causes earth's "fields and regions" to "Breathe forth *Elixir* pure" (one form of the *lapis*) and "Rivers" to "run / Potable Gold" (another form of the *lapis*) (III, 606–608). With one "touch of the "Arch'Chimic" sun's "vertuous" or life-giving ability "so many precious things / Of colour glorious and effect so rare" are produced (III, 608–612). The implications of natural alchemy are extremely important: they concern the notion of unfallen, healthy, spontaneous creativity. And, significantly, Milton communicates this idea through alchemical terminology.

Direct or explicit reference gives rise to implicit reference. For example, the radiant light of the sun has its divine counterpart in God's holy light, the source of inspiration celebrated in the proem to Book III, and the "vertuous" powers of the radiant light have their counterpart in the Spirit of God's brooding on the Abyss and infusing "vital vertue" and "vital warmth" (VII, 236). The connection is apparent enough, but it is especially important since it associates God with the alchemical act of transmutation. Edgar Duncan certainly views the connection in this way. The "Elixir" that the sunlight produces is associated, according to Duncan, with the Spirit of God,[5] so that divine light in *Paradise Lost* performs the transmutational act when it vivifies through revelation.

Milton himself suggests an alchemical relationship between the sun and God in the description of the Son "all armed" in his "Celestial Panoplie" with "radiant *Urim*, work divinely wrought" (VI, 760–761). Milton, it will be remembered, associates Urim with the sun's alchemical transmutations; it is a natural product of the sun's sublime radiance. That

[5] "Natural History," pp. 418–420.

Urim has a paramount place in the Son's equipage tends to associate the Son, at least implicitly, with the alchemical operations of the sun. If Milton had more in mind than an implicit relationship, however, he likewise had at his disposal a well-established alchemical tradition associating Christ and the Philosopher's Stone.[6]

The Son's affinity with the *lapis* is perhaps further substantiated by the Chariot that carries him on his "destructive" mission. According to Jung, the Chariot of Ezekiel's vision, from which Milton's account is drawn, is a standard alchemical symbol, and the lightning it shoots forth (compare VI, 849) indicates the transforming and generative powers

[6] See Jung, *Psychology and Alchemy*, for a detailed discussion of this tradition. Jung notes that in religious and alchemical literature, Christ is a "paradigm of sublimation" (p. 354). See also Jung, *Aion: Researches into the Phenomenology of the Self*, p. 225. Interestingly, Milton works with certain images and figures that are basic to alchemical lore. I refer to the number four (Jung terms it the quaternity), its multiples and configurations in such figures as the square and its associations with Ezekiel's vision. Harry F. Robins ("Satan's Journey: Direction in *Paradise Lost*," pp. 92–95) has already established, quite conclusively, I think, the square shape of Heaven, and I have noted elsewhere (Chapter 4, esp. n. 1, above) how that figure is repeated in the angelic phalanx to represent the holy union. In alchemical work, according to Jung (*Psychology and Alchemy*, pp. 119, 225–228), the quaternity symbolizes the unity of the four original elements produced through the womb containing the prime matter. If such an idea is in any way relevant to Milton, then the holy union as a quaternity is related to the alchemical work. What may be concluded from this assumption is that since in *Paradise Lost* the Son is generated as a product of the holy union with the Father, the Son, on this score, bears some affinity with the *lapis*. The idea of the quaternity, moreover, manifests itself in other contexts. It is seen not only in the Son's Chariot, a "fourfold-visag'd Four" that is "convoyd / By four Cherubic shapes" (VI, 845, 752–753), but in something so domestic as the description of Adam and Eve's table in Eden. "Rais'd of grassy turf / Thir Table was, and mossy seats had *round*, / And on her ample Square from side to side . . ." (V, 391–393; italics mine). Alchemically, such a description corresponds to the circumambulation of the square or the alchemical squaring of the circle (*Psychology and Alchemy*, p. 221; and cf. 1 Kgs. 7:23: "And he made a molten sea, ten cubits from the one brim to the other: it was round all about . . . and a line of thirty cubits did compass it round about.") Finally, one might explore the overtones of the "quaternion" as it appears in Adam and Eve's morning prayers: "Air, and ye Elements the eldest birth / Of Natures Womb, that in *quaternion* run / Perpetual Circle multiform . . ." (V, 180–182; italics mine). Unfallen Nature perfects itself with its own perpetual combinations.

which reduce the imperfect material before rebirth in the stone.[7] But we hardly need Jung to tell us about the alchemical ramifications of the Chariot, for those ramifications are present in the epic. As previously noted, the Chariot is "distinct" with a "multitude of eyes" (VI, 846–847 and 755), which cause the Chariot to become a revelation of God's blessed vision (from which the rebel angels will be cut off when they are plunged into darkness). Blessed vision is in turn the result of God's holy light; to be deprived of it is to be blind, so that the poet prays for its illuminating powers in the proem to Book III. But Milton, according to Duncan, associates holy light with alchemical transmutations, and at the end of Book VI it flashes from the eyes of the Chariot. Significantly, according to Jung, the philosophical vessel or *rotundum* in alchemical literature is a vehicle "distinct with eyes."[8]

If one were to interpret the Son's actions alchemically, he would have to deal with the idea that the Son sets out to destroy the rebel angels, to uncreate them, to return them to the state of Chaos, as an ultimate means of re-creation when the universe is purged of all impurities and "exists" in the sublime state of the "All in All." In alchemical terms, such an act is nothing less than the transmutation of corrupt matter to its *nigredo* state as a prelude to regeneration. If such is the case, then the rebel angels in their fall are returned to the Chaos of *prima materia (substantia)*, which, for the alchemist, is the world of the "uncreated" (Jung's term also), out of which the *lapis* is generated.[9] In *Paradise Lost*, however, transmutation has even further correspondences. Moving from the War in Heaven to the original image of the sun as a transmutational and vivifying power, we can likewise

---

[7] *The Archetypes and the Collective Unconscious*, pp. 294–295, 319–320, 335n.; and *Psychology and Alchemy*, p. 368. Jung associates the Chariot's liberating force with Moses' potent rod (*Archetypes*, pp. 294–295), and according to Duncan ("The Alchemy in Jonson's *Mercury Vindicated*," *SP*, XXXIX [1942], 633), the caduceus is the alchemical symbol of the stone. See also Read, pp. 106–107.

[8] *Archetypes*, pp. 294–295.

[9] Blackness is the "initial state," the Chaos present from the beginning, and is

see how the alchemical metaphor has possible repercussions throughout the Miltonic universe.

If, as Evelyn Underhill says, alchemy in its true sense is a spiritualizing art involving a movement from the physical to the spiritual, an "ascension to that perfect state" which is God,[10] then in *Paradise Lost* natural alchemy is everywhere. On the human level, it might be said to operate in the association of Adam and Eve, who need only join with one another in a union of love in order to rise in absolute purity and refinement (VIII, 589–592).[11] A similar idea is repeated on the cosmic level. For instance, the sun (Sol), the natural alchemist, is traditionally an alchemical symbol of gold, whose "marriage" or cohabitation with the moon (Luna), the alchemical symbol of silver, generates the Philosopher's Stone.[12] Raphael speaks of the "Male and Femal" joining between the "Light" of the sun and moon as the "two great Sexes" that "animate the World" (VIII, 148–151). Simultaneously, their union is nutritional. The moon, as the first Ethereal fire that receives sustenance in the purgative

produced by the separation of elements. Cf. Jung's *Psychology and Religion*, p. 109, and *Psychology and Alchemy*, pp. 218–219, 304. The alchemist is the creator whose purpose is to bring order out of Chaos (Edgar Duncan, "The Yeoman's Canon's *Silver Citrinacioun*," *MP*, XXXVII [1940], 246). See also Duncan, "Donne's Alchemical Figures," p. 275; and Mazzeo, pp. 105 and 109.

[10] *Mysticism: A Study in the Nature and Development of Man's Spiritual Consciousness* (Cleveland, 1955), p. 143. In Donne, moral refinement has its counterpart in alchemical refinement, a conventional association found in such alchemists as Paracelus (Duncan, "Donne's Alchemical Figures," pp. 271–275).

[11] The Platonic basis of such an idea is, of course, essential to its understanding. (See Irene Samuel, *Plato and Milton* [Ithaca, 1947], pp. 152 and 164. Even Professor Samuel, however, finds that "something of hermetic mysticism remains . . . in *Paradise Lost*," p. 35.) I am merely suggesting what is possibly a further dimension having its correspondence in the imagery. See *Psychology and Alchemy*, pp. 37 and 55. In the alchemical work "ascent" is synonymous with sublimation. Jung also notes the decisive role played by the idea of "opposites" in alchemy. The ultimate phase of the alchemical work is one in which the union of opposites becomes the archetypal form of the chemical marriage. Thus Jung says: "Here the supreme opposites, male and female . . . are melted into a unity purified of all opposition and therefore incorruptible" (p. 38).

[12] F. Sherwood Taylor, *The Alchemists* (New York, 1949), p. 148. The alchemical marriage of Sol and Luna is envisioned, according to Taylor, "with a frankness of sexual symbolism unacceptable in a modern published work."

process, gives sustenance by exhaling her vapors to "higher Orbs" such as the sun (v, 421–422). The process is universal. As Raphael says:

> of elements
> The grosser feeds the purer, Earth the Sea,
> Earth and Sea feed Air, the Air those Fires
> Ethereal, and as lowest first the Moon.
>
> (v, 415–418)

Sustenance, purgation, and coition thus ensue in the "marriage" of all these elements in what approximates an alchemical union. The sun, which is the symbolical height of the purgative or sublimational operation receives sustenance or "alimental recompence" (v, 424) from all, like God, who receives tribute, and in return "imparts" light to all. The "alimental recompence" takes the form of "humid exhalations," which correspond precisely to the alchemical process; in this process the "vaporous exhalation is the cause of all metals, fusible or ductile things, such as iron, copper, gold."[13]

The natural alchemy that pervades the entire Miltonic universe was created, of course, as the result of the Spirit of God's having brooded upon the "vast Abyss" out of which the world arose. If one considers that both the brooding of the Spirit and the rising of the world out of Chaos are alchemical symbols,[14] he will not be surprised to find that in their concern for cosmic creation the alchemists view the opening chapter of Genesis as the "most important source for the study of nature."[15] Interestingly, both for the alchemists and for Milton the process of separation and division involved in the Genesis account of the creation of the universe (see, for example, Gen. 1:6–7) has extremely

---

[13] Taylor (*The Alchemists*) citing Aristotle, p. 13.

[14] Duncan, "Natural History," p. 418; and Allen G. Debus, "Renaissance Chemistry and the Works of Robert Fludd," *Alchemy and Chemistry in the Seventeenth Century* (Los Angeles, 1966). p. 17.

[15] Debus, p. 16.

important ramifications. If the alchemists refer to such a process to characterize their own work,[16] the activity of separating one thing from another becomes central not only to Milton's description of cosmic creation (VII, 237–241) but to the creation of Pandaemonium (I, 700–709; as I shall discuss, Pandaemonium has alchemical associations), as well as the Son's promise to separate the pure from the impure in the War in Heaven (VI, 742–743; see also XI, 48–53). The correspondence extends still further, however, since both the alchemists and Milton cause the act of "brooding" to imply both incubation and meditation, causing birth and thinking.[17] That is, they both work with the same metaphors. In this last instance, the poet as creator is especially significant.

The complex set of associations discussed in the first chapter is present in the alchemist and his art. Like the poet, the alchemist returns himself to Chaos, to the corrupt or *nigredo* state through meditation (the alchemical idea of digestion or feeding on thoughts) in order to produce the work of art, the *lapis* out of its own corruption. By means of meditation, the alchemist, like the poet, participates in a creative dialogue with his inspirer in order to infuse more spirit into the stone (compare the concept of inspiration as a breathing of spirit into that which is to be animated[18]), so that "it will become still more spiritualized, volatized, or sublimated."[19] In both instances, the creator has the qualities of a Redeemer: both the poet and the alchemist, one through the poem and the other through the *lapis*, reveal to man the means of redemption.

What the return to the underworld means for the poet,

[16] Ibid., pp. 11–13.

[17] Jung, *Psychology and Alchemy*, pp. 235, 261–262.

[18] According to Shawcross ("The Metaphor of Inspiration in *Paradise Lost*," p. 75), "inspiration is literally a breathing into, and for Milton as Christian poet it is the breathing of the *anima* of God into him as mortal. Such 'animation' supplies the life-giving force which will bring about creation." Cf. also *PL*, XI, 1–5; Ezek. 11:19; and Ps. 114.

[19] *Psychology and Alchemy*, p. 263. Cf. also Mircea Eliade, *Rites and Symbols of Initiation*, pp. 123–124.

it also means for the alchemist. Their experiences are most similar. If the poet's venturing down and moving upward implies the encounter with Sin and Death in Hell and with the warring elements in Chaos, the alchemist's experience implies a similar encounter with the "nether regions" ruled by evil, on the one hand, and with the *prima materia*, on the other. In his "journey" the alchemist confronts a female figure, woman above and serpent below, and that figure, appropriately, has incestuous relations with her son.[20] For the alchemist, the female figure represents, in part, the feminine aspect of his fallen state, the "darkness of inanimate matter" (compare Milton's *substantia*), from which he attempts to redeem his lost or uncorrupt nature.[21] In more general terms, the return to this dark place has affinities with the idea of returning to the "womb" (compare the "womb" of both Sin and Chaos) as a means of re-creation.[22] The return to the underworld and the movement out of it have both Christian and alchemical implications in the idea of re-encountering the consequences of one's fallen condition with the possibility of redemption.[23] In coming to terms with his fallen nature, the alchemist undergoes much of the poet's plight of "initiatory torture, death, and resurrection"[24] discussed in the first chapter. In alchemical terms, such is the suffering, death, and rebirth to which the mineral substances are subject in the transmutational process.[25]

[20] *Psychology and Alchemy*, pp. 291–293.

[21] Ibid.

[22] Eliade, *Rites and Symbols*, p. 57.

[23] In the context of his attempt to generate in himself an image equal in glory to that of God, Satan's further attempt to "create" himself by traveling through Chaos in Book II also has alchemical implications. For by then the uncreated Satan confronts the element of uncreation itself, the Chaos or *prima materia* of the alchemist. He attempts while in an uncreated state to regenerate himself by exiting out of the alchemical Anthropos or *rotundum* containing the *prima materia*. His exit is, of course, illusory: the birth partakes of the excrement, the corrupt matter, that the alchemists so often work with (*Psychology and Alchemy*, p. 248).

[24] Eliade, *Rites and Symbols*, p. 123.

[25] Ibid.

Whatever the extent of its implications in *Paradise Lost*, alchemy, as noted previously, is dialectically conceived. Up to this point, I have been considering the positive facets of alchemy expressed through God, unfallen nature, unfallen man, and the fallen but regenerate poet. In these instances, Milton, I feel, makes use of the original associations of alchemy as a noble art, in which the quest for the Philosopher's Stone had a spiritual significance as well as a practical one. But at his disposal Milton also had the degenerate tradition, alchemy as a charlatan's art used to dupe others for the purposes of material aggrandizement. If Chaucer dramatized such an idea in his Canon and Jonson in his Subtle, Milton made that idea an integral part of his Satan.

The debased approach to alchemy returns us to the idea of equating materiality with spirituality and the consequent failure to achieve the spiritual by means of the material. Such false productivity is associated, on the one hand, with the "vain" attempts to "bind / Volatil *Hermes*, and call up unbound / In various shapes old *Proteus* from the Sea" (III, 602–604) and, on the other, with the sooty art of mining. We think, for example, of the "Empiric Alchemist," who with "fire" from his "sooty coal"

> Can turn, or holds it possible to turn
> Metals of drossiest Ore to perfet Gold
> As from the Mine.
>
> (V, 441–443)

The first association implies the insubstantiality, transience, and deceptiveness; the second association, the artificiality and filth of the alchemical act devoid of true guidance. Both associations find expression in Satanic creativity.

Satan's production of gunpowder, for example, is clearly alchemical in its implications, first because, in its resorting to the world beneath the surface of Heaven, it is a mining activity and second because the manufacture of gunpowder is directly related to the alchemist's art.[26] With the use of his

[26] Debus, p. 12.

gunpowder, Satan is mimicking God's thunder and lightning, which, to the alchemist, "were no less than an explosion of aerial sulphur and niter duplicating gunpowder on a grand scale."[27] Like alchemists, then, the rebel angels perform the forbidden act of transmutation:

> Sulphurous and Nitrous Foam
> They found, they mingl'd, and with suttle Art
> Concocted and adusted they reduc'd
> To blackest grains, and into store convey'd.
> (VI, 512–515)

The "concocting," "adusting," and "reducing" to the *nigredo* state of "blackest grains" are aspects of the alchemical process, here performed for the purposes of deception and fraud. Satanic deception, however, does not end in Heaven.

The many dimensions of perverse creativity are represented also in the building of Pandaemonium. That is, Satan's assault upon Heaven's "Originals" in order to build weapons is repeated within Hell. The construction of Pandaemonium is clearly alchemical,[28] and its debased implications are unmistakable. Sexual and alchemical imagery are, as I shall attempt to demonstrate, combined to reveal further the uncreative nature of Satan's world. The "Hill," into whose depths the fallen angels venture, stands as a parody of God's holy Mount and as a debasement of God's throne:

> There stood a Hill not far whose griesly top
> *Belch'd* fire and rowling smoak; the rest entire
> Shon with a *glossie scurff*, undoubted sign

---

[27] Ibid.

[28] Duncan, "Natural History," p. 393. See also W. A. Murray, "Donne and Paracelsus: An Essay in Interpretation," *RES*, xxv (1949), 116, for the idea that mining and alchemy are closely associated. Milton's association of Vulcan with Pandaemonium (I, 740) is also appropriate, since Vulcan is an alchemical figure. He figures prominently in Jonson's *Mercury Vindicated from the Alchemists at Court* as the personification of alchemy, and "is to be found more than once in an alchemical setting" (Duncan, "The Alchemy in Jonson's *Mercury* . . .," p. 629).

> That in his *womb* was hid metallic Ore,
> The work of *Sulphur*.
>
> (I, 670–674; italics mine)

To understand the full implications of the imagery, one must recall the earlier description, in which "combustible /And fewel'd entrails" burst forth and caused a "stench" (I, 228–237). What fuses the oral ("Belch'd") and vaginal ("womb") nature of the above quotation with the anal nature of the earlier description is their common reference to Typhoeus, who also appears in Milton's "In Quintum Novembris" (ll. 31–39) spewing sulphur. Through the one allusion, then, Milton makes use of a number of debased associations. Such a method is by no means unusual for Milton, since he employs the same means of describing the explosion of gunpowder in Book VI (576–590).

Our first indication that the image has alchemical implications is the mention of "glossie scurf," which suggests the presence of "gold-bearing ore."[29] "Glossie scurf," incidentally, is also interesting because it derives from that same debased environment alluded to in Typhoeus' spewing, belching, and excreting activities. In this context, "glossie scurf" connotes, in support of its alchemical associations, the dried remains of anything foul that adheres to a diseased surface. The description, after all, is only one small facet of what Milton calls Satan's filthy and indecent world. It is also apt for the alchemical idea, since the natural conditions of the debased alchemist are those of waste and putrefaction.

The second indication that we are in the presence of an alchemical work is the mention of "metallic Ore, / The work of Sulphur," whose transmutational effects are conceived in a generative manner (alchemists believed in the breeding or growing of gold [compare IV, 220]). According to David Masson, the "metallic Ore" is the

> offspring and production of sulphur . . . [in] which . . .
> the subterranean fire concocts and boils up the crude

[29] Duncan, "Natural History," p. 393.

and undigested Earth into a more profitable consistence, and by its innate heat, hardens and bakes it into metals.[30]

The alchemical "science of the Middle Ages, inherited by Paracelsus, based itself on a doctrine that sulphur and mercury were the two all-pervading substances in nature . . . *generating* all things between them" (italics mine).[31] Sulphur, mercury, and forms of nitre, which are all important to the alchemist's art, are variously referred to in a generative sense in *Paradise Lost*.[32]

As a fit symbol of the lust for wealth represented by the degenerate alchemist's attempt to create the *lapis,* the fallen angels are led by Mammon, the "least erected Spirit" in Heaven. As previously noted, the materiality of the diabolic quest for magnificence is fittingly contrasted with the spirituality of the divine quest. The fallen angels would re-create the glory of Heaven through the alchemical transmutation of baser metals into gold. And Mammon is their leader (compare Jonson's Sir Epicure Mammon in *The Alchemist*).

The first association with Mammon is that of robbery; thus it was through Mammon's "suggestion" that men

> Ransack'd the Center, and with impious hands
> Rifl'd the bowels of thir mother Earth
> For Treasures better hid.
>
> (I, 686–688)

The act of ransacking the earth for hidden treasures approximates the alchemical act of extracting the buried stone.[33] In their desire for wealth, men rob, that is, in Milton's terminology, violate sacrilegiously the generative area of the earth,

---

[30] *Milton's Poetical Works*, III, 130n.

[31] Ibid. Of the previous image ("whose combustible / And fewel'd entrails thence conceiving Fire, / Sublim'd with Mineral fury . . ." [I, 233–235]), Merritt Y. Hughes (ed., *Paradise Lost*, p. 12n.) notes: "Milton had sulphur mainly in mind as one of the three or four basic minerals of the alchemists, for whom 'sublimation' meant the refining of metals by the hottest possible fires."

[32] See, for example, VI, 512–515; III, 603.

[33] Jung, *Psychology and Alchemy*, p. 187.

which as a "mother" reproduces the treasures within it. The "rifling" of the mother's bowels has distinctly debased and distasteful connotations.

In like manner is Satan's crew described as having "Op'nd into the Hill a spacious *wound* / And dig'd out *ribs of Gold*" (I, 689–690; italics mine). The creation of an opening (a pattern previously discussed) yields the birth of gold, and the act of extracting the gold causes the "wounding" of that which produces the object. That Satanic mode of creation stands in fit contrast to God's *wounding* of Adam and consequent creation of Eve from Adam's *rib* (VIII, 465–467). Through association, then, the creation of Eve takes on alchemical implications. The artifice of golden ribs, which are cold and lifeless, is contrasted with the natural qualities of Adam's rib, which is flowing with warmth and life and is conducive to birth. Furthermore, whereas the creation of Eve is a natural act, the construction of Pandaemonium suggests that which is not only unnatural but deceptive.

Indeed, the deceptive aspect of Satan's creativity, which, as previously discussed, characterizes the Arch-Deceiver as a trickster, is central to the traditional idea of the alchemist as charlatan.[34] The impossible sleight of hand that underlies all Satanic production is also true of the alchemical metaphor. As the consummation of the busy construction work that goes into the building of Pandaemonium, "Anon out of the earth a Fabrick huge / Rose like an Exhaltation" (I, 710–711). The substances and artifices of the entire ingenious construct are based finally on a magician's trick. Again, in alchemy we see that illusion is the result of materiality, and substance is insubstantial at best. Such deception is the crowning feat of the degenerate alchemist.[35] Consequently, in Milton's handling of Pandaemonium, we can discern the culmination of

[34] Jung, *Archetypes,* p. 255. The trickster is associated with the "alchemical figure of Mercurius."

[35] Jung, *Psychology and Alchemy,* pp. 241, 462. "Exhalation" has a number of references. As an alchemical term, it suggests the "breath" that causes life to be generated out of substances, and as such it was for the alchemists "at once the root and the active principle of all things" (Taylor, *The Alchemists,* pp. 12,

alchemy as a debased art. If Satanic debasement manifests itself in Hell and Heaven, however, it certainly can be found on earth. There, Tubal Cain, among others, carries on alchemically the work of Satan.

According to Lynn Thorndike, the assumed antiquity of alchemy goes back to Tubal Cain, who, like Vulcan (the Architect of Pandaemonium), is designated an inventor of alchemy.[36] Since both Tubal Cain and Vulcan engage in similar activities, Milton appropriately creates an earthly setting containing a number of details found in the construction of Pandaemonium. For instance, as Pandaemonium was constructed on a "Plain" (I, 700), so it is on a "Plain" (XI, 556) that Adam sees

> one who at the Forge
> Labouring, two massie clods of Iron and Brass
> Had melted

> .   .   .   .

> the liquid Ore he dreind
> Into fit moulds prepar'd; from which he formd
> First his own Tools; then, what might else be wrought
> Fusil or grav'n in mettle.

> (XI, 564–573)

The use of fire, the founding of ore, and the draining into molds all recall the building of Pandaemonium (compare I, 700–707). Those who pursue this type of work are by their

13–14). But "exhalation" may also have negative connotations. In *Paradise Lost*, for example, it has implicit affinities with the idea of death or the expelling of the spirit, as opposed to "inspiration" or of breathing into as a quickening act. Such negative overtones are, of course, common (see Lynn Thorndike, *A History of Magic and Experimental Science* [New York, 1958], VII, 213). Even from the alchemical perspective, "exhalation" has a decidedly unrefined quality about it. According to Jonson's Subtle in *The Alchemist* (*Elizabethan and Stuart Plays*, ed. Charles Read Baskervill, et al. [New York, 1934], II.iii.145–149), the alchemist's material (of which Pandaemonium is composed) is "of one part, / A humid exhalation, which we call / *Materia liquida*, or the *unctuous water*; / On the other part, a certain crass and viscous / Portion of the earth." When viewed alchemically, Pandaemonium loses much of its stateliness and magnificence.

[36] *History of Magic*, VIII, 364.

fallen natures outcasts from God. Their creativity is part of the artifices of Satanic creation, such as metallurgy, mining, and engineering.[37] Like Satan, the race of him "who slew his Brother" (XI, 609) appear "studious" of "Arts that polish Life, Inventers rare" (XI, 609–610). Paying no heed to their Creator and caring only for this life and its satisfactions, they are bent on creating pleasure meaningful only to the present.

In that way, they become part of the tradition of those whose purpose is to attain gratification solely through the material and thereby fulfill on earth that manner of Satanic creativity found, during the rebellion, in Heaven, and, after the fall, in Hell. As creators, they contrast implicitly with the natural form of creativity seen in God and unfallen man. I hope to have shown, however, that the contrast is not merely generative; that if natural creativity manifests itself in alchemical terms, debased creativity, here as elsewhere, reveals itself in a similar way. If such is the case, then we must say that alchemy and creativity become interdependent modes of expression in *Paradise Lost;* that their interdependence both provides an important means of viewing the many facets of Milton's epic and becomes part of an intricate dialectical design unifying the poem on all levels.

---

[37] Mining and metallurgy and many of the other industrial sciences were originally closely related to the alchemical art (Taylor, *The Alchemists*, p. 193; and Thorndike, VII, 298).

Bibliography

Bibliography

ADAMSON, J. H. "The War in Heaven: Milton's Version of the *Merkabah*," *JEGP*, LVII (1958), 690–703.

ADLER, MORTIMER J. *Dialectic*. New York, 1927.

ALLEN, DON CAMERON. *The Harmonious Vision: Studies in Milton's Poetry*. Baltimore, 1954.

BAILEY, MARGARET L. *Milton and Jacob Boehme: A Study of German Mysticism in Seventeenth-Century England*. New York, 1914.

BANKS, THEODORE H. *Milton's Imagery*. New York, 1950.

BODKIN, MAUD. *Archetypal Patterns in Poetry* (1934). New York, 1958.

BOYETTE, PURVIS. "Something More About the Erotic Motive in *Paradise Lost*," *Tulane Studies in English*, XV (1967), 19–30.

BROADBENT, J. B. "Milton's Hell," *ELH*, XXI (1954), 161–192.

BROWN, NORMAN O. *Life Against Death: The Psychoanalytical Meaning of History*. New York, 1959.

BURKE, KENNETH. *A Grammar of Motives and a Rhetoric of Motives*. Cleveland, 1962.

CAMPBELL, JOSEPH. *The Hero with a Thousand Faces*. Bollingen Series XVII. New York, 1949.

CASSIRER, ERNST. *Language and Myth*, trans. Susanne K. Langer. New York, 1946.

CHAMBERS, A. B. "Chaos in *Paradise Lost*," *JHI*, XXIV (1963), 55–84.

COLERIDGE, SAMUEL TAYLOR. "Milton" (1818), *Milton Criticism: Selections from Four Centuries*, ed. James Thorpe. New York, 1950.

COPE, JACKSON I. *The Metaphoric Structure of Paradise Lost*. Baltimore, 1962.

CORCORAN, SISTER MARY IRMA. *Milton's Paradise with Reference to the Hexameral Background*. Washington, 1945.

CURRY, WALTER CLYDE. *Milton's Ontology, Cosmogony, and Physics.* Lexington, Kentucky, 1957.

DAICHES, DAVID. "The Opening of *Paradise Lost*," *The Living Milton: Essays by Various Hands*, ed. Frank Kermode. London, 1960.

D'ARCY, M. C. *The Mind and Heart of Love.* 2nd ed. rev. Cleveland, 1962.

DAVIE, DONALD. "Syntax and Music in *Paradise Lost*," *The Living Milton: Essays by Various Hands*, ed. Frank Kermode. London, 1960.

DEBUS, ALLEN G. "Renaissance Chemistry and the Works of Robert Fludd," *Alchemy and Chemistry in the Seventeenth Century.* Los Angeles, 1966.

DI CESARE, MARIO A. "Advent'rous Song: The Texture of Milton's Epic," *Language and Style in Milton*, ed. Ronald David Emma and John T. Shawcross. New York, 1967.

DUNCAN, EDGAR. "The Alchemy in Jonson's *Mercury Vindicated*," *SP*, XXXIX (1942), 625–637.

———. "Donne's Alchemical Figures," *ELH*, IX (1942), 257–285.

———. "The Natural History of Metals and Minerals in the Universe of Milton's *Paradise Lost*," *Osiris*, XI (1954), 386–421.

———. "The Yeoman Canon's *Silver Citrinacioun*," *MP*, XXXVII (1940), 241–262.

ELIADE, MIRCEA. *Cosmos and History: The Myth of the Eternal Return*, trans. Willard R. Trask. New York, 1959.

———. *Rites and Symbols of Initiation: The Mysteries of Birth and Rebirth*, trans. Willard R. Trask. New York. 1958.

ELIOT, T. S. "A Note on the Verse of John Milton," *Milton: A Collection of Critical Essays*, ed. Louis R. Martz. Englewood Cliffs, New Jersey, 1966.

ELLIS, HAVELOCK. *Studies in the Psychology of Sex.* Vol. VII. 3rd ed. rev. Philadelphia, 1928.

EMPSON, WILLIAM. *Some Versions of Pastoral.* London, 1935.

———. *The Structure of Complex Words.* Norfolk, Conn., n.d.

FERRY, ANNE DAVIDSON. *Milton's Epic Voice: The Narrator in Paradise Lost*. Cambridge, Mass., 1963.

FISCH, HAROLD. "Hebraic Style and Motifs in *Paradise Lost*," *Language and Style in Milton*, ed. Ronald David Emma and John T. Shawcross. New York, 1967.

FLETCHER, HARRIS FRANCIS. *Milton's Rabbinical Readings*. Urbana, Illinois, 1930.

FRENCH, JOHN MILTON. "Milton as Satirist," *PMLA*, LI (1936), 414–429.

FREUD, SIGMUND. "The Relation of the Poet to Day-Dreaming," *On Creativity and the Unconscious*, ed. Benjamin Nelson. New York, 1958.

FRYE, NORTHROP. *The Return of Eden: Five Essays on Milton's Epics*. Toronto, 1965.

GARDNER, HELEN. *A Reading of Paradise Lost*. London, 1965.

GILBERT, ALLAN. "Milton's Defense of Bawdry," *SAMLA Studies in Milton*, ed. J. Max Patrick. Gainesville, Florida, 1953.

———. *On the Composition of Paradise Lost*. Chapel Hill, North Carolina, 1947.

HINKLE, BEATRICE M. *The Re-Creating of the Individual*. New York, 1923.

HUGHES, MERRITT Y. "Milton and the Symbol of Light," *SEL*, IV (1964), 1–33.

HUNTER, WILLIAM B., Jr. "Eve's Demonic Dream," *ELH*, XIII (1946), 255–265.

———. "The Meaning of 'Holy Light' in *Paradise Lost* III," *MLN*, LXXIV (1959), 589–592.

———. "Milton's Urania," *SEL*, IV (1964), 35–42.

———. "Prophetic Dreams and Visions in *Paradise Lost*," *MLQ*, IX (1948), 277–285.

———. "Some Problems in John Milton's Theological Vocabulary," *HTR*, LVII (1964), 353–365.

HUNTLEY, JOHN F. "Aristotle's Physics as a Gloss on *PL* VIII. 152," *PQ*, XLIV (1965), 129–132.

JONSON, BEN. *The Alchemist, Elizabethan and Stuart Plays*, ed. Charles Read Baskervill, et al. New York, 1934.

JUNG, CARL GUSTAV. *Aion: Researches into the Phenomenology of the Self*, trans. R. F. C. Hull. Bollingen Series XX. New York, 1959. (Vol. IX, Part 2 of *The Collected Works of C. G. Jung.*)

——. *The Archetypes and the Collective Unconscious*, trans. R. F. C. Hull. Bollingen Series XX. New York, 1959. (Vol. IX, Part I of *The Collected Works of C. G. Jung.*)

——. *Psyche and Symbol*, ed. Violet S. de Laszlo. New York, 1958.

——. *Psychology and Alchemy*, trans. R. F. C. Hull. Bollingen Series XX. New York, 1953. (Vol XII of *The Collected Works of C. G. Jung.*)

——. *Psychology and Religion*. New Haven, 1938.

——. *Psychology of the Unconscious*, trans. Beatrice M. Hinkle. New York, 1916.

KELLEY, MAURICE. *This Great Argument: A Study of Milton's De Doctrina Christiana as a Gloss upon Paradise Lost*. Princeton Studies in English, XXII. Princeton, New Jersey, 1941.

KRANIDAS, THOMAS. *The Fierce Equation: A Study of Milton's Decorum*. The Hague, 1965.

LANGDON, IDA. *Milton's Theory of Poetry and Fine Art*. New Haven, 1924.

LE COMTE, EDWARD. "Milton as Satirist and Wit," *Th'Upright Heart and Pure: Essays on John Milton Commemorating the Tercentenary of the Publication of Paradise Lost*, ed. Amadeus P. Fiore, O.F.M. Duquesne Studies 10. Pittsburgh, 1967.

——. *Yet Once More: Verbal and Psychological Pattern in Milton*. New York, 1953.

LEWALSKI, BARBARA KIEFER. *Milton's Brief Epic*. Providence, Rhode Island, 1966.

——. "Structure and the Symbolism of Vision in Michael's Prophecy, *Paradise Lost*, Books XI–XII." *PQ*, XLII (1963), 25–35.

LEWIS, C. S. *A Preface to Paradise Lost* (1942). New York, 1961.

MAC CAFFREY, ISABEL GAMBLE. *Paradise Lost as "Myth."* Cambridge, Mass., 1959.

MC COLLEY, GRANT. *Paradise Lost: An Account of Its Growth*

and Major Origins. Chicago, 1940.

MAZZEO, JOSEPH A. "Notes on John Donne's Alchemical Imagery." *Isis*, XLVIII (1957), 103–123.

MILTON, JOHN. *The Complete English Poetry of John Milton*, ed. John T. Shawcross. Anchor Seventeenth-Century Series. New York, 1963.

———. *Complete Prose Works of John Milton*, gen. ed. Don M. Wolfe. Vols. I and II. New Haven, 1953 and 1959.

———. *Milton's Poetical Works*, ed. David Masson. Vol. III. London, 1874.

———. *Paradise Lost*, ed. Merritt Y. Hughes. New York, 1962.

———. *Paradise Lost: Books I and II*, ed. Frank Templeton Prince. London, 1962.

———. *Paradise Lost: Books I and II*, ed. Balachandra Rajan. Bombay, 1964.

———. *Paradise Lost: Books I and II*, ed. E. M. W. and P. B. Tillyard. London, 1956.

———. *The Prose of John Milton*, gen. ed. J. Max Patrick. Anchor Seventeenth-Century Series. New York, 1967.

———. *The Works of John Milton*, gen. ed. Frank Allen Patterson. Vol. XV. New York, 1933.

MURRAY, W. A. "Donne and Paracelsus: An Essay in Interpretation," *RES*, XXV (1949), 115–123.

PATRICK, JOHN M. *Milton's Conception of Sin as Developed in Paradise Lost*. Logan, Utah, 1960.

PECHEUX, MOTHER MARY CHRISTOPHER. " 'O Foul Descent!' : Satan and the Serpent Form," *SP*, LXII (1965), 188–196.

POPE, ALEXANDER. *The Poems of Alexander Pope,* ed. John Butt. New Haven, 1968. (The Shortened Twickenham.)

PRINCE, FRANK TEMPLETON. *The Italian Element in Milton's Verse*. Oxford, 1954.

———. "On the Last Two Books of *Paradise Lost*," *Essays and Studies*, XI (1958), 38–52.

RAJAN, BALACHANDRA. *Paradise Lost and the Seventeenth-Century Reader*. London, 1947.

READ, JOHN. *Prelude to Chemistry: An Outline of Alchemy,*

Its Literature and Relationships. 2nd ed. London, 1939.

RICKS, CHRISTOPHER. *Milton's Grand Style.* Oxford, 1963.

ROBBINS, FRANK EGLESTON. *The Hexaemeral Literature: A Study of the Greek and Latin Commentaries on Genesis.* Chicago, 1912.

ROBINS, HARRY F. *If This Be Heresy: A Study of Milton and Origen.* Illinois Studies in Language and Literature, LI. Urbana, Illinois, 1963.

———. "Satan's Journey: Direction in *Paradise Lost,*" *Milton Studies in Honor of Harris Francis Fletcher,* ed. G. Blakemore Evans, et al. Urbana, Illinois, 1961.

ROSS, MALCOLM M. *Poetry and Dogma: The Transfiguration of Eucharist Symbols in Seventeenth-Century English Poetry.* New Brunswick, New Jersey, 1954.

SAMUEL, IRENE. *Plato and Milton.* Ithaca, New York, 1947.

SAURAT, DENIS. *Milton, Man and Thinker.* New York, 1925.

SCHULTZ, HOWARD. *Milton and Forbidden Knowledge.* New York, 1955.

SHAWCROSS, JOHN T. "The Balanced Structure of *Paradise Lost,*" *SP,* LXII (1965), 696–718.

———. "The Metaphor of Inspiration in *Paradise Lost,*" *Th'Upright Heart and Pure: Essays Commemorating the Tercentenary of the Publication of Paradise Lost,* ed. Amadeus P. Fiore, O.F.M. Duquesne Studies 10. Pittsburgh, 1967.

———. "The Son in His Ascendance: A Reading of *Paradise Lost,*" *MLQ,* XXVII (1966), 388–401.

SPENSER, EDMUND. *The Poetical Works of Edmund Spenser,* ed. J. C. Smith and E. De Selincourt. Oxford Standard Authors. London, 1912.

STEIN, ARNOLD. *Answerable Style: Essays on Paradise Lost.* Minneapolis, 1953.

SUMMERS, JOSEPH. *The Muse's Method: An Introduction to Paradise Lost.* Cambridge, Mass., 1962.

SVENDSEN, KESTER. *Milton and Science.* Cambridge, Mass., 1956.

SWIFT, JONATHAN. *Selected Prose and Poetry,* ed. Edward Rosenheim. New York, 1959.

TAYLOR, F. SHERWOOD. *The Alchemists: Founders of Modern Chemistry*. New York, 1949.

TAYLOR, GEORGE COFFIN. *Milton's Use of Du Bartas*. Cambridge, Mass., 1934.

THORNDIKE, LYNN. *A History of Magic and Experimental Science*. Vols. VII and VIII. New York, 1958.

TILLYARD, E. M. W. *The Miltonic Setting, Past and Present*. London, 1938.

UNDERHILL, EVELYN. *Mysticism: A study in the Nature and Development of Man's Spiritual Consciousness*. Cleveland, 1955.

WATKINS. W. B. C. *An Anatomy of Milton's Verse*. Baton Rouge, Louisiana, 1955.

WEIDHORN, MANFRED. "Dreams and Guilt," *HTR*, LVII (1965), 69–90.

WERBLOWSKY, R. J. Z. *Lucifer and Prometheus*, intro. Carl Gustav Jung. London, 1952.

WESTERMARCK, EDWARD. *The Future of Marriage in Western Civilization*. New York, 1936.

————. *The Origin and Development of the Moral Ideas*. Vol. II. London, 1908.

WHITING, GEORGE WESLEY. *Milton and This Pendant World*. Austin, Texas, 1958.

————. *Milton's Literary Milieu*. Chapel Hill, North Carolina, 1939.

WILLIAMS, ARNOLD. *The Common Expositor: An Account of the Commentaries on Genesis, 1527–1633*. Chapel Hill, North Carolina, 1948.

WOODHOUSE, A. S. P. "Notes on Milton's Views on the Creation: The Initial Phases," *PQ*, XXVIII, (1949), 211–236.

Index

147, 176, 177, 212, 232, 233; as a Re-creator, 87, 122, 123, 205, 212, 213, 214, 215, 216, 217, 218, 219, 220

Hinkle, Beatrice, 44n15
Hughes, Merritt Y., 38n1, 67n11, 182, 241n31
Hunter, William B., Jr., 23, 38n1, 191n3
Huntley, John, 59, 60

Invective: in the prose, 10–13, 14, 15; in the poetry, 13, 14, 15

Jonson, Ben, 242n35
Jung, Carl Gustav, 26n10, 51, 52, 53, 94, 94n18, 101n21, 105n22, 109n1, 132, 144n4, 145n5, 155n12, 163n2, 168n5, 232, 232n6, 233, 233n7, 233n9, 234n11, 236, 237, 237n23, 241, 242, 242n34

Kelley, Maurice, 81
Kranidas, Thomas, 3n2, 5n4, 77n22

Langdon, Ida, 46n17
LeComte, Edward, 10n11, 86n7
Lewalski, Barbara K., 38n2, 205n1
Lewis, C. S., 26

MaCaffrey, Isabel G., 19, 69
McColley, Grant, 10n10
Masson, David, 180, 219, 241
Mazzeo, Joseph A., 229n2, 233n9
Milton, John: as polemicist, 3, 4, 12, 13, 14, 15, 28, 120; as satirist, 10n11, 11, 12, 13, 14; and the composition of *Paradise Lost*, 46, 47, 51, 73, 74; as Christian poet, 47, 54, 122, 123, 205, 236n18; and critical approaches to *Paradise Lost*, 222, 223, 224, 225; and criticism of his poetic practices, 223, 223n3, 223n4, 224; and the texture of *Paradise Lost*, 225; *Areopagitica*, 4–6, 54n39, 229n2; *The Reason of Church-Government*, 5n4, 39, 110n2, 229n2; *Of Reformation*, 10, 11, 12, 229n2; *Animadversions*, 12, 162n1; "Psalm 2," 13, 81n1; *An Apology*, 14, 14n12, 229n2; *Pro se defensio*, 14n12; "Lycidas," 31n16, 53, 54, 93n17; *Christian Doctrine*, 38, 39, 40, 42n10; *Commonplace Book*, 47n21; "At a Solemn Musick," 49;